THE LADIES' ROOM

Other books by Carolyn Brown

The Dove
The PMS Club
Trouble in Paradise
The Wager
That Way Again
Lily's White Lace
The Ivy Tree
The Yard Rose
All the Way from Texas
A Falling Star
Love Is

The Angels & Outlaws Historical Romance Series:
From Wine to Water
Walkin' on Clouds
A Trick of the Light

The Black Swan Historical Romance Series:
From Thin Air
Pushin' Up Daisies
Come High Water

The Broken Roads Romance Series:
To Hope
To Dream
To Believe
To Trust
To Commit

The Drifters and Dreamers Romance Series:
Morning Glory
Sweet Tilly
Evening Star

THE LADIES' ROOM

ROOM

•

Carolyn Brown

AVALON BOOKS
NEW YORK

*This one is for
Shirley Marks and Carolyn Hughey
With many thanks!*

Published by Avalon Books,
an imprint of Thomas Bouregy & Co., Inc.
160 Madison Avenue, New York, NY 10016

Library of Congress Cataloging-in-Publication Data

Brown, Carolyn, 1948–
    The ladies' room / Carolyn Brown.
        p.   cm.
    ISBN 978-0-8034-7602-8 (acid-free paper)   1. Married
women—Fiction.   2. Families—Fiction.   3. Inheritance and
succession—Fiction.   4. Dwellings—Remodeling—Fiction.
5. Domestic fiction.   I. Title.
    PS3552.R685275L33 2011
    813'.54—dc22

                                                2011018706

PRINTED IN THE UNITED STATES OF AMERICA
ON ACID-FREE PAPER
BY RR DONNELLEY, BLOOMSBURG, PENNSYLVANIA

Chapter One

If I wiggled again, Great-aunt Gert was going to sit straight up in that pale pink coffin and give me an evil glare the way she used to do when I was a child and couldn't sit still in church. Not even in death would Gertrude Martin abide wiggling at a funeral, especially when it was hers. She'd been an outspoken, caustic old girl the whole time she was alive, and I had no doubt she could resurrect herself at the faintest whisper of queen-sized panty hose rubbing together as I crossed and uncrossed my legs.

I should have gone to the ladies' room before the service began. But my four cups of coffee that morning and the thirty-two-ounce Coke I'd drunk on the way to the church hadn't made it to my bladder until the preacher cleared his throat and began a eulogy that sounded as if it would go on until six days past eternity. If the poor man was trying to preach Aunt Gert through the pearly gates, we'd all starve to death before he finished. Thank goodness I had a Snickers candy bar and a bag of barbecued chips in my purse and twenty extra pounds of pure cellulite on my thighs. At least I wouldn't be the next one knocking on heaven's door.

I crossed my legs yet again and tried to concentrate on what the preacher was saying to take my mind off the pressing matter. After two minutes nothing worked. The space between the far end of the pew and the wall was just barely passable for an anorexic teenager, so I had to walk sideways. It was unforgivable enough that I was leaving in the middle of the funeral sermon, but to trouble ten members of the congregation to get

1

to the center aisle would have had Aunt Gert doing more than sitting up. The tirade she'd have produced would've withered my poor bladder into a dried-out raisin.

I trotted all the way to the ladies' room. By the time I was inside one of the two stalls, I already had my tight black skirt jerked up. I grabbed the top of the ultracontrol panty hose and tugged hard, only to push a thumbnail through the fabric. I'd thought that they were made of the same stuff that was used to construct space shuttles and that neither excess weight nor blistering fire could destroy the material.

I was carefully pulling up my ruined hose when the door opened, and Marty and Betsy, my cousins, rushed into the small room. I recognized them the minute they began to talk. They've smoked since they had to hide behind the barn to do it, and their voices proved it—plus they smelled as if they'd just walked through the sulfurous fires of Hades.

"We'll just blend in when the service is over, like we got there late and sat in the back pew," Marty said.

How stupid was that? Everyone would know they hadn't been at the service. Of course, everyone would also know I'd left in the middle of the sermon, but at least I'd been there through part of it. I wished I had the nerve to really fuss at them for being late and hiding out in the bathroom, but I didn't. Not at a funeral. Not even in the ladies' room. It wasn't the place or the time. I had my hand on the stall lock when I heard my name mentioned. I quietly put the lid down on the toilet and sat down.

"Did Trudy come to this thing?" Betsy asked.

"Of course Trudy is here. God knows she'll do what's right. Good old dependable Trudy. She's never rebelled and never will. She'll be the good child to her dying day. Only reason I'm here is to hear the will," Marty said.

"What if Aunt Gert leaves that house to you? What are you going to do with it?" Betsy asked.

"I'll hire a bulldozer to raze the thing and sell the lot to pay the bill. I wouldn't go through all the old junk in that house for a one-night stand with Brad Pitt."

Betsy giggled. "If she leaves it to me, I'm callin' an auction company. They take a healthy cut of the money, but they do all the work. I'm going to auction everything off in one day. Then when I get my share, I'm going on a cruise."

I heard the flick of a cigarette lighter before Marty commented. Thank goodness there were no windows in the bathroom, or lightning would have zigzagged in and zapped her dead for smoking in the church house.

"That place won't bring enough for a cruise anywhere, unless you want to hire a fishing boat on Lake Texoma. But it'll either be me or you or Trudy. We're the only living heirs, except for Trudy's mother. And she's got Alzheimer's, so Gert wouldn't leave it to her."

"Poor Trudy. Bless her heart," Betsy said.

I leaned forward and strained my ears until my head hurt. It would be too awkward to open the door now. There would definitely be a confrontation, and I've always hated that kind of thing. Besides, I wanted to know just what I'd done to be *poor* and *blessed.*

"It's sad, isn't it? But she's always been that way. Even when we were kids, we could convince her of anything. She's so blind. She's like an ostrich with her head in the sand and that big bubble butt in the air," Marty said.

A lump caught in my throat. I swallowed a dozen times before it went down. If they hadn't been so intent on talking about me, they'd have heard the gulps.

Betsy giggled. "Maybe not blind. Just naïve. Hasn't got a clue as to what really goes on around her. She actually liked Gert."

"Anyone who liked that salty old witch deserves to be running around in the dark. Let her live in ignorance. They say it's bliss. Besides, Trudy's always had it all, and I've been jealous. She deserves to have to get her hands dirty. If she gets the place, she'll work her chubby little rear end off getting it all organized. There won't be a doily or an ugly knickknack that she doesn't categorize," Marty said.

My face burned, because that was exactly what I'd been thinking since I'd heard Aunt Gert was dead. Her prized stuff might not bring much, but it could be given to a good charity.

"That's Trudy—her head so far into good deeds, she doesn't see what's right before her eyes." Betsy chuckled. "Give me a drag off that. Does God strike people dead for smoking in a church? We'll have to go out and blend in with the crowd in a minute, and it'll be an hour before we can smoke again."

My skin prickled with hives. Was I that predictable?

"God won't strike us dead for smoking, but Gert would have. Maybe Drew will talk sense to Trudy and make her bulldoze the place," Marty said. "He's a smart lawyer. Guess Trudy don't care what she has to put up with for that fancy house and all that money."

Cigarette smoke drifted under the toilet-stall door. I clamped a hand tightly over my mouth to keep from coughing. Talk about a disaster. It would be the beginning of a family war for sure if I got caught now. And Aunt Gert would rise up out of that coffin if we got into it in the bathroom while her funeral was going on.

"Do you think she knows about either her husband or her daughter's shenanigans, or has her head been in the sand so long that she's never coming up for air?" Betsy asked.

"If she doesn't know, she's dumb, not blind. Everyone knows about Drew," Marty answered. "How could Trudy not? It's been goin' on ever since the week after he married her."

My eyebrows furrowed so tightly, I felt the birthing of a dozen new wrinkles on my forehead. What was it that everyone except *poor Trudy, bless her heart* knew about Drew? And what did they know about my grown daughter, Crystal, that I didn't know?

Marty lowered her voice slightly. "Remember when Trudy did that overnight sleepover in Dallas with Crystal and her little friends on—what was it?—Crystal's seventh birthday so the kids could go to see Disney On Ice? Lori Lou came over to my house and borrowed my casserole recipe for hot chicken salad. I caught her coming out of Drew's house the next morning when I delivered the newspaper."

My stomach did thirty-nine flip-flops before it settled down to plain old nausea. If I got sick, they'd hear me, and then I'd have to endure a gazillion apologies with excuses about how they should have told me but really thought I knew and was ignoring it to keep my marriage intact. Hearing the words was so much worse than the niggling little suspicions I'd had through the years. My two cousins had turned on the lights and showed me exactly what Drew was, and now I had to deal with it.

I wished I had that little .22 pistol from my nightstand. When the custodian came to clean the church bathrooms after the funeral dinner, there would be my two female cousins, one bullet in each. If only I'd had the good sense to carry a gun in my purse instead of candy bars.

My ears hurt so badly, it sounded as if Betsy was yelling, but she was really just talking in a conversational tone. "Lori Lou wasn't the first, you know. He was looking over the crowd and flirting even at his and Trudy's wedding reception. Only person who doesn't know that Drew is a rich, good-looking, philandering fool is Trudy. She just thinks he's rich and good-looking. I've always said that if she doesn't know, then I'd let her live in bliss. I heard his newest toy is that new twenty-year-old blond teller at their bank. Her name is Charity something. Trudy gets older and frumpier every day, and his toys get younger and prettier. You've seen her, haven't you?"

"Know exactly who you're talking about. My oldest son asked her out on a date. She turned him down cold. Now I know why. Donnie James doesn't have the money to buy her one of those brand-new Thunderbirds like Drew shelled out the money for."

A moment passed before Marty continued. The cloud of smoke attested to the fact that she was busy burning an inch off the cigarette before she spoke. "Charity is young enough to be his daughter. Hey, so what did you think about Crystal's sneaking off to marry that worthless boyfriend of hers in Las Vegas?"

"Just a minute," Betsy whispered, and I heard the bathroom door squeak.

Maybe I could strangle them with the legs of my ultracontrol panty hose. It would be so satisfying to see their eyes bug out and their faces turn blue. If I put the hose back on after I'd committed justifiable homicide, no one would ever be able to find the murder weapon.

Betsy whispered, "They're all coming out of the church. We can blend in now. Put on your sad face, and for God's sake put a mint into your mouth. I can still smell the smoke from way over here."

The door shut, and I released my breath. I hadn't even realized I was holding it until it gushed out in a great sob. I leaned my head against the cold metal of the stall wall. Its coolness kept me from fainting dead away. It didn't, however, prevent me from curling up in a ball of anger, pain, and tears until my chest ached.

I had always had the perfect family, while my two cousins had messed up their lives with five unwise marriages between them. Now I had found out that the only real difference was that my family had had a sugar coating and theirs didn't.

I talked my jelly-filled legs into supporting me, and a glob of cheesy cellulite bubbled out through the hole in my panty hose as a runner inched its way down to my knees. If I didn't cross my legs, *poor, frumpy* Trudy might make it through the dinner without a run all the way to her ankles. A conspicuous run would certainly be a disgrace.

My reflection in the mirror almost sent me right out to my car. Big black mascara streaks ran through pink blush. My eyes were swollen. My chin wouldn't stop quivering. I took a deep breath and looked into my own green eyes. My long black hair was a fright. What was I going to do?

The first step was to make myself presentable. I'd focus on one thing at a time and get through the graveside part of the service. After that would be the dinner and the reading of the will. Then I'd deal with what I intended to do about my husband.

I walked out of the ladies' room with my shoulders straight and a fake smile on my face. A lady kept up appearances and never lost her dignity—even when her world had just shattered around her in the stall of the women's bathroom.

Marty, Betsy, and I were required to ride together in the limousine to the cemetery for the final bit of the service. They were whispering when I crawled inside. At least the fat escaping through the hole in my panty hose reminded me that I had a murder weapon at hand. I could strangle them and then shove half my Snickers bar into each of their mouths after they were dead and swear they'd both choked to death while weeping for Great-aunt Gert. No one would doubt frumpy old Trudy's word.

"How you holdin' up?" Marty asked.

"I'm just fine," I told her.

"Well, you look like warmed-over sin," Betsy said.

"And you look absolutely beautiful," I said sarcastically.

Marty became the buffer. "Don't take that tone with her, Trudy. What's the matter with you? She's just tryin' to make you laugh. We didn't know Aunt Gert meant so much to you. We're just happy the old gal finally kicked the bucket and we can go to the grocery store without checkin' around the end of the aisles to make sure we're not goin' to run into her."

"That's not any way to talk about the dead," I said.

"Why not? You're being hateful to the living," Marty snapped.

I turned my head and looked out the window.

They figured I was mourning or in a snit and went back to the latest gossip: whose kid was in trouble with the law, who was sleeping with whom. I didn't care about the latest gossip, but I would have liked to have that list of home-wrecking women they knew all about. I wanted to see the names of the women in Tishomingo, Oklahoma, and the surrounding areas that my husband had slept with. Peace always seemed to come at a high price, and the way my stomach was hurting, the cost of keeping quiet was going to be a full-fledged ulcer.

At the cemetery we were escorted from the limo by three of the men from Gert's church. They acted as if they expected us to go into some kind of wailing fit and were a little disappointed when we didn't.

The pallbearers set the pale pink casket on the fake-grass-covered rise, and everyone gathered in the tent. Three chairs waited for the bereaved great-nieces to sit in right in front of the casket. Sweat poured off my neck and ran in rivers down every wrinkle it could find, wetting the wide strip of elastic at the edge of bra that was biting holes into my rib cage. The fat bubble on my thigh stuck through the panty hose on the other side, and no amount of wiggling would unhinge it.

Through the pain, all I could think about was killing the messengers of the horrible news that my husband had been cheating on me most of my married life. They should have told me the day they found out rather than laughing about it behind my back.

"We are gathered here at this site to remember one more time the life of Gertrude Elizabeth Martin. She lived a long, happy life and has gone on to a better place. She has folded up her tent and gone on home to Jesus," the preacher said.

Jesus had better be ready for a different lifestyle once Gert got to heaven, because there were going to be some major changes up there. Saint Peter could get rid of his little black book with the names of the worthy written in it. Aunt Gert would arrive with a new and updated version tucked under her arm.

The singers began to sing "Amazing Grace," but I didn't hear a word of it. The preacher said a prayer, and as soon as he uttered "Amen," there were people all around us.

"You be strong, Trudy," Daisy Black said. "Gert wouldn't want to see you grieving a long time. Lean on your happy memories."

If I did that, I'd fall on my bubble butt pretty quickly. Was the woman daft?

Another little gray-haired lady hugged me and whispered, "Gert was a great lady. You'll have a time filling her boots."

"Dinnertime," Betsy whispered into my ear, and she headed toward the limousine that would take us back to the church.

"I sure hope someone made hot chicken salad," I said.

She did have the grace to blush. "I never knew you liked hot chicken salad. I mean, I know you make it for Drew, because you told me, but I didn't know it was your favorite."

"Of course I like hot chicken salad. I make it every week for Drew. If he doesn't have it on Tuesday night, it's grounds for divorce." It was amazing how easy it was to dump ashes upon her head and how much I enjoyed it.

I could have sworn I heard Gert's voice whispering that a true lady could weather tragedy and heartache and keep her pride and dignity. I suppose she was trying to tell me to be careful, but I didn't really care about all those old southern-isms she'd spouted all the time. I wanted to roll down the windows of the limo and yell toward the single white cloud up there in the ultrablue summer sky, *Don't be telling me any-thing about pride and dignity! I want to kill someone, and I'll gladly start with Betsy or Marty—either one. So take your advice on to the pearly gates and rearrange heaven. Don't be whispering into my ear. You probably knew Drew was cheat-ing, and you didn't bother to tell me, either!*

I didn't do it. Instead I sank down into the heavy silence. What on earth was I going to do? My salary at the school wouldn't pay rent and bills on a one-room shanty on the edge of the Washita River. Did I swallow my pride, wrap myself in a robe of dignity, and shut my eyes? After all, evidently he'd been cheating for years. Everyone in town knew and "blessed my little heart" on a daily basis.

If Aunt Gert could have been in that limo right then, she would have told me to stop blaming my cousins and blame the party responsible. She would have said for me to go take care of business so I could hold my head up. She would have kicked my hind end for wanting to kill the messengers when the per-son I should be thinking of murdering was my lying, cheating, two-timing husband.

Marty cleared her throat to get my attention. "What are you thinking about? You look like you've seen a ghost."

"Aunt Gert," I answered.

Betsy pulled out a compact and applied a fresh coat of bright red lipstick. "What're you going to do if you get that horrid house? We've already decided what we'd do with that eyesore."

I paused.

"Well?" Marty asked testily.

"She'll probably leave it to the church, and we'll all get some of her jewelry. The church can take care of the sale of the place and use the proceeds to buy new carpet or a new piano." Betsy stopped herself. "I can't believe I'm sayin' this. She's not even covered up in her grave yet."

Marty set her mouth in a firm line and narrowed her eyes.

"Stop acting like you're sorry she's gone. She was a pain. I hope she doesn't leave me her jewelry. That's the last thing I'd want. All that awful junk she bought at yard sales. I wouldn't be caught dead in any of it."

Betsy sighed loudly. "What we'll probably get is a bill for ten years' back taxes and a house full of termites to split three ways. We'll end up in debt because of our inheritance."

"Don't count your chickens before they're hatched," I snapped.

Marty gasped. "You sounded just like her. I swear, that was even her voice. Did her spirit stick around and crawl inside you?"

The glare I gave her apparently erased all doubt. She shivered and looked out the side window the rest of the way to the church. When the funeral-home limo parked, Betsy giggled in an attempt to ease the tension, but it came out as a high-pitched squeal. "Here we are! Dinner and then the will. Are we ready?"

They couldn't get out of the limo fast enough. I didn't know either of them could run in three-inch pumps, but run they did. If I'd tried to keep up with them, I'd have fallen flat on my face right there in the church parking lot.

I slowly walked toward the fellowship hall for the dinner. Charity was that teller with the tight little body and straight blond hair, I remembered. Short blond hair at that. I liked to wear my hair short and kinky, but Drew hated it, so I kept it long and fought with straightening irons and hair dryers every single day.

Go to the bank and hit him where it hurts, Gert's voice said.

We had a joint checking account and at least one joint savings account. If I wiped out those two accounts, I wouldn't have to end the marriage; he would.

Was I ready to live in the same town with him and watch each new plaything drive a new Thunderbird? Blast it all, I was driving a five-year-old Chevrolet Impala.

Some folks can't eat when they're stressed out. Not me. For me, food cures everything. Depression. Boredom. Anger.

Chocolate cake can take care of ingrown toenails, and potato chips can eradicate acne. I've told my fat cells things like that for so long, my body believes all of it.

The ladies of the church had prepared every Great-aunt Gert recipe they had in their files. There was potato salad. Barbecued chicken. Turkey, cooked long and slow with a stick of pure butter in the cavity to keep it tender. Corn bread dressing. Hot rolls with butter smeared on the tops when they're fresh out of the oven. Chocolate cake topped off with an inch of homemade fudge icing. Baked beans. Hash brown casserole.

Folks lined up for the buffet and talked about how Aunt Gert had made this for Thanksgiving or always brought that when someone died. It was as if they were trying to use her favorite foods to give her the strength to face the afterlife. Those poor folks didn't know that Gert didn't need any extra strength. She could take on Lucifer himself and come out the winner.

My plate needed sideboards by the time I finished loading it, but I just got *frumpier every year,* so it didn't matter how I comforted my aching heart. By the time I got through the line, the only place left for me to sit was right across from Marty and Betsy. There I was with the best plate of food since last Thanksgiving, and just looking at my cousins nauseated me. It wasn't fair that they'd shattered my whole world and taken my appetite too.

"Feelin' better?" Betsy asked.

I pushed my plate back. "I'm not hungry. I need some air. I'll see y'all at the reading of the will."

Marty whispered but not low enough. "What's gotten into her?"

Great-aunt Gert was barely in the grave, and the dirt was loose enough that she could still claw her way out of that pale pink coffin if I made a public scene, so I kept my mouth shut and didn't tell them *what had gotten into fat Trudy, bless her heart.* I meandered into the sanctuary and sat down in the pew where she'd always sat. Who cared if my mascara left black streaks, anyway? It was a funeral, and I was the only one in the sanctuary, so I gave way to tears and wiped at them with the back of one hand.

Suddenly I could feel her presence so powerfully that I hesitated before I turned to look to my left. Naturally, there wasn't a ghost sitting there in the oak pew beside me; it was more like a feeling, and it wasn't a happy one, either. It was the same feeling I'd had the time she caught me buying a frozen turkey for Thanksgiving. I had gotten the entire thirty-minute tirade about how a person should buy the live turkey directly from the farmer and dress it herself if she wanted a perfect Thanksgiving dinner. I had stared dumbly at her. Dress a turkey? I wouldn't know where to start with a live bird. I could sense that she had a lecture all prepared for me but I sure didn't want to hear it.

I blinked and allowed the feeling to pass. My tears dried up. I wanted to destroy something. I could have torn the pulpit down with my bare hands and then started on the oak pews. Forget about killing the messengers, Betsy and Marty. I'd deal with them later. Drew Williams was a different matter. He had vowed to be faithful right there in a church house in front of my parents, God, and even Great-aunt Gert. I could see him telling a lie to my parents and maybe even God, but he was a fool of the worst kind for lying to Aunt Gert. She'd get even, and she had a heck of a lot more power now that she was on the other side. He'd best be getting his affairs in order, because there was a good chance he'd be standing on a street corner with an empty Campbell's soup can begging for pennies before it was all said and done.

Was Miss Charity keeping him company on his business trip, or was she at the bank that day? I was definitely going to wipe out those two accounts. Wouldn't it be a hoot if she waited on me? She'd do just fine for a taste of my anger until Drew got home.

"Excuse me. Are you all right?" a masculine voice said right at my elbow.

My cheeks burned scarlet, and I hoped none of my thoughts had been whispered aloud.

The voice was deep and faintly familiar. I jerked my head up to look into Billy Lee Tucker's crystal blue eyes.

"I'm fine," I said.

"Well, I was sitting back there thinking about Gert when

you came in, and I just wondered if you were all right. It looked like you were crying," he said.

Billy Lee Tucker was a nerd with a capital *N* back when we were in school, and afterward he became Tishomingo's oddball. We had all started school together—Billy Lee always wearing his overalls and thick glasses. My friends and I largely ignored him, and he quietly found a corner to be alone, usually with a book in his hands.

He didn't grow out of it. He just got taller, and his glasses got thicker. The other boys wore tight jeans, and he continued to wear bibbed overalls—always clean and starched, right along with his chambray shirts. He didn't play football, so that was another strike against him in Tishomingo, Oklahoma. He didn't play basketball. Strike three. He didn't drink or smoke or chase around town on Saturday night in a pickup truck. Strikes four, five, and six.

His voice was a whisper of respect. "Mind if I join you?"

I didn't answer, but he sat down in the corner of the pew. "It just don't seem right. Everyone is in there eating and laughing. How can they act so happy, like it's a normal day?"

Billy Lee hadn't changed all that much. His angular face had a few wrinkles, but he was my age, and wrinkles come along at about that time. He was still thin, but the thing that almost took my mind off Drew was the suit he wore. If it wasn't Armani, I would eat my hat—tulle, fake black rose, and all.

"What way do you think it should be?" I asked.

"Gert was a lady. They should be sitting quietly and thinking about her and the way she brought happiness into the world."

Gert, a lady? What rock had he been hiding under all these years? Poor Billy Lee was several bricks short of a wagonload, bless his heart. And Gert bringing happiness into the world? Was the man crazy? She had brought lots of things into the world. Opinions. Bossiness. Bitterness. But happiness?

"They should be in here with us, not out there carrying on like they're glad she's gone," he said.

Maybe he didn't have *any* bricks in his wagon. They *were* glad she was gone.

"She was the wisest woman I knew and the best neighbor a man could ask for." Billy Lee kept talking.

They say birds of a feather flock together. He and Gert were both slightly odd.

"I didn't realize you still lived in your grandparents' house." "Nice" wasn't difficult for me. Conflict was, and I was wondering how to get out of the sanctuary without being rude.

He shrugged. "I was born in that house and have lived there my whole life."

"I see. Then you knew Gert very well?"

"Of course. She was my next-door neighbor and my best friend."

Even though I'd had my head in the sand and my big bubble butt stuck up in the sky, I knew what had happened to almost every kid in my graduating class all those years ago—where they lived, where they worked, how many kids they had or if they had divorced, how many had had affairs and how many times—most everything Marty and Betsy knew. Or I thought I had until that morning. Evidently I didn't know Drew Williams at all. Or Billy Lee Tucker.

My husband's name on the edge of my conscience jerked me right back into the present. I absolutely hated conflict. How would I ever psych myself up enough to confront him?

"I guess I should go on back into the dinner," I said.

"I'm staying right here."

"Trudy? You in here?" Betsy whispered loudly.

"I'm right here."

What would Betsy tell Marty about poor, pitiful Trudy sitting with Billy Lee Tucker in a semidark, quiet church? I didn't need to wait to take action. There was a pulpit in front of me and a congregation in the fellowship hall. Maybe I'd call them all in and preach them a sermon on two-timin' husbands.

She talked too fast and too loud as she walked toward the pew. "We are gathering in the children's Sunday school room for the reading of the will. The lawyer is some fancy-pants out of Dallas. Don't know why Gert couldn't use Drew for her business."

"Guess she knew too much about him," I sniped.

"Hello, Betsy," Billy said.

"Do I know you?"

"Probably not. I'm Gert's next-door neighbor."

"Oh, I thought she lived next door to Billy Lee Tucker."

"That's right."

"Well, I'll be danged. Didn't recognize you with a suit on, Billy Lee. Sorry about that. It's time for the judgment, Trudy. Have you been prayin' that she doesn't leave you that eyesore of a house? If I hadn't been starvin', I would have joined you, and I haven't prayed in years." Betsy was trying to be amusing.

"I was not."

Betsy shot me a mean look. "You have been horrid all day long. You are acting just like Gert."

Anger replaced the sadness in Billy Lee's blue eyes.

I looked up at Betsy, standing there with her hands on her hips in defiance, and said, "You're right. I have been praying, and I really don't see a change coming anytime soon. Let's go hear the will. Billy, would you like to join us?"

"I would love to."

Betsy shot me another hateful look. "Why would he want to be there?"

"Who knows? Maybe she left her house to him, and he gets to decide whether to burn it down or not."

"I hope she left it to you, Trudy. I hope you get all hot and sweaty cleaning out that mess," Betsy said. "You've really been horrible today."

"And just think, my dear cousin. Today is the first day of the rest of my life, and I may never change." I led the way out of the sanctuary and into the room where the lawyer and Marty waited.

Chapter Two

This is ridiculous," Marty said.

Betsy folded her arms over her chest and snarled at the sight of the tiny chairs and tables. Billy Lee pulled one out and sat down, his knees drawn up practically to his chin.

"Let's go into the sanctuary or the adult Sunday school room," Betsy said.

The lawyer ignored her, opened his briefcase, and took out a single sheet of paper. "I am Steven McRae. Gertrude asked that her last will and testament be read in this room. It won't take long to take care of the business."

He picked up the single piece of paper and adjusted his reading glasses. My stomach growled loudly. Marty stared at me. Betsy actually giggled. It wasn't fair to be hungry and not be able to swallow a bread crumb. Drew might have to pay for that as well as his philandering.

"Will you get on with it? I want a slice of that sour-cream pound cake before it's all gone," Marty said impatiently.

"It won't take long," the lawyer repeated. Then he began reading aloud. *"Hello, you three girls. This is my letter to you, and if Steven is reading it, then I'm dead. It'll be over soon, and you can all go home, and two of you can rejoice that you don't have to deal with my house and all its contents."*

Billy Lee chuckled for the first time all day.

Marty shot him and me both one of her famous "drop dead" looks.

I fired one right back at her and eased down gently into a

kiddy-sized chair and hoped it didn't fold with me. Surprisingly enough, it was sturdier than it looked.

Steven McRae went on. *"First of all, I chose this room because it's where I taught Sunday school for the past sixty years. Not that it makes a bit of difference, but even as I write this, I can hear Marty whining and Betsy refusing to sit in one of the little chairs.*

"You've all three been named after me, so I couldn't decide to leave my belongings simply to the one who had my name. I dislike all three of you, but I have to be honest and say that I dislike Trudy the least. At least she doesn't hide from me in the grocery store, so I'm leaving it all to her. Lock, stock, and barrel. Makes it right simple. If she's of a mind to give you other two a piece of my jewelry or a keepsake, then she can do it with my blessings. If not, then so be it. Go home and pout. I really don't care.

"And it is signed, notarized, and witnessed, so it is legal," Steven McRae concluded. "Mrs. Williams, this file contains your copy of her will and all her financial records. If you have any questions, she has paid my firm a retaining fee for the next thirty days to render any help you need, so feel free to call."

"Thank God. Let's go home, Betsy," Marty said.

Betsy shot me another hateful look. "Good luck."

"You are welcome to have anything you want." The whole time I was making the offer, I was wondering if Aunt Gert still kept arsenic under the kitchen sink to kill field rats.

"I wouldn't be caught taking out the garbage in any of that dime-store jewelry," Marty said.

"I don't want a single thing. You need me to sign anything to make that legal?" Betsy said.

Mr. McRae headed toward the door. "No, that's between you and Mrs. Williams."

"Then, Trudy, get this straight. We don't want anything, but by the same token we don't want you to be callin' on us to help clean out that junky place," Betsy said.

They were hurrying to the door when I said, "I won't ask

either of you for help. You've done enough already. And thank you, Mr. McRae."

Billy Lee had a big grin on his face, and his eyes twinkled. Why was he so amused now? Minutes before, he had been bewailing the fact that there was too much merriment going on in the fellowship hall, suggesting that everyone in Johnston County should be tearing at their hair and gathering ashes to put on their sackcloth clothing because Aunt Gert had died.

"So what are you going to do with the old place?" Billy asked.

I made the decision. "I'm going to live there."

I now owned a piece of property in Tishomingo, Oklahoma, lock, stock, and barrel. A two-story house with peeling paint, a sagging front porch, no air-conditioning, and an odd next-door neighbor.

His face registered pure shock. "Is Drew moving in with you?"

"No, he is not. But I suppose I'll be seeing you, since we'll be neighbors."

"Probably so." He grinned.

I walked through the fellowship hall, ignored Betsy when she called out my name, and continued right out the door without a backward glance. She didn't follow, but I hurried to my car in case she changed her mind. Twenty years of marriage had just burned to the ground. Sadness, weeping, anger, and pain were all rolled into one big unhealthy ball of raw nerves.

I could stay with Drew. That was an option and the easiest one. After all, it wasn't a new thing he'd done. But I couldn't! My pride was already in ashes. Staying would push my dignity right down there among them.

I drove slowly because there were little red dots flashing in front of my eyes. I didn't know if severe anger could produce a heart attack or a stroke, and there were things I had to do before I dropped dead. I pulled up in the yard and stared at the sprawling ranch-style house. It had been my home for more than twenty years, and I'd raised Crystal there. How could I entertain notions of leaving it?

I got out of the Impala, opened the front door of the house, and headed down the hallway to the master suite. I opened my closet and pulled the biggest suitcase I owned from the top shelf, then stood there in front of the rack of clothing while tears dripped from my cheeks onto the lapels of my black jacket.

What did I take, and what did I leave behind? I couldn't decide, but I was hungry, so I went to the kitchen, made myself a banana and strawberry smoothie, and hit the message button on the phone. Betsy wanted to know why I'd been so rude at the dinner. Marty said that she should come over to my house and kick my butt for being so hateful at a funeral. Drew called to say he'd be staying another day on his trip.

I took one sip of the smoothie, and it tasted horrible. I set it on the counter and peeled out of my skirt right there in the kitchen, leaving it in a pile on the floor. Just that meager act of rebellion gave me courage to keep going.

Next the ruined panty hose came off. I removed my wide gold wedding band, tied it to the leg with the big hole, and carried it back to the bedroom. I stood on the bed and looped the hose around a blade on the ceiling fan. I hoped Drew would flip on the light switch and the thing would knock him upside the head. I took off my jacket and threw it onto the floor and slung my hat against the far wall. When Drew came home, he could find the first mess in his house since we'd married. Good little wives kept a nice, clean home for their husbands. They kept his shirts ironed perfectly. They had his dinner on the table.

Apparently good little husbands cheated, and everyone in Tishomingo knew about it. Except his wife. Okay, so a few times I'd wondered about a phone call or when Drew worked late, but didn't all women?

Thinking about all those shirts I'd ironed and he'd worn while he flirted with other women infuriated me. I went through his closet like a wild woman, jerking them all off the hangers, wadding them up into tight little balls, and throwing them at the walls. Then I stripped the closet of his suits and slung them down the hall. After that I threw myself down onto the bed and watched my wedding ring make lazy circles around and around.

I'd take nothing out of the house. There was precious little of me in the place, anyway. I looked at the clock: one thirty. Could it really have only been three hours ago that I was wiggling around in a pew? If I could go back and live in blissful ignorance, would I? No, I would not! I should have been told years ago, and my cousins should have been the ones to tell me.

I opened the closet doors again. Wouldn't it be a hoot if I showed up in public in overalls? I didn't own overalls, but I could improvise. I chose a pair of faded denim Capri pants I wore to work in the flower beds, and a bright yellow shirt with a hole in one sleeve and a spaghetti stain right on the front. I picked out green rubber flip-flops and tied my hair back with a red and white University of Oklahoma bandanna. I was tempted to draw freckles across my nose with an eyebrow pencil and tie my hair up in pigtails but figured someone might call in the boys in the white jackets to carry me off to a mental institution if I went that far. I checked my reflection in the mirror and was content with the effect. Between my showing up in town looking like a bag lady and his losing enough money to buy more fancy cars for his bimbos, Drew should come close to having full-fledged cardiac arrest. I hoped he didn't die instantly but was fully awake when they socked those electric paddles onto his chest.

I picked up my purse, walked out the front door, and took a long look at all I was leaving behind. Then I slammed the door hard enough to rattle the windowpanes and didn't even look back. In ten minutes I was at the bank, standing in Charity's teller line. She was a pretty little thing. Not even old enough to get into a bar without an ID. Blond hair cut in one of those multilayered styles that was shorter in the back and framed her delicate face. Neither cellulite nor gravity had attacked her body, and every inch looked firm and taut. Did she iron shirts and make two meals a day? She'd better learn if she didn't, because Drew Williams didn't pay for a maid or a cook.

"And what can I do for you today?" she asked when I reached her.

"Would you please check the total amount in my family's savings account?" I was proud of myself for not grabbing a handful of that blond hair and jerking her through the opening in the teller station. It wouldn't be difficult to send her sailing through the plate-glass front window like a giant Frisbee.

"Your account number, please."

I told her, and she poked a few buttons, then sucked air for a few seconds before she looked up at me again.

"Mrs. Drew Williams? Do you have identification?"

I flipped open my wallet and presented my bank card. "Right here. How much is in that account?"

"Fifty thousand, four dollars, and twelve cents," she said.

"I'll be withdrawing all but the twelve cents right now."

"But, but . . . oh, dear. I'll have to make a phone call." She reached for the phone.

I slapped my hand onto hers and looked her right in the eye. "I want a cashier's check for fifty thousand, four dollars. And then you'll see what's in my joint checking account. I want to withdraw all of it except thirteen cents. Do you understand me, Charity?"

"I think you'd better talk to the bank president. I can't authorize such a large withdrawal."

I yelled at the teller all the way at the other end of the row. "Hey, Mindy, go get Horace, and bring him up here. I want to take money out of my accounts, and Charity can't take care of my business."

Mindy nodded toward Charity. "Give her what she wants. That's Trudy Williams. She and her husband are among our best customers."

Charity gasped as if she'd been tossed over the side of the Washita River bridge in nothing but her sexy little thong underpants and concrete shoes. It was ten minutes before two, and all bank business was concluded promptly at two o'clock. I'd made sure that my transactions would go into that day's business and she couldn't call Drew to warn him until the deed was already done.

"Mindy, tell her to hurry up. I want these transactions done before the two o'clock business goes in," I said.

"Get a move on it, Charity," she said.

Charity handed me two checks just as the clock ticked off the two o'clock deadline.

"Thank you for your help. Now you can call Drew on his cell. Tell him he's a lucky man. I only wiped out what I could. The two bits I left are for you. Seems fittin', don't it?"

The ringtone on my cell phone let me know Drew was calling when I crawled into the car. Miss Two-bit Charity hadn't wasted much time. The cat was out of the bag now, and there was no turning back. If I regretted my hasty decision in ten years and found myself living in a tar-paper shanty on the Washita River, my newly found hot temper would be to blame. I tossed the phone out the window.

The bank president at the other bank in Tishomingo met me in the foyer and ushered me into his office. "Trudy Williams, I was hoping you'd come here after the funeral."

He was new in town, and his instant warmth scared the bejesus out of me. What if Drew had called him with instructions to keep me there until the mental institution could send a helicopter to take me to a padded cell in Norman?

He motioned toward one of the leather chairs. "Please have a seat, Mrs. Williams."

I didn't want to even think about the name *Williams,* much less be called it. "Trudy. My name is Trudy."

"Thank you. I'm hoping you will want to keep your business here. Gertrude was one of our bank's biggest customers, but I know you and your husband keep your affairs at the other bank in town."

I laid the cashier's checks on his desk. "I'm going to keep everything right here from now on. I've got a couple of checks, and I'd like to open a checking account and savings account in this bank."

He smiled. "That is wonderful. Just wonderful. I've prepared a list of Gert's assets just like she told me to do."

I wondered why he'd be so eager to keep Aunt Gert's miserly amounts of money in his bank. She'd barely made it on her Social Security income. Worn secondhand clothes and jewelry.

Used coupons at the grocery store. Wouldn't even put in a window unit for air-conditioning.

"I'm not here to move anything," I assured him.

The papers he shoved across the desk were inside a manila folder. I opened it carefully, expecting to find a hundred dollars in her checking account and half that in savings. What I saw almost stopped my heart. What I'd brought from the other bank was a mere drop in the ocean compared to the figures before me.

"As you can see, your Aunt Gertrude was a very wealthy woman. Her folks had money, invested well, and left it all to her. She and her lawyer came in here a few months ago with instructions that I was to hand you this report after she passed and the will was read," he said.

I was in total shock. I pinched my leg. It hurt like the devil, so I wasn't dreaming.

"The interest off the money should provide a healthy monthly income. Will you be selling the house on Broadway Street?"

I was surprised I could even utter a sensible word. "No, I'm moving into it tonight."

"Good. I'm sure that would make her very happy. She hoped that you might . . . let's see if I can remember her exact words . . . come to your senses and face what was right in front of your eyes and do something about it—though I'm not sure what she was talking about."

"I am."

"Good. Then I've passed on a message from her. You'll be drawing on the money to repair the old place?"

"Yes, I will. And thank you for your help today. You'll take care of these two deposits?"

"Yes, I surely will. I'll take care of them personally. How do you want to handle this?"

"I can write checks on Aunt Gert's account starting right now?"

"Trudy, you could have written checks on her accounts six months ago, when she found out about the cancer. Everything was taken care of then."

"Then put them both into a savings account."

He pulled paperwork from a drawer in his desk and showed me where to sign. Then he took the checks to a teller window and deposited them into the new account. He brought back a deposit slip and handed it to me along with his business card. "Thank you again for keeping your business here. We will do anything we can to be of assistance to you. Feel free to call anytime."

I nodded toward the folder as I stood up. "Thank you. I can take this with me?"

"Yes, ma'am. Gert came in here on the first day of every month for a folder like that. You'll probably find them all stashed somewhere in her house, filed neatly and labeled by the year. She was a stickler for keeping good records."

I shook his hand. "That sounds like Aunt Gert. Thanks again."

I must have sat there sweltering in the broiling heat with the car windows rolled up for ten minutes before I turned the key to start the engine as well as the air conditioner. I actually shivered when the icy cold air rushed over all the sweat on my arms and face.

It was only five minutes from the bank to Aunt Gert's house on Broadway Street. Her parents had built the two-story house somewhere around 1910, right after statehood, and back then it was one of the more prosperous homes in the area. But in the sixties things started falling apart, and she ignored them. For fifty years very little maintenance had been done on the place, and it showed.

I parked in the gravel driveway and stared blankly at my new home. For a minute I almost wished the helicopter bearing those boys in the white jackets would appear on Gert's overgrown lawn. A padded cell, whether in a state-run facility or a private one, was looking better by the minute. I left all the paperwork I'd been given that day lying on the car seat and opened the door to a blast of summer heat. If the end of May felt like this, then what would July and August be like with no air-conditioning?

I marched stoically across the unkempt yard and had barely

reached the porch when everything began to look like the special effects in a movie running in slow motion. I'd fainted one time in my life, back when I was first pregnant with my daughter, so I recognized the symptoms. I eased down onto the porch steps and put my head between my legs. It was midafternoon, and I hadn't eaten since breakfast. I'd gotten rid of the coffee, soft drinks, and my ignorance in the ladies' room at the church.

When I raised my head, Billy Lee Tucker was sitting beside me.

"Still moving in here sometime in the future?"

"I'm moving in right now, and I hope she's got a can of soup in the pantry, because I'm hungry."

"When are the movers bringing your things?"

"No movers. I've got a purse and a bunch of papers in the car, and that's it."

He raised an eyebrow and held out his hand. "Here's keys to the place and her car. I was going to bring them out to your house this evening, but I saw you drive up, so I came on over. You all right? You're as white as a ghost."

"I'm just hungry. Thanks for bringing over the keys. This house is a mess, isn't it?"

"It is right now, but it won't be for long. I've been hired to redo the house from top to bottom if you decide to move into it, so I suppose we'll be working together real soon," he said.

"Who hired you?" I asked.

"Gert. Gave me an envelope I was to open only after she died. She said I was to remodel this place if you moved in. If you didn't, then I could count on getting what was inside as my inheritance for being her favorite neighbor."

"Well, thank you." I found enough strength to get up and cross the front porch. I had to keep my body and soul together long enough to spit in Drew's eye and get even with my two cousins.

He followed me to the door. "Foundation is good. House was built right in the beginning. It's got the potential to be a real beauty."

Inviting him inside would be stretching my depleted supply of manners entirely too far. Being nice had netted me misery beyond description. Besides, I'd already been nice enough to leave my cousins alive that day. Plus the prissy little bimbo down at the bank still had all her blond hair and not a mark on her face. That was enough "nice" for one day.

I stopped at the door. "I'm glad to hear it, Billy Lee. Come around in a few days, when I've had a chance to think, and we'll talk about it."

He nodded. "My phone number is on the refrigerator. Let me know when you want me to go to work. I'll outline what I've got in mind for the exterior. I think we can make this look like it did in its heyday. I'm glad to have you for a neighbor, Trudy."

He whistled as he left. I wanted to slap him. No one should be happy when my world was in shambles.

Not one thing had changed since the last time I'd walked through the front door of Aunt Gert's house. Every square inch of the place was covered in mismatched furniture and cheap collectibles. Every table sported a lamp sitting on a crocheted doily. None of the lamps were plugged in, because there were very few electrical outlets. Ceramic ducks, cows, and lots and lots of birds surrounded the lamps. Chairs and sofas had mismatched hand towels pinned to the backs and washcloths on the arms.

I walked right past it all without even a shudder. Whoever said that a person, especially an overweight one, could live for weeks with no food had rocks for brains. I was about to join the ranks of the recently departed if I didn't find something to put into my mouth. When I reached the kitchen, I was amazed at the contents of the refrigerator. Milk, still inside the expiration date. Lunch meat. A whole loaf of bread. Lettuce. Tomatoes. Cheese. Real mayonnaise that was even my favorite brand.

I made a sandwich, devoured it, and made another. I finished the second one and had a tall glass of milk before I went out to the car to get the paperwork. I carried it to the house and wondered why Aunt Gert had let things go to rot and ruin with all that money in the bank.

I climbed the stairs and laid the papers on the bed in the

guest room where I planned to sleep that night. The second floor had three bedrooms and a bathroom. When the house had been built, the bathroom was down the back path toward the rear of the lot. According to Momma, the family modernized the place after her grandfather died. The heat was oppressive, so I opened a window and begged for a breeze, but there wasn't a bit of wind between me and the Gulf of Mexico.

The sweat pouring off me had as much to do with nerves as the weather. A cool shower might keep me from melting into a puddle of lard on the floor. I opened the bathroom door and almost cried. The wall-hung sink was listing to the front. The toilet was crazed and cracked. The tub was as old as God and pitted. There was no shower above it. This would definitely be the first place I started when Billy Lee and I sat down to talk about remodeling.

When I finished bathing, I wrapped a towel around my body and wandered through the other rooms. Aunt Gert's bedroom was cluttered with more stuff than the rest of the house. Knick-knacks and old pictures. The guest room where I'd left my paperwork was clean but smelled unused and slightly musty. Then there was Uncle Lonnie's room, with a padlock on the outside.

I didn't remember there being a lock on the door the last time I was in the house, but then, that was probably back when Lonnie was still alive. Why had Aunt Gert closed up the room, and how long had it been locked?

Aunt Gert was a few inches taller than I, but her elastic-waist jeans and shirts fit me fairly well. The nightgowns in her dresser drawer looked inviting, but it wasn't time for bed. I had a lot of reading to do to understand what all Aunt Gert had left behind.

I dressed in a pair of Aunt Gert's pants and a faded T-shirt, made a pot of coffee, and sat down at the kitchen table to read through all of the paperwork. But the lock on that bedroom door kept bugging me. Why had she put a padlock on the outside of a bedroom? What was in there that she needed to protect?

I sighed and tried to mentally rehearse what I would say to

Drew when he got back to town, but my curiosity got the better of me. I went to the foyer table where I'd tossed the keys Billy Lee had given me. Sure enough, there was a padlock key on the ring.

No chilly air brushed past me as Lonnie's ghost left the room when I opened the door. Nothing jumped out from under the bed to scare me. The hair didn't stand up on my arms, nor did any scary music play in my head. It looked exactly as I remembered from back when I was a little girl. Which was completely out of place. All the other rooms in the house were filled with junk, but this room was stark and plain with a nightstand on each side of a full-sized bed. No knickknacks anywhere. A calendar dated the year he had died back in the nineties was the only thing hanging on the walls. Plain white curtains framed the single window overlooking the front yard. A rocking chair with a worn red plaid pad in the seat stood nearby. Uncle Lonnie's polyester pants and jackets still hung in the closet along with cotton shirts, his wing-tipped shoes and bedroom slippers lined up neatly on the floor.

The room was spotless, not even one lonesome old dust bunny hiding under the bed. Why would Aunt Gert clean the room on a regular basis and then put a padlock on the outside? But just in case there was a ghost in there that only came out at a certain time, I snapped the padlock shut when I left. By the time I got back downstairs, the phone was ringing.

"What the devil are you doing?" Marty asked when I answered it.

"Taking a look at my inheritance," I answered.

"I don't mean that. Why were you in town looking worse than the garbage collector?"

"That is none of your business."

"Drew is going to kill you. I heard you went into the bank and made a big withdrawal from his accounts and then went to the other bank to deposit it. Is that true?"

I stretched the phone cord, but it wouldn't reach to the kitchen, so I couldn't see if there was any rat poison under the sink. "Doesn't the town have anything else to talk about today? They could be discussing dear old Aunt Gert."

"It's your funeral they're going to be discussing when Drew comes home."

"I'm sure you and Betsy will console him after he kills me. Maybe you can make him some hot chicken salad like Lori Lou did."

Dead silence on the other end of the phone line.

"Are you still there, Marty?"

"What are you talking about?"

"He might not be too choosy, especially if the affair with Charity goes south. And it will. She'll get tired of him. Maybe you can make him some hot chicken salad, and he'll buy you a new car. I think you have to be about Crystal's age to get a Thunderbird, but then, I might be wrong."

Nothing felt better than listening to her gasp when I hung up the phone.

Chapter Three

"They've been talking about you," Momma whispered when I stopped at the nursing home on my way to Durant the next morning. I'd slept poorly. Different house. Different bed. I needed it to be a good day with Momma.

"Who has?" I asked.

"You know who. They said you moved into Gert's house. She's dead, you know. She won't be there to keep you company."

"I know, Momma. I went to her funeral yesterday, and she left me the house. I'm going to remodel it and live there."

We were sitting in the little garden behind the nursing home. A dove flew up, alit on the low branches of a tree, and cocked its gray head toward us. The thermometer on the side of the porch post that morning had read eighty-five degrees, and the weatherman had said it would be in the high nineties before the day was finished. A soft, warm breeze flowed through the garden, and Momma lifted her head to catch the sun's rays. She still had a lovely complexion, and the home's beautician kept her hair dyed the same shade of dark brown that she'd had when she was a young woman. Her eyes were the same shade as Crystal's, that lovely summer sky blue. She was a perfect size four before she married Daddy, and she'd maintained that size all her life.

When she brought her chin down, her eyes had gone blank. Past, present, and future would be mixed up together as if she'd tossed them into a blender and pushed the puree button. She whispered, "Gert should have known better than to marry that Lonnie. Forty is too old to be a bride, and him ten years younger. He wants her money, but she's a smart girl, that Gert is."

"Nice warm morning," Lessie said as she sat down in a chair next to Momma. Her back was as straight as it had been when she was fifteen, and her hair boasted very little gray.

Momma smiled at Lessie. "It is, isn't it? Did you know that Gert died and left Trudy her house? Trudy was married at one time, but her husband died. She keeps a lock on his bedroom door. I never figured out why, but she does."

Lessie sat down beside Momma and winked at me. "Yes, I was sorry that Gert died. Marty also told us you've moved into her house."

"Marty was here?" I was amazed.

Lessie nodded. "Last night. Came to see about a job. This place needs an activities director. Someone to fix up a party once a month and to help us old codgers paint flowerpots. Your mother and I were sitting in the lounge watching a rerun of *The Golden Girls*. That one where Blanche's daddy dies and she gets crossways with her sister and won't go to the funeral. Marty stopped and visited for a minute on her way out. I think she was too late. They hired someone yesterday morning."

Lessie's mind was still good, but she had diabetes, congestive heart failure, arthritis, and a whole host of other physical problems. Momma's little body was in perfect shape, but Alzheimer's had robbed her of her mind.

"Blanche was sorry she didn't go to Big Daddy's funeral. I'm sorry I didn't go to Drew's funeral, but I never liked that man. I might have spit in his dead face," Momma said seriously.

"Momma, you always loved Drew," I reminded her.

"I'm a good pretender." She shot me a puzzled look. "Who are you? I'm waiting for Trudy. She'll be home from school for lunch soon. I'm making her grilled cheese sandwiches and real fried potatoes." She turned to Lessie. "Are you the new maid? If you are, then be sure and clean the toilet better than you did last week."

Lessie took her arm. "Yes, ma'am, I am the new maid. You come on with me, and we'll go look at that toilet right now." She whispered to me, "I'll get her back to her room. Tomorrow might be a better day."

"I hope so," I said.

"Glad to hear you're going to live in Gert's house. There ain't no use in talkin' about the reason you made that decision. Just get on with your life. You're still young and pretty."

At ninety plus, Lessie would probably classify any almost-forty-year-old woman as young and pretty, but I appreciated the compliment.

I hit a button that opened the back door into the activities and physical therapy room, and we all three filed into the nursing home. Lessie and Momma slowly made their way across the room and down the hall to the right. I went on through the visitors' lounge and punched in the code to open the front door, only to find that the code had been changed. A nurse's aide came along and poked in the right numbers to let me out.

While she pushed the buttons, I checked my reflection in the door glass. I hardly recognized the woman looking back at me. She wore Aunt Gert's jeans rolled up at the hems and a T-shirt with a sequined butterfly across the chest. A few sequins had long since flown away in the Oklahoma wind, but several hanging threads gave testimony to the fact that they'd once sparkled there. Her long brown hair was tied back in a ponytail at the nape of her neck with a red silk scarf, and her green eyes looked tired. I rather liked the new, strange woman in the glass, even with the tired eyes, but it wasn't any wonder that Momma hadn't recognized me.

"Thank you," I told the aide.

She smiled. "You're welcome. Your mother is a sweetheart. I love her style."

"I just wish she had more good days."

"Even when she doesn't know any of us, she still looks like a fashion queen. You do well keeping her all dolled up," she said.

I could have hugged the woman. "Thank you for noticing. You have a nice day."

"You too," she said as the door closed between us.

When I opened the car, a blast of heat hit me in the face, blowing strands of hair to stick to my cheeks and forehead. It didn't take long to get the engine going, the air conditioner running full speed, and to decide that I was cutting my hair. The only reason I had kept it long was for Drew.

I drove through Milburn, Emit, and Nida, which was basically a church and a few scattered homes. Then it was on to Durant. The idea of stopping to talk to Crystal about her decision to get married on the sly did cross my mind, but I had a war to fight with her father, and I couldn't do battle on two fronts at once.

When I arrived at Walmart, there was no waiting line in the beauty shop. I waltzed in, hopped up into a chair, and pointed to a picture on the wall of a young girl with too much eye shadow and bright red lipstick. She wore black leather and looked like a rock star. "I want it all cut off like that."

The hairdresser flipped a plastic cape around my shoulders. "Are you sure?"

"Absolutely. Only don't leave so much on the sides. Cut it above my ears. I want to be able to wash it and go. I'm sick of straightening irons and blow-dryers."

"You have a lot of curl for that cut. It's going to kink up all over your head."

"And I'm going to love it. I wore it like that in high school."

She removed the red silk scarf and brushed out a tangled mess of long, frizzy curls. "Why did you let it grow long?"

"Because my husband liked long hair."

She giggled. "Fighting with him, are you?"

"No, but I'm going to be very soon."

I flinched when she gathered up my long hair and laid the scissors to it.

"Want to change your mind?"

"No. Cut it off."

In twenty minutes it was short and kinky. My head felt lighter than it had in years. Too bad my heart was still a heavy chunk of rock in my chest. I paid the woman and added a tip, found a shopping cart, and was headed toward the clothing section when I heard my daughter's voice.

"Mother, what have you done?" Crystal gasped.

"I had my hair cut. What do you think?"

"Daddy is going to have a fit. He hates your hair short. That's why your senior picture isn't hanging in the hallway. I'm not coming home to visit you two until you grow it out again."

The battle had arrived whether I was ready or not. It was either fight or slink into a corner, and I was tired of that business. "Too bad, then. I'm keeping it this way forever."

Her nose wrinkled up in disgust. "And your clothes? You look like Aunt Gert."

"That's because these used to belong to Aunt Gert. I missed you at the funeral yesterday."

My daughter wore a cute little pair of jean shorts, a Vegas T-shirt, and fancy sandals, and she carried a purse that likely would have cost half of my teacher's-aide paycheck. Her light brown hair had been recently cut and highlighted with blond streaks.

"Was that yesterday? I wouldn't have come even if I'd remembered. I hate funerals. But why are you wearing her clothes?"

"You got time to have lunch with me? I'll tell you all about it." When opportunity knocks, you don't leave it standing on the doorstep. You invite it in and feed it chocolate cake. That's what Aunt Gert used to say.

She blushed. "No, I've got . . . Actually, I'm just picking up some shampoo and conditioner and . . ."

"Oh, don't get your panties into a wad. I know you and Jonah went to Vegas and got married. I don't like it, but evidently my opinion doesn't matter."

She tilted her head up and looked down her aristocratic nose at me. "I can't have this conversation now."

"Me, either. I've got underwear to buy. I'm at Aunt Gert's— no, I can't say that anymore. I'm at *my* house, but it's still listed under Gertrude Martin in the phone book. Call that number if you need me." I pushed my cart around her.

She grabbed the cart and glared at me, those pretty blue eyes flashing enough anger to light up the whole Walmart store. "You're going to tell me right now what is going on!"

I gave the cart a jerk. "I'm not having this conversation here. If you want to talk, you can come to lunch with me. Otherwise, run along and buy your shampoo. We'll discuss it another day."

I left her digging in her purse for her cell phone, no doubt to call her father, but right then she could have been tattling to Saint Peter and I wouldn't have cared. On my way to buy underwear, I passed the window air conditioners, hauled the cheapest one down off the shelf, and set it into my cart. I'd be cool in the guest bedroom at night until central heat and air-conditioning was installed. Billy Lee would most likely tell me the whole place had to be rewired before we could think about something that luxurious.

Cato's dress shop was located next to Walmart. A few minutes in there netted me a couple of dresses to wear to church: a bright red one with a parrot embroidered on the hem and across the back of the jacket, and a more subdued canary yellow with a Hawaiian-print, short-sleeved jacket. No more black silk for this girl. Lessie had said I was young and pretty. Besides, look what expensive black suits had gotten me: a husband who cheated with girls who wore bright colors.

I bought red leather slides with kitten heels and a pair of cute little flats in hot pink that matched a flower in the Hawaiian print. I wasn't slinking into church the next day. The old Trudy had died in the church bathroom. She was now a new woman who didn't need to be "poor" anymore or have her heart blessed, either. That's when I saw a beautiful hot pink hat. It would provide the crowning glory to my new outfit, so I bought it too.

I wouldn't have noticed the rack of Capri-length bibbed overalls if there hadn't been a line at the checkout counter. I found two pair in size sixteen and grabbed a couple of sleeveless tank tops to wear under them, one orange and one turquoise.

It was two o'clock when I got back to Tishomingo, and I hadn't had anything to eat since breakfast. I whipped into the SONIC and ordered a foot-long hot dog with chili and cheese and a side order of Tater Tots. I rolled down the windows and ate in the car rather than taking the food home.

When I pulled up under the carport in the backyard, Billy Lee was coming through the opening in the hedge with a notebook in his hands. I took a long look at the house and seriously contemplated buying a box of dynamite, blasting the place, and letting it rain pieces all over town. Then I'd cash in all those assets Aunt Gert had left me and disappear off to a beach with white sand and no cellular service. That way I wouldn't have to have a conversation with Drew, Crystal, my cousins, or Billy Lee.

"Hey." Billy Lee's pale blue eyes lit up.

He stopped beside the car and flipped open his notebook on the hood. "So, you ready to see my ideas?"

"I guess I am." I looked at the air conditioner in the backseat and longed for a cool breeze. The wind blows constantly in Oklahoma until the first day of June, and then a body can't buy, borrow, or steal a gust of it until after Labor Day. That's because it's so hot in June, July, and August that any amount of wind would cook the flesh off our bones. Daddy used to say that even the lizards carried canteens over one shoulder and a machine gun over the other during the summer months. The machine gun was to take out anyone who looked sideways at the water jugs.

Billy Lee nodded toward the house as he pointed to his drawings. "The way I see it is that we have someone come in first and redo all the windows. They're older than Methuselah, and we need central heat and air. All that bought air will escape out those old wooden sashes. I've got some estimates here on new ones that open to the inside for easy cleaning and will still keep the look of the house."

He already had that "we" business down pat. I forgot all about dynamite when he flipped a few pages and showed me a before-and-after picture in a brochure of a house where that kind of windows had been installed. He had my undivided attention after that.

"While the window people are here, the electricians can be rewiring the whole place and getting it ready for air-conditioning. I see you've got one of those little units in your backseat. Guess that's for your bedroom. You'll have to run an extension cord from the outlet attached to the light fixture in the ceiling, since there are no plugs on the walls in any of the upstairs rooms. Gert had one put in the kitchen so she could hook up a microwave. The rest of the house is wired only for lighting."

"Good grief!" I was glad I'd had my hair cut. I would have had to unplug the microwave every morning to plug in my hair straightener.

"If you'll trust me to get the ball rolling, I can probably get things started on Monday morning."

"Fine," I agreed.

With one word I had just put my trust in Billy Lee—after I'd vowed never to trust another man for anything.

"While they're working on that, I'll start rebuilding the front porch. It's a wonder Gert didn't fall through those rotten boards. And all the gingerbread around the eaves and dormers needs to be removed and stripped of all that nasty peeling paint and refinished. You'll need to decide what colors you want to use on the house and the trim while I get it ready to paint. Hopefully we'll get all that done by fall, and then we'll begin on the inside. That'll give you lots of time to clean it out. By the way, why are you living here without your husband?"

"I want the house a soft yellow and all the trim white like it was in the beginning. I want to take out the wall between the living room and dining room and make it airy and light. I want a new bathroom upstairs, so we will need a plumber, and I want a bathroom put in downstairs. Part of the back porch off the kitchen can be turned into a bathroom, can't it? And I'm divorcing my husband, Billy Lee."

"Sorry if I stepped on sore toes. You sure you want to move in here?"

"Very, very sure."

"Want me to carry that air conditioner upstairs and get it running for you?"

I could have kissed the man right between his pretty blue eyes. Billy Lee had simply accepted my decision and moved on. And everyone thought he was an odd duck!

He picked up the air conditioner box as if it was a feather pillow and started into the house. "Tomorrow is church. Shall we begin the work the next day?"

I carried my other bags and opened the door for him. "I'd like that."

He found a long brown extension cord in a kitchen drawer, laid it on top of the air conditioner box, carried both upstairs, and plugged the cord into an apparatus with a plug on each side that was screwed into the lightbulb socket. He weaved the cord around the end of the iron bedstead, under the throw rug on the hardwood floor, and over to the window. In minutes cool air blew into the room.

"Keep the door shut, and this room will cool down by bedtime. I've got a rack of ribs smoking for supper. Dinner at six?"

My expression must have been scary, odd, or plain crazy, because he threw up his hands in defense. "What's the matter? Did I say something wrong? Do you hate ribs? I used to bring Gert food all the time."

Evidently I'd taken Gert's place in the scheme of things. As the wife of a small-town lawyer I'd been at the top of the social ladder, but now I was on the same level as crazy old Aunt Gert. That deflated my ego as much as the news in the ladies' room had.

"No, Billy Lee, you didn't say anything wrong. I'd love to have ribs for supper. Thank you."

"Good. I'll go on home and check on them. They're in the smoker. I'll be here at six, then?"

I nodded.

He closed the door behind him.

I plopped down onto the bed and enjoyed the wonderful cold air flowing over my body. After a while, I flipped over onto my stomach. That's when I saw the old wooden jewelry box sitting on the nightstand. I rolled off the bed and picked it up. It was heavy enough that it could have been holding gold nuggets, and after my bank trip nothing would surprise me. I opened it carefully. It was brimful of gorgeous jewelry that I'd never seen Gert wear and that sure hadn't come from a dollar store.

I picked up a brooch shaped like a daisy with a long golden stem. The petals were white elongated opals, the center a lovely golden topaz of at least three carats. I flipped it over to find a date written on a tiny piece of masking tape attached to the back. June 3, 1958. That would have been a year after she'd married Uncle Lonnie. Why hadn't she ever worn this lovely piece?

A beautiful, heart-shaped pendant was the next thing I pulled out. The diamonds around its outer edge sparkled in the light. The single dangling diamond in the middle was a carat or maybe more. It was dated August 1959. Uncle Lonnie had died the year Drew and I married, and there was a piece for every year up until then.

Why had he given Gert one costly piece of jewelry a year, and why hadn't she worn any of them? They couldn't be anniversary presents, because they'd married in June of 1957, and not all the dates on the jewelry were in June. She'd told me at my wedding, which was also in June, that she'd married in the same month and that I was not to expect a happily-ever-after marriage just because I'd chosen that most traditional month to marry.

I scattered the jewelry on the bed all around me. The topaz and opal pin looked familiar; I'd seen one like it before, but where? I picked it up, and then it dawned on me. Daisy Black wore one pinned to the lapel of a black suit almost every Sunday. Why would Aunt Gert and Daisy have identical fancy brooches?

I untangled a pendant with a fine gold chain and looked at the diamond cross and remembered that Patsy Banner had had one like it. She had died a couple of years ago and had passed it down to her daughter, Loretta, who wore it all the time to remember her mother.

A square-cut emerald ring caught my attention. As I laid it back in the box, I noticed the corner of something sticking out from the felt bottom. It was a certificate for the diamond pendant from a famous jewelry store in Oklahoma City.

What a mystery! Either Uncle Lonnie Martin had purchased the necklace for Gert, and she'd been too mean-spirited to ever wear it, or she had bought the jewelry for herself and maybe kept it a secret from Lonnie. If the designer was still living, the jewelry store that sold it could probably tell me something about the pieces. Finding the jeweler took a little longer than typing the address into the laptop I'd left behind with all my other belongings, but the telephone operator finally located it for me.

The phone rang twice before a nice voice asked if she could be of assistance.

"Hello, this is Trudy Williams. I've just inherited several pieces of jewelry from my aunt, Gertrude Martin . . ."

"Just a minute, ma'am. You'll need to speak to my husband. Please hold on while I transfer you to his office."

A deep voice promptly answered. "Hello, Mrs. Williams. My name is Paul Fisher. I understand you have inherited a collection of jewelry from your aunt. I wasn't even aware that Gert had passed on. Please accept my condolences."

"You knew Gert?" I was amazed.

"Oh, yes. I only met her once, but we've talked several times on the phone. I've been trying to buy back those pieces ever since Lonnie died. It's the only complete set of my work. Name your price."

"Mr. Fisher, I know of at least two more pieces you designed right here in Tishomingo. Two different women each own a piece exactly like these," I said.

"Yes, they do. There are thirty-seven pieces in all, and I made two of each design. But Gert had the only complete set."

"Why did Gert have them all and these other women have one each?"

"Because Lonnie had two pieces done each time he came in. I didn't ask questions. I was here to design and sell jewelry."

"That rat!" I changed my mind about Gert.

"Could be. I didn't ask what he did with the two pieces when he walked out of here. I just knew that after Lonnie died, Gert came here toting a wooden box with all that jewelry and asked me what it was worth. I made her a generous offer, but she laughed at me. Every year I beg, and every year she tells me the same thing."

"Which is?"

"Verbatim?"

"That would be nice."

" 'I'll keep these until I die. The world is going to the devil in a handbasket. These will keep me and my family from starving.' So, are you selling?"

"Not today, but if I decide to, I won't sell to anyone else. You've got my word."

"If it's as good as Gert's word, then that's all I need. Call me when you get ready to give them up."

A cuckoo clock in the living room clicked six times, and Billy Lee knocked on the door at the same time I hung up the telephone. When I opened it, he was standing there with a container of food.

"Suppertime," he said.

"Have you eaten?"

Crimson flooded his cheeks. "No, me and Gert always ate together."

"Then bring it in. I've got sweet tea in the fridge."

"Gert and I ate in the kitchen on the bar. Is that all right with you?" He followed me through the living room and dining room and into the kitchen.

"How did Gert stand you? You're too nice to get along with her."

He squared his shoulders and set his jaw. "I'm not always nice. I speak my opinion. I just didn't want to offend you on your first day here."

"I'm not going to be nice all the time, and I don't want you to be. I'd rather have honest than nice. So we'll always speak our minds. Deal?" I stuck out my right hand.

"Deal." He set the food on the counter and shook.

He opened the plastic containers, and I popped ice out of

those old aluminum trays that have a handle on top, filled two glasses, and added tea. The aroma of barbecue and baked beans filled the kitchen, and my mouth began to water. He opened cabinet doors and removed two plates, took out silverware from a drawer, and pulled the paper-napkin holder over to the middle of the breakfast bar.

"Dig in," he said.

The ribs had just the right blend of smoke and sauce. The baked beans had been slow-simmered until they were thick, and the biscuits were light and fluffy.

"Tell me something," I said between bites.

"Long, slow cooking over a low flame."

"No, not about supper. This is better than a five-star restaurant's food, and you ought to run a barbecue joint. But that's not what I wanted to know. Do you know much about the relationship between Uncle Lonnie and Aunt Gert?"

He shook his head. "I was off at college when Lonnie died. I didn't know Gert really well until after that. She didn't talk much about him. Matter of fact, the only time we talked about Lonnie was a couple of years ago. I was helping her with some plumbing and noticed the padlock on that door up there."

"What did she say?"

"She said that what was in the past was best left there and that talking about it was like stirring a fresh cow pile with a wooden spoon. Didn't accomplish a thing, and only made the stink and the flies worse and the spoon useless for anything else. Then we came downstairs and had a beer and talked about the new president. His inauguration was on television."

"You remember exactly what you talked about?" I asked, amazed.

He shrugged. "Sure. I'd stepped on her toes pretty badly, so I remember it well. Gert was a fine old girl."

"What else is this old place going to tell me?"

He smiled, and his whole face lit up. "Whatever it is, I hope you like it."

The phone rang, so I dashed off to the foyer table where the ancient blue object was located.

I hoped it was Crystal, but the minute I picked up the receiver, Drew started yelling, "Have you gone as crazy as your mother, woman? I'll be home on Monday, and you'd better have a good excuse for what you've done. Why did you take all that money out of the bank?"

"I'm not having this conversation right now." I hung up on him.

The phone rang again immediately. I picked the receiver up. "I took the money out of the bank and buried it in the backyard under Aunt Gert's apricot tree. I left two bits in the accounts for your newest fling. I'm having supper with a friend, so leave me alone."

Drew was yelling and cussing as I hung up on him. I made a mental note to ask the phone company about getting caller ID when they came to add a jack to every room.

I returned to the kitchen and loaded another helping of barbecue onto my plate.

"Hey, I forgot to tell you this afternoon. I love your new haircut. It looks just like it did when we were in high school," Billy Lee said.

"Thank you." I smiled, and it felt dang good that he remembered.

"Was that Drew?"

"Yes."

"Want to talk about it?"

"No."

"Then we won't."

I'd never appreciated a person as much as I did Billy Lee right then.

Chapter Four

I'd never been claustrophobic in my life until I shut the bedroom door the second night. Every knickknack in the room seemed to stare at me with those never-closing eyes. Shelves were covered with everything from cats to elephants waiting for me to shut my eyes so they could come alive like in a sci-fi movie. Poorly painted ceramic ducks on the windowsills had cacti growing out of the holes in their backs. I imagined them jumping off the sills and throwing cactus needles at me like porcupines.

The cold breeze from the air conditioner caused the wooden thread spool attached to the end of the light cord to sway. Would the menagerie of glass-eyed critters blink and begin to breathe if I yanked on the cord? Why was I suddenly afraid to turn off the light?

A little introspection said it wasn't all that junk that bothered me but the fact that Drew was coming home in two days. We'd never fought. Not one time. I'd figured out early how to keep him happy and made a full-time job of it. The wind-up clock beside the bed sounded a tick-tock warning in singsong fashion: *Drew is coming home. You are dead. You will never out-argue a lawyer. He'll talk you into going back with him . . . yes, he will!*

I vowed that the next morning the animals and the clock were all going to the Dumpster or Goodwill. It was their last night to look at me with black-enameled eyes and evil little smirks on their faces or for the clock to tick out a message.

I was in charge of my future, and Drew wasn't going to win, lawyer or not.

I pulled the cord, but all the dark did was bring on acute insomnia. I tossed and turned and finally groped around for the cord and turned the lights back on. All the animals were exactly where they'd been, and Drew was still coming home. I went to the kitchen and had a cookie. That led to another cookie and a glass of milk. While I was pouring the milk, I dropped the jug and drenched the front of my nightgown. I cleaned up the mess, then went back upstairs to find another nightgown in Aunt Gert's dresser. I pushed aside the flannel gowns searching for a cotton summer one, and found a manila envelope addressed to Gert.

The jewelry box had taught me not to throw anything away unexamined, so I carried the envelope to my bedroom. I removed my wet gown, put on the fresh one, and crawled into the middle of the bed. The envelope was dated the previous March, and the postmark said it had come from Hollis, Oklahoma. The return address label had *Harriet Stemmons* on it, but the handwriting was big and masculine.

I turned the envelope upside down, and letters tumbled out in front of me. Aunt Gert's precise, small writing on the outside of the letters addressed them to either Harriet O'Brien or Harriet Stemmons. A single sheet of paper among them explained that Harriet had prized their friendship and had kept a few of the letters she had received through the years. But Harriet had passed on the month before, and the sender was now returning those letters to Gertrude. He hoped she'd enjoy remembering all the good times they'd had when they were the two new teachers in the Milburn school system and the letters they'd shared since then. The letter was signed *Thomas O'Brien, Harriet's son.*

I shuffled them into order by date and opened the one dated December 10, 1944. In it, Aunt Gert wrote about riding a horse nine miles each day so she wouldn't have to use her gas ration stamps. She mentioned her sister, who would have been my grandmother, and then told Harriet how much she missed her beau, Miles, who was fighting in the war.

It was hard to think that Aunt Gert had ever been that young or happy, but there it was on the page. One letter turned into two, three, and four until I'd read all of them.

Gert didn't go into much detail, but there was a splotch that looked like a teardrop on the letter she wrote saying that Miles had died in the war and that she'd never marry.

Letter number twelve was dated May of 1957, and she was almost giddy. She was in love, and she was going to be married. He worked at the local Chevrolet dealership and was ten years younger than she. She hoped that in the near future she and Lonnie Martin would make a road trip to western Oklahoma to visit Harriet and Rick.

Number thirteen, written in December of 1957, was a very different letter. Gert's tone had changed drastically. She apologized to Harriet for not writing since the wedding but confessed that the marriage had been a very big mistake.

The fourteenth letter was the one that caused my eyes to pop wide open. It was dated June of 1958, a year after she'd married Lonnie. It started out:

Dear Harriet,

I made a mistake. If I could figure out a way to kill my husband, I'd do it in a heartbeat, but I'm stuck with him until he dies. He married me because he thought I had money, and he's cheating on me, and the crazy thing is, most of the women he goes after are my friends. Daisy Black and I were friends from the time we were just little girls, and now she's sleeping with my husband. He even gave her a fancy piece of jewelry just like one he gave me. I saw her wearing it at church and knew immediately what was going on. When I confronted him, he laughed in my face and said that when I gave him access to all my money instead of a monthly allowance, he'd stop giving his mistress the same jewelry he gave me. Until then I could expect to see lots of jewelry just like mine in Tishomingo. If I divorce him, he'll get at least half my property. What am I to do? If I toss him out, everyone will think I was just a silly old woman who

*played into the hands of a con artist. If I don't, I'll be
miserable.*

I wish I'd never married him.

I took a deep breath. It's a wonder the man lived another
thirty years. No wonder she'd grown bitter. I yawned twice and
turned off the light. A full moon filtered in through the lace
curtains, and I thought about Lonnie's spirit being locked up in
the room across the hall. If I heard chains rattling in Uncle
Lonnie's old room, I was hightailing it out of that house and
buying dynamite the next morning.

I had just shut my eyes when I heard a sound like a freight
train headed right toward my pillow.

How on earth the train had jumped the tracks in Ravia and
made it five miles to Tishomingo was a mystery, but clearly it
was on Broadway Street and coming on strong.

I sat up so fast, it made me dizzy, and I tried to jump out of
bed, but my legs were tangled up in the sheets. My life flashed
before my eyes as I got ready for the impact.

If I died, Drew would automatically get everything Aunt
Gert had left me. I'd rather suffer the wrath of Lucifer than
Aunt Gert in those circumstances. I hit the floor in a run and
made it to the door when I realized it wasn't a train but Gert's
alarm clock, which I'd set the night before so I wouldn't be
late to church.

The cursed thing had two bells on the top and no volume
button. It took me several minutes to find the off button on
the back, and the silence did nothing to stop the ringing in my
ears. I grabbed the clock and slung it against the far wall, but
it kept ticking. I kicked it like a soccer ball against another
wall, and it still kept ticking.

I picked it up and marched downstairs, out the back door,
and to the garage. The cursed thing was not going to live to ring
another day. The noise it made when it hit the concrete floor
was pitiful but still not enough to kill it. Until that moment, I
hadn't known that inanimate objects could be immortal.

I searched for something to use to destroy it. I uncovered
ant poison in a bag with the top rolled down and secured with

two clothespins. Would alarm clocks be susceptible to ant poison? Probably not. I pushed around a dozen cans of paint with labels dating them back at least fifty years. It would take an act of God to get any of the lids off, so lead poisoning was out too. There had to be a hammer somewhere. Finally I spied a rusty metal toolbox pushed up under an old chrome kitchen table. I bloodied a knuckle trying to open it, but finally a good, solid cussing popped the lid, and there was a hammer, right on top. I picked up the clock, set it on Uncle Lonnie's worktable, and smashed it with the first swing.

It felt so good that I hauled off and hit it again, then once more as I envisioned Drew's face between the bells. He was still smiling, so I gave him a couple more licks for good measure.

"That clock do something to make you mad?" Billy Lee asked from the doorway.

I was wearing one of Aunt Gert's cotton summer nightgowns in Pepto-Bismol pink. My hair kinked all over my head. My bare feet were dirty from trekking out across the dusty yard, and rising blood pressure was no doubt turning my face red and blotchy. But I did not care. For the first time in my entire life I was liberated.

I pointed at him. "Yes. Scared the devil out of me. It won't do that again."

"You don't give second chances?" He grinned.

"Not anymore."

He stepped aside and, I guess, returned to the peace of his own home when I marched past him and into the house. I wasn't living one more second doing what society expected. That had gotten Aunt Gert a life of misery until Lonnie died, and by then she was so set in her ways, she couldn't change. I had just destroyed the first thing to upset my brand-new life. I was brave enough now to take Drew on.

I put a Band-Aid on my knuckle and ate leftover ribs for breakfast—cold, right out of the refrigerator, licking the sticky sauce off my fingers instead of using a napkin or even a paper towel. The phone rang as I started up the stairs to get ready for church. I picked it up on the third ring.

"Hello."

"Trudy, are you still there? You *will* go home right now. Mother is mortified. Dad is ready to commit you. You've proven your point. You've embarrassed me. I'll be home tomorrow, and you'd best be there," Drew said.

"You can kiss my naturally born southern hind end, Drew Williams." I hung up. That felt even better than murdering the alarm clock had.

The phone rang again, but I gave it a threatening look and reminded it that the hammer was still out in the toolbox. It stopped on the fourth ring. Guess I made a believer out of it.

I held up the two new dresses hanging in the closet and decided on the red one. I liked the yellow with the Hawaiian-print jacket, but I would want to wear the hat with it, and today I wasn't covering up my hair. Not one resident of Johnston County, Oklahoma, was going to say I wore a hat out of shame for a bad decision.

I slipped the red dress over my head. It was as comfortable as one of Gert's nightgowns. The jacket didn't bind me up, and the shoes felt pretty darn close to house slippers.

Billy Lee was sitting on the porch when I opened the door. He wore bibbed overalls and a short-sleeved chambray shirt. Both were crisply ironed, and his shoes were polished.

"You going to church?" he asked.

"Yes, I am."

"Which one?"

"Same one I always go to. The one on Main Street. You?"

"I go to the same one me and Gert always went to. The one on Broadway Street. Thought if you were going to our church, we might ride together."

It looked like the property came complete with Billy Lee Tucker in all phases—work, eating, church. "Maybe another time. You want to come with me today?"

He shook his head so hard that if he'd been wearing glasses, they would have been flung to a far corner of the yard. "No, thank you. But it's an open invitation if you ever want to go with me."

"Thanks. I just might do that someday."

Carolyn Brown

He followed me out to the Impala and opened the door. "You look lovely. Is that a new dress?"

"Yes, it is, and thank you," I said.

"Red is a good color for you. It goes well with your hair."

I had a panic attack in the church parking lot. I wasn't even sure I could get into heaven if I didn't uphold the standards set by my mother. What would happen to the rich and shameless if I didn't wear black Versace and control-top hose to church on Sunday mornings?

Eyebrows almost hit the ceiling, and there was a steady drone of whispers, but no one brought out a rope with a noose on the end when I walked inside. Betsy wore the same black suit she'd worn to Aunt Gert's funeral, and her bleached hair had been cut. Marty wore a black sheath-style dress with a lacy jacket, and her red hair was swept up with a clip. If they had their hearts set on a new Thunderbird, they'd best call in a plastic surgeon. A new hairdo wouldn't be enough to do the trick. I slid into my normal place, leaving room for Drew out of habit.

Betsy leaned over and whispered into my ear. "What in God's name are you wearing?"

"A new bra, panties, no hose, a dress with matching jacket, and shoes," I whispered back.

Marty leaned past her and gave me a dirty look. She should be careful with those mean glares. A dead alarm clock could testify that I was never taking any guff again, and the hammer was in the toolbox, ready and waiting.

The Sunday school director made a few announcements. The choir director led us in a hymn, and the preacher took the pulpit. He preached on about forgiveness. He was one funeral late and two cousins short. I'd forgive my cousins if they apologized from the depths of their evil souls. I would forgive Drew when he was lying in a casket with his hands draped over his cheating heart.

"Drew is going to kill you, coming to church looking like that," Marty said the minute the benediction was delivered.

"Crucify, is more like it," Betsy said.

"Which one of you wants Aunt Gert's house when he does?" Marty shivered.

Betsy's eyes bugged out.

"Then you'd better protect me, because I swear to God, I'll leave it to one of you. You'll be sure to take care of it for me, won't you?" I reached the door and shook the preacher's hand. He blinked fast a dozen times before he called me by name. I'm sure he was in shock, but I don't reckon it was fatal, since he didn't drop graveyard-dead.

I was glad for air-conditioning when I got into my car and drove west through town toward the Western Inn's restaurant. I cruised past the funeral home, the H&R Block, the flower shop, drugstore, E-Z Mart, a bank, clothing stores, and all the makings of a small town with a four-block business area and two red lights.

I knew most of the people in the restaurant, and a few mumbled a cautious hello. They didn't want to get too close to the crazy woman, since scientists hadn't yet proved whether crazy, like stupid, is inherited or contagious.

The waitress brought a glass of water to my booth and asked if I wanted to see a menu or if I would be having the buffet. I chose the buffet, so she told me to help myself. Mabelle Strong slipped in behind me as I was loading my plate with fried chicken, mashed potatoes, gravy, green beans, and hot rolls and eyeing the fried okra on the other side.

Mabelle had wispy blue gray hair that barely covered her scalp. Her lipstick had run into the wrinkles around her mouth, and a bed of crow's-feet cradled her bright blue eyes.

"Trudy Williams, you need to go home and stop this non-sense. You look like a cheap floozy. Have you lost your mind, girl? Gert would be ashamed of you," she said, without lowering her voice a bit.

"How are you doing, Mabelle? I suspect that Gert would be standing on a tabletop clapping for me this morning. That is a lovely brooch you're wearing. I believe my Uncle Lonnie bought that for you back before he died. Now, what were you saying about my state of mind?"

She turned sixteen shades of red, one of which matched her

lipstick perfectly. It looked as if she was going to succumb to acute cardiac arrest, but she managed to suck in enough air to keep her heart pumping. It would have been terrible if she'd dropped right there, because it would've slowed down the line, and the fried okra was on the other side of the buffet.

I ate alone and wondered if Billy Lee was having Sunday dinner with some of the folks from his church. Did they tell him he looked like a dirt farmer and to go home and change his clothes? I didn't think so. Compared to Gert, Billy Lee probably didn't even qualify as an oddball.

After lunch I went home and changed into my new overalls and orange sleeveless knit shirt and started cleaning out my bedroom. I carefully wrapped all the ceramic animals in old newspapers and filled two empty boxes I found in the garage. After I taped the lids shut, I carried them down to the living room. I'd haul them down to Durant to the Goodwill store the next time I went that way.

I found a flat-edged screwdriver in the toolbox out in the garage and went after the shelves and their cornice boards with the gusto of a hungry hound dog. But the screws had been there since the sixth day of creation and wouldn't budge. I leaned into the screwdriver with all my might, and a cornice finally let go. I started to back that sucker right out of there, only to have the one on the other end of the shelf let go and the whole shelf crash down on my bare right foot.

I threw myself across the bed and beat the pillows while it throbbed. How was I ever going to get this house cleaned out and remodeled if my foot rotted off? Its arch was turning purple, but I could still wiggle all my toes and put weight on it. It appeared that nothing was broken—thank goodness! I needed that foot to kick Drew.

I lugged the shelf to the top of the stairs and chucked it to the bottom. It clattered and rattled all the way down, landing only a few inches from a table with a huge lamp shaped like a Siamese cat. I was going to have to practice my aim. With luck, by the time I threw the last shelf, I'd break the cat into a million pieces. I wouldn't even fuss about having to clean up the mess if I could accomplish that feat before nightfall.

It was dark when I finished in the bedroom. If Drew knew what was good for him, he'd catch the red-eye home tonight instead of waiting until the next day. My arms ached so badly that I could hardly make a sandwich, but my aim hadn't improved a bit. I hadn't hit the cat lamp even though I'd tried. If he came home now, I wouldn't have the energy to even utter angry words in argument, much less kick him with my sore foot. I might have the energy to pull a trigger if I hadn't left my .22 behind in my fit of anger. Apparently Gert had known better than to tempt the devil, because either she didn't keep guns in the house or I hadn't found one.

I made a ham and tomato sandwich slathered thickly with mayonnaise and liked it so well, I ate another one. My tired muscles protested when I started up the stairs, but I didn't listen to them. After a soaking bath, I went to bed in a nice, cool room completely devoid of animals with beady little black eyes.

I laced my hands behind my head and thought about the next day. My stomach didn't knot up. Drew's clothes and the house were in shambles. I'd faced off with Charity down at the bank and basically told everyone where they could go and which poker to ride. I wasn't taking one step backward. From now on everything was full speed ahead and damn the torpedoes, even if one was named Drew.

Chapter Five

Billy Lee and I were in my bedroom measuring for new carpet and talking about paint when the doorbell rang and the door creaked open. Heavy footsteps crossed the foyer and moved up the staircase. I hopped up and peeked out the bedroom door into my husband's uplifted eyes when he put his foot on the third step.

I shook a finger at him. "You stop right there, and don't take another step."

My tone shocked him so badly that he backed up and stopped in the foyer. That gave me courage to go on. He was not bringing the fight to me on his terms. I was taking it to him . . . on mine.

I leaned on the banister and took the steps two at a time, even though my foot ached. "You have no right to walk into my house as if you were welcome. Out on the porch! I'm not discussing anything with you in here."

At about that time, Billy Lee stepped onto the landing.

Drew's face registered pure disgust. "What is that nitwit doing here? Have you been . . ." He narrowed his eyes at me. "Trudy, what have you done? And what have you done to your hair? You know I hate it short."

I opened the front door and pointed.

He stomped out onto the porch, and I followed.

He opened his mouth, but I took off before he could say anything. "Number one, don't you ever call Billy Lee Tucker a nitwit or any other name again. He's got more integrity in one toenail than you've got in your whole body. Number two, I'm working on remodeling this house to live in it. Number three, I really don't care if you like my hair or not, Drew."

It was his turn to shake a finger at me. "I'm going to have you sent off to a mental institution. Are you shacking up with the village idiot too?"

I got so close to his nose that I had to look at him cross-eyed. "What's it to you if I am? You're messing around with the village bimbo. And you are not sending me anywhere. I'm saner than I have been since the day I made the biggest mistake of my life and married you."

"You mean you regret Crystal?" he snapped.

"That is a stupid question! My only regret is that I cursed her with a lying, cheating father."

He glared at me. "You are as crazy as Gert. That was the thing about you that worried my folks."

"You should have listened to them. But Gert was a lot smarter than me. She figured out the first year what kind of man she'd married. I didn't figure out things until a couple of days ago, so I haven't gotten a thing but a reputation for being a naïve fool. She got jewelry every time Lonnie had an affair. Your newest toy has a brand-new Thunderbird. I didn't get one, did I?"

He crossed his arms over his chest and glared at me. "I'd say what you got out of the bank would compensate for anything I've done."

If looks could kill, he wouldn't be anything but a greasy spot on my rotting porch. "What I took amounts to five thousand dollars a year. I don't think that compensates for anything you've done."

For the past three days I had been busy figuring out ways to kill Drew. Now that he stood before me, merely arguing seemed to be killing him quicker than a dose of rat poison or a bullet between the eyes. He didn't have any idea how to fight with his wife; but then, he'd had no experience. I'd never stood up to him or called him names before. He was in brand-new territory without a compass.

He dropped his arms to his sides and hung his head. "I'm so sorry, Trudy. I messed up bad. You are a good woman, Trudy. Can't you forgive me for one little mistake?"

He almost had me there for a minute—until I realized that he was lying about the number of infidelities and that he hadn't said anything about loving me. Had he ever?

I shook my head. "The old Trudy was a good woman. I'm not, and I will not forgive you."

His tone went from warm to cold instantly. "Come on, Trudy, be sensible. This fling was my first one," he lied. "It's a male-menopause thing. I am past forty, and my life is slipping away. I hate getting old. I'll buy you a new car tomorrow. So, what do you say?" He touched my arm.

Cockroaches crawling across my skin couldn't have been more repulsive. I picked up his hand and removed it from my arm.

That's when he lost it. Daggers shot out of his eyes. His face turned the color of day-old liver, and I thought for a minute he was going to fall down on my porch and start slobbering. And my cell phone was lying in a ditch, so I'd have to go inside to call 911. Of course, I could sit down on the steps and see if he came out of it on his own before I went inside the house and called. But, dang it all, he started yelling again. Some days I couldn't catch a lucky break.

"I never wanted to marry you," he said icily.

"I'll make it easy for you to be footloose and fancy-free, then. Either you file for divorce, or I will."

"The money you stole from me won't last you a lifetime, and that nit . . ." He stopped and took half a step toward me.

"Don't finish that, or I'll kick you off this porch," I said.

He backed up two steps. "Billy Lee can't give you what you are used to. This is your last chance, woman. Either walk your fat rear end out there and get into my car, or I'll have divorce papers served tomorrow morning."

I smiled. "My fat rear end will be glad to get them. The only thing I'll fight to the death for is my maiden name back. I don't want to be affiliated with the cheating, slimy name of *Williams* ever again. I'd take a job picking the white tops off chicken droppings before I took another penny of your precious money, so I won't even fight you for half of what you've got."

He smirked. "It wouldn't do any good. I'm a lawyer, and I'll . . ."

"Don't threaten me, Drew. I didn't even want my clothes, so why would I want anything more? Besides, it'll take more and more money each time you get involved with a younger woman, so you'll need it all just to keep up."

He drew back a fist, and I got right into his face. "Take your best shot, and give it all you've got, and then I'm going to wipe up this porch with you. There's enough mad in me right now that you don't really want to take the chance. But if you are idiot enough to do it to soothe your damaged pride, then hit me."

He dropped his hand and stomped off the porch. "The papers will be here tomorrow. Sign them, and stay away from me."

"Signing them will be the highlight of my day. Staying away from you will be the easiest thing I've ever done."

I watched him drive away, and a nervous giggle bubbled up from my chest. By the time he pulled out of my driveway, I was sitting on a porch step, tears running down my face and laughter echoing up and down Broadway Street.

He shook a fist at me as he drove away. I wished for my digital camera to take a picture of that sight, but it was back at Drew's house, lying in the nightstand drawer beside my little pistol.

Billy Lee sat down on the top step a few feet from me. "You okay?"

"You didn't rush right out to my rescue, did you? Some neighbor you are, and after I took up for you too. Left me to fight the battle all by myself."

"You are a strong woman. You just proved it. I was standing in the doorway. If he'd tried to hit you, I'd have been there."

I didn't know whether to thank him for all that confidence or to slap him for getting out of helping me. "Okay, that's over and finished. Let's go back up to the bedroom. I hate white woodwork. What's it going to take to get it all stripped and stained, and is it worth the effort, or do we just buy new?"

I went back inside the house, and he followed me up the stairs.

Halfway up he said, "Thanks for taking up for me."

"Who said I was taking up for you?"

"You did. And you told him not to call me a nitwit."

I turned and looked back at him a few steps behind me. "Maybe I was taking up for me. I don't befriend nitwits. My friends are all first-class people. Maybe I thought he was questioning my judgment."

Billy Lee grinned. "Thanks, anyway."

By then we were in the bedroom, and he went right back to talking about the job. "Refinishing or buying new depends on how much work you want to do. I chipped a chunk of paint away in a corner of your bedroom. Looks to me like the woodwork is burled oak, so it's worth the time and effort."

"Then let's move the furniture out of the room, tear up the carpet, and get started."

"Right now?"

"You got somewhere else you have to be?"

"No, ma'am. It's Billy Lee at your service until we get this old place into shape, but we'll need to make a trip to the lumberyard for supplies after we tear up the carpet. I imagine there's oak hardwood under it."

"Then let's go to the lumberyard right now before we get all sweaty and hot."

"I'll go get my truck and pick you up on the corner," he said enthusiastically.

"Me and my fat rear end will be waiting."

"I don't listen to derogatory remarks about my friends, either. And you look just fine to me, Trudy."

He walked across the back lawns and returned in minutes with his pickup truck. He got out and opened the passenger's door for me. I felt like Cinderella in the pumpkin-chariot in that beat-up Chevy truck that had to be at least twenty years old. It had been red at one time, but now it had rust spots and splotches of primer gray where Billy Lee had tried to keep it together with putty and paint.

We bought paint stripper, varnish, and two kinds of wipe-on stain for the woodwork, but we held off on lumber, just in case we lucked out with the flooring under the carpets. By noon we'd moved the furniture from the guest room I was using to Uncle Lonnie's old room. I'd be sleeping in Aunt Gert's room until mine was finished. I wasn't looking forward to the possibility of sharing the room with her spirit if it hadn't gone on to rearrange heaven. But the other option was Uncle Lonnie's old room. I wasn't about to stretch out on the bed where lousy Lonnie had slept.

Sweat had slicked up every inch of my overweight, over-forty body by the time we pulled up the carpet, but I danced a jig when we found oak hardwood floor, the movement of my feet sending dirt flying up around my sneakers and settling into the grooves of my turned-down bobby socks. Suddenly I could see the house in all its potential glory, just waiting to be turned from the girl in ugly rags to a princess, the belle of the ball.

"Don't take much to make you happy, does it?" Billy Lee chuckled.

"It's going to be a grand house when we get done."

"I've wanted to do this for years, but Gert wouldn't have any part of it. She said she was too old to be in the middle of remodeling, and she'd grown to like her life the way it was."

"I can see a vision of it finished, and you can too. It's plain as day in your eyes. Speaking of which, when did you stop wearing glasses? Did you get that new surgery?"

"No, just contacts. The doctor says I'm not a candidate for the surgery, or I'd have it."

"Not me. If I was nearsighted, I wouldn't have it."

"Why not?" he asked.

"If I was nearsighted, then I could choose what to see or not see."

"Trust me, it doesn't work that way," he said. "If I don't have my contacts in, I stumble around like a drunk."

My stomach growled loudly. I hadn't had food since break-fast, which was something new for me. I always had tea and cookies midmorning.

"Sounds like you're about to starve," he said.

"Let's go up to the SONIC and get some lunch before we clean the dust away and start to work for real."

"Want to go over to the park across Pennington Creek to eat?"

My stomach set up an unladylike howl. "I'd eat in the truck."

"Truck's hot. We might catch a breeze in the park."

I smiled, and it felt good. "I wouldn't waste a breeze."

We ordered foot-long cheese Coneys with extra onions, Tater Tots, and one of those big drinks that hold a quart of Coke. While we waited for the waitress to bring our food, Daisy Black and her daughter pulled up beside us in a late-model Cadillac. From the passenger seat, Daisy looked at me as if I was something she had tracked in from a pig lot.

She was the one who'd gone to church with Aunt Gert and had slept with Uncle Lonnie. But then, maybe she'd had a come-to-Jesus experience and repented of her sins. Jesus might instantly forgive her, but it was going to take me a while longer.

"How you doin', Miz Daisy?" I asked.

"I'm doin' just fine. I heard you moved into Gert's house and that you and Drew had a big argument on the porch this mornin'. It's not too late to undo what you're doin' and go on back to Drew."

"No, thank you."

"Think about it before you make a bad decision. How's your momma doin'? I been meanin' to get out to the nursing home to check on her, but I don't drive since I had my knee replaced."

"Momma's fine. Some days are better than others, but that's the way of her illness. She gets things all confused at times," I said.

"Well, when she's having a good day, you tell her that I asked about her, and I'll get on out there one of these days," Daisy said.

"Momma always likes company."

They brought out her milkshake. She and her daughter drove away.

"She was one of Uncle Lonnie's women, one of the first ones. What gives her the right to give me advice?" I asked.

"Age."

I looked at him quizzically.

He shrugged. "Old folks have seen more than we have. They know more."

"Are you telling me to go back to Drew?"

His eyebrows shot up. "I am not! You should have made this decision years ago."

"I might have if someone had stepped up to the plate and told me what was going on. Why didn't you?"

"Would you have believed me?"

I had to think about that. By the time I had an answer, our food had arrived, and he was driving down Main Street. "No, I wouldn't have believed you, Billy Lee."

"Who did you finally believe?"

I got the giggles and told him about the ladies' room, and we were both laughing when he parked the truck beside a picnic table under a shade tree. He got out and hurried around the truck to open the door for me.

"World is a strange place we live in," Billy Lee said as we laid our food out on the table.

I narrowed my eyes at him. "You knew, didn't you? You knew that Uncle Lonnie cheated on Gert back in their younger days too."

He cleared his throat. "Some things don't have to be written in a book down at the courthouse for everyone to know."

"Such as how Lonnie and Drew were just alike?"

"I ain't goin' there with you. I'll just say that what's past is past. Let it go, and get on with your life. You always were too good for Drew Williams." He changed the subject abruptly. "I'm glad to see you eatin'. I was afraid that episode this morning would ruin your appetite. Never did like a woman who didn't appreciate a good meal."

Now, wasn't that a hoot? Drew thought I had a fat rear end, and Billy Lee wanted me to eat. I polished off every crumb of the hot dog, didn't leave a single Tater Tot in the paper bag, and kept at the Coke until the straw made slurping noises at the bottom of the cup.

Chapter Six

I saw the Disney movie *Bambi* when I was seven years old. It was the day before deer season opened in Oklahoma. When my dad began to clean his gun in preparation for the big hunt, I set up a howl. My father wiped away my tears and explained that the state game commission had a big refuge for deer and other animals. On that refuge those animals could never be shot, and we had such a place right there in Tishomingo. He promised to take me for a drive through it so I could see all the wild creatures. But outside that place, he said, if hunters didn't kill deer sometimes, there would be too many of them, and that made a problem with nature's balance.

I wanted to believe him, but a little part of me always wondered which story was true. Bambi's tale of the evil man who killed his mother, or my father's? Thirty-three years later, the idea of deer hunting came to mind as I read through the divorce papers the sheriff had delivered to my house that morning. It was really quite simple. Drew got everything "in his possession," and I got everything in mine.

I picked up the pen and signed my name at the bottom with a flourish.

In his mind, he'd just bagged a trophy divorce.

I laughed until my sides hurt. If he'd known what I was worth, he'd have been fighting me for half of *my* possessions!

My mind went back to *Bambi*. If there were too many deer, then hunters were given the opportunity to shoot them. Cheating husbands were also a problem in the balance of nature, and there were far too many of them. Why couldn't there be open season on cheating husbands? Deceived wives could purchase a gun, take lessons, and receive a cheating-husband hunting license complete with a big red *A* label to tie to the man's zipper after the kill. Open season could be scheduled months in advance to give the husbands a fighting chance. They could hide in refuges or stay home and take their chances at being shot through the living room window as they watched Monday Night Football.

The licenses would bring in tax revenue, and resorts could hire employees to cater to cheating husbands during the open season. The staff could put up a razor-wire-topped chain-link fence, guard it with attack dogs and ex–Navy SEALS, feed the husbands home-cooked food like their wives made, iron their clothing, charge them a fortune, and send them home when the season was over.

As I carried the divorce papers out to the car to take back to Drew's office, I wondered how many women I could get to march with me in Washington, D.C., to lobby for just one day a year of open cheating-husband season.

I spotted Aunt Gert's old adult tricycle in the garage. How much trouble could it be to ride four blocks to Main Street, three back east to his office, and then up to the nursing home to visit Momma?

I was so happy, I forgot that every muscle in my body ached. Billy Lee and I had filled two galvanized buckets with soapy water and set about removing ten layers of wallpaper once we cleaned all the dirt from the floors. We'd thought it best to start at the top and work our way down, which seemed like a good idea at the time. I had stretched as high as I could, then I'd sat Indian style and bent every which way. No gym could have ever given my muscles such a workout.

Someone had said that fat cells were like globs of bacon grease and had no feeling. Whoever said it had lied. Every fat cell seemed to have a sensory fiber attached to my eyelids, which sent out screaming signals when I opened them that morning.

Standing up was agony. They should send criminals into Aunt Gert's house and make them strip wallpaper from daylight to dark. That would sure enough reform them.

I figured a short cycle trip to Drew's office would work out the kinks and embarrass him even further. By the time I'd gone a block, though, my thighs were quivering, and the muddy water in the puddles left by a late-night rain began to look good. But I was on a mission, and, by golly, I would get it done, and I would not die! Because if I did, Drew would get all my money to spend on his teenage queens. I'd taught the alarm clock a lesson; the bike was next.

Heat waves rose from the road, and the humidity was at least ninety percent. I felt like a turkey in the oven on Thanksgiving morning. Three blocks later, sweat poured down my neck and hit the dam made by the elastic of my bra. There it lay in salty glory, eating away at the fabric. Next week I'd have to make another trip to Durant to buy more bras.

I parked the bike in front of his office in full view of Drew's secretary, Georgia. She was the only woman I was sure he'd never had a fling with. She wore her gray hair in a tight bun at the nape of her neck and always came to work in a no-nonsense suit, either navy blue or black, with a paler blue or a gray silk blouse to match.

I stepped inside the cool office and almost swooned at the wonderful central air-conditioning. "Good morning, Georgia."

She eyed me from the toes of my ratty sneakers up to the top of my sweaty, kinky hair. "What are you doing out in public looking like that?"

I dropped the divorce papers onto her desk. There were a few smudges of sweat on the front page, but I'd signed all the lines that had had the little markers. "Bringing you this."

Her eyes bugged out, and she gasped. "You signed that farce?"

"Yep, I did. He keeps what is his, and I keep what is mine, and I take my maiden name back. Right?"

She nodded. "But you are entitled to—"

"I don't want his money. I took what I wanted out of our joint accounts last Friday. It doesn't compensate me for twenty years of infidelity, but it embarrassed him. Not as much as I was when I learned what he'd been up to for most of our married life, but it made me feel better. So here it is, signed and delivered. When is he sending you to file it?"

"This afternoon."

"The sooner the better. I am now officially a Matthews again. Off with the old, on with the new. Good-bye, Georgia."

"Trudy, should you be riding that old tricycle on Main Street, dressing like . . ."

I finished the sentence for her. "Dressing like a woman who intends to go back home and apply stripper to baseboards all day or finish removing the last of the wallpaper from a bedroom wall? One who has a house to remodel? I don't reckon I need a Liz Claiborne or a Versace suit to do those jobs, do I?"

"Is it true that you are already keeping company with Billy Lee Tucker?"

I shot her one of Marty's patented "drop dead" looks. "I'll answer that when you supply me with the long list of names of the women you've sent flowers and expensive gifts to with Drew's name attached, the way you did for me on anniversaries and my birthdays."

She was still sputtering when I walked out the door. Getting back onto that bike was no picnic, but a whole cheesecake waited at the Sooner Food's grocery store on the way back home as a reward. Thinking of the first bite helped, but I still groaned when I pushed the pedals to get started toward the nursing home.

Mother was sitting in the lobby when I arrived. Lessie shook her head when I walked in the door. It wasn't a good day, and I'd so hoped it would be. I wanted to tell my mother about the divorce. I pulled up a folding chair, sat down, and patted Momma's hands. "Hi, Momma. How are you today?"

She jerked her hands back and blinked several times as if trying to put my face in focus. "Who are you? I'm not your mother. You stink. You should have taken a bath before you came to my home."

"Miz Clarice, this is Trudy, your daughter," Lessie said.

She eyed me seriously. "My daughter doesn't stink, and she has long hair. She married a man named Lonnie—no, that's not right. Gert married Lonnie."

I reached out and touched her shoulder. "I cut my hair, Momma."

She shrugged me away. "I've only got one daughter. Her name is Crystal. She's going to college."

"I see. Well, maybe I'll come back tomorrow."

"You take a bath before you come back to my house. I'm going to my bedroom now to take a little nap."

She stood up and disappeared down the hallway toward her bedroom. Lessie laid a hand on my shoulder. "Don't worry. Tomorrow might be a good day. She's about due for one." She shook her head sympathetically. "You know, I used to clean your Aunt Gert's house. After Lonnie died, she hired me to work for her on Wednesdays. She never went into that room of his again. She'd hand me the key and tell me to lock up after I'd dusted it. Last year I had to give up my home and check into this place because of my ailments, but I remember Gert right well. She loved your momma."

"What else do you remember about Aunt Gert?"

Lessie smiled sweetly. "She was a fine woman in her day. Looked like a million dollars walking around town. Held her head up high and was always a lady. Then that fool of a man talked her into marrying up with him. A sad day that was. About twenty years ago she come down with the pneumonia and spent three weeks in the hospital. Next month after she went home, he died. She shut the door to his room and hired me to dust and vacuum every week while she was ailing. I just kept going even after she got well. We were pretty good friends. I wish I could've gone to her funeral, but I can't sit that long anymore in a hard pew with these old bones."

I touched her arm. "I know she'd understand."

Lessie shook her head. "I don't know about that. Gert was outspoken."

"Well, I was there, and the church was full to the limit. Every good recipe she ever used was at the dinner, and . . ." I paused.

"And most folks was just glad she was gone, right?"

I nodded honestly.

"Billy Lee Tucker was sad," I whispered.

"Oh, that boy would miss her, all right. He was the child she never had. They was a good pair. I like Billy Lee. Most folks, they don't understand him. He's not strange. He just . . ." It was her turn to pause.

"He just doesn't care what other people think," I said.

"You got that right, girl. We'd all be better off if we had a bit of Billy Lee in us. You go on now, and I'll see to it your momma is in the right room. It makes me feel useful to have someone to take care of. Body needs to feel useful. If they don't, they soon wither up and die."

I hugged her and went back out into the heat. I stopped at the grocery store on the corner of Main and Byrd Streets and purchased a Sara Lee cheesecake, a pound of bologna, a gallon of milk, and a loaf of bread. It all fit very well in the basket of the bike from hell. Then I pushed off toward the middle school, a block off Main and half a block from the grocery store.

When Momma was in school back in the sixties, the middle school was the high school. I stopped pedaling and walked the tricycle over to a big tree in front of the building. I sat down beneath the tree and tried to imagine my parents when they were young and in high school. Instead of seeing them laughing and talking during lunch, though, I had a vision of Billy Lee come to mind.

It was graduation night, and he wore a red robe. For the first time he looked like all the rest of his classmates, until I looked down and saw the legs of his striped overalls. He'd delivered the valedictorian speech that night, but we'd been too excited about getting out of school to listen to him. If I could go back, I think I would have paid attention to what he had to say.

It was either get back on the bike or walk, so I hefted myself up and set off toward home. It would have been so much easier to go back down to Drew's office, snatch that divorce decree out of Georgia's little paws, and rip it to shreds than to ride that stupid tricycle home, but I couldn't do it. I wouldn't live with a man I couldn't trust.

Someone should have been waiting with a brass band, a medal on a ribbon, or at least a round of applause when I parked the three-wheeled monster in the front yard. I had conquered it. I'd lived. I would never get on it again. I'd learned my lesson, and I still might take the hammer to it before nightfall.

All I got was Billy Lee leaning against a porch post with a silly grin on his face.

"You a glutton for punishment? I figured you'd be moaning about sore muscles this morning," he said.

"I didn't know how far it would feel to bike to town or to the nursing home, or I would have taken the car," I huffed.

"Had a little fit and decided to humiliate Drew, did you?"

He knew me too well after only a few days. How had that happened?

"The divorce papers have been signed and delivered. It's up to the court to put the seal on it. I brought bologna and cheese-cake, so we won't have to go out for lunch. Thought I'd throw a roast into the Crock-Pot for supper tonight. Are the window people on the way?" I changed the subject.

"They'll be here in thirty minutes to start work. It'll take them three or four days to finish. The electrician is coming by this afternoon to give you an estimate." He carried the two bags of groceries into the house for me.

"I don't care about an estimate. I want this place rewired so we can put in central heat and air, and we need plugs in every single wall. I don't care what it costs," I said.

We? My conscience picked up on that word so fast, it made my head swim.

He leaned on the doorjamb into the kitchen. "You ready to start removing paint?"

"I am." I lied so well, I almost convinced myself.

We climbed the stairs, each carrying a bucket filled with putty knives, a can of paint remover, and sandpaper.

"I'm really surprised you aren't sore," he said.

"Who says I'm not?" I asked.

"Well, at least you aren't a whiner." His tone held respect.

After that, how could I say a word? In Billy Lee's eyes I wasn't a whiner. I'd worked all day, then gotten up the next morning and ridden the monster tricycle to town and back. It might not be a lot in anyone else's opinion, but right then I needed a champion, and I'd gladly take Billy Lee.

He set his bucket down. "Way this works is that we pour the remover into one of the buckets, paint it on a foot at a time, let it set for a few minutes, and use the putty knives to take off what we can. It'll probably take several applications to get down to raw wood."

"So we're not going to get this room completed today?"

He'd already begun to pour some of the smelly liquid into a bucket. "You in a hurry?"

"If I live to the promised three score and ten, I figure I've got about thirty years. Same as you. So I don't reckon I'm in a big hurry. Can't promise I'll be lucid the last ten, though. Momma started losing it at sixty. Think we can get this room done by then, so I can enjoy it for a few days before I have to check into the nursing home?"

"Trudy, you are not going to that place," he said seriously.

"And what makes you so sure?" I asked.

He quickly changed the subject. "I'll open the windows and get some ventilation in here. Fumes get pretty strong after a while. Hey, the window people just pulled up."

He raised the windows. One looked over the backyard and his little frame house next door, and the other overlooked Broadway Street with all its killer potholes.

"You are the official contractor on this job, so would you go show them where to start?"

"Wow, I get a title." He grinned.

"Want me to make you a fancy name tag?"

"Sure." He nodded on his way out of the room.

Two men and Billy Lee were back in a few minutes with a window. I'd expected them to measure, rub their chins, measure again, and do all the stereotyped things men do when they're discussing a job. But Billy Lee had already given them measurements of every window in the house, and they went right to work.

Billy Lee showed me how to apply the paint stripper, and I found out really quickly that it could make fat cells whine and cry like little girls. I dropped a chunk of saturated paint off the putty knife onto my bare leg, and it dug in like a leech and in seconds was burning so badly, I thought for sure I'd see bone when I wiped it off. But there was barely a red mark. I sucked up the screaming and saved the whining until later, when I was all alone.

One of the men asked Billy Lee how his business was doing with the economy in trouble, and he brushed the guy off with an evasive answer. My curiosity alert went into high gear. Just what kind of business did he have? I figured he lived on some kind of inheritance his grandparents had left him and doing odd jobs like this one when he could get them.

"You'll have a nice place here when you get done. I'm glad to see you restoring rather than just remodeling. By the way, I'm Roy, and this is Melvin." The window man made introductions.

I nodded toward them. "Nice to meet both of you. I've got this idea in my head about how I want things to look when it's all done. I love the warmth of wood and bright colors. Billy Lee is my contractor, but I'm helping where I can."

"Don't know how you got him to work for you, lady, but you got the best there is. I'd gladly pay him double top wages to remodel my house. I didn't know he'd come out of his shop building for anyone. How'd you do it?"

I raised an eyebrow at Billy Lee.

He blushed. "Gert was my friend, and she asked me to do this."

"I'm your friend. When you get finished, will you work for me?" Melvin asked.

Billy Lee shook his head.

"Is that a no?" Roy teased.

"That's exactly what it is," Billy Lee said.

"Can't blame a man for trying. These are going to be beautiful framed out in oak," Roy said.

I stopped long enough to wait for the stripper to do its job. "I hope so."

"So you like the . . . What did you say? The warmth of wood?" Billy Lee asked.

I wiped sweat from my forehead with a paper towel and nodded. "I didn't realize how much until these past few days. I'm a country girl at heart, not a modern one. I want a house full of color and laughter."

"That's the way you were when we were little. You liked red and yellow and blue when we colored out on the back porch, and you were always laughing," he said.

"You remember me as a child?"

"Sure. Y'all used to visit Gert, and I'd sneak through the hedge. Your mother always had a bag with crayons and two coloring books, and Marty and Betsy got one, and you always colored with me."

Talking about it jarred my memory. "And you colored so perfectly, you made us girls look bad."

"But you made everything so much fun. You colored hair purple or blue, and sometimes the sky was green. You've always loved color, Trudy. I'm glad you're going to keep the wood natural and use bright colors in the house. It'll be you."

"I may dye my hair purple or blue next week to prove the real Trudy has been resurrected."

"Please don't do that. Leave it brown. It's you just like it is now."

"And who is me?" I asked.

"You are Trudy Matthews with kinky, curly hair and a beautiful smile."

"Flattery will get you out of lots of explaining," I teased.

At noon Billy Lee and I washed up side by side in the kitchen sink. Our hands touched in the basin as we rinsed off paint speckles and dirt. There weren't any tingles, though, and the floor didn't wiggle a bit. I wasn't surprised. I never expected to feel anything romantic again.

"Mayonnaise?" I asked.

He pulled paper plates and napkins out of the cabinet. "Mustard, please."

"On bologna, lettuce, and tomatoes?"

"And dill pickles. Ever try it?"

I shook my head and left the mayonnaise in the refrigerator; might as well do something different to celebrate my freedom. "Is it good?"

He opened the bread wrapper and took out four pieces. "If you don't like it, I'll eat yours and mine. Here, I'll make them."

"What kind of chips and soda do you want?" I asked.

"Barbecue is good with bologna. And I'll have sweet tea if you have it made up."

I took a bag of mesquite-barbecued chips from the pantry,

put them on the bar, and fixed two glasses of sweet tea. By that time he had the sandwiches finished.

He dragged a bar stool around and sat down across from me. "We ready? You saying grace or me?"

"Go ahead."

His prayer was very brief. He thanked God for good friends and the health to enjoy them. Then he thanked Him for the food and a beautiful day. When he said "Amen," I looked up to find him with his sandwich headed toward his mouth. I did the same and was amazed. Pickles and mustard were meant to go together.

"Where'd you learn to make a sandwich like this?" I asked.

"Gert always made them with mustard. Mayonnaise was for ham and cheese. Mustard for bologna."

"Wise old coot, wasn't she?"

"That she was." He nodded and kept after the sandwich until it was gone. Then he made himself two more.

On occasion I've let myself have two sandwiches—like when I'm upset enough to chew up railroad ties and spit out Tinker Toys—but not too often. Not with my propensity to pack weight onto my hips and thighs.

He took in the whole house with a sweep of one hand. "You still want to strip all this wood?"

I nodded and swallowed. "Did Gert really leave you enough money to work that long? I can pay you, Billy Lee. She left me well-fixed for life. I can pay whatever you charge. Just give me a bill once a week, and I'll write you a check."

High color crept up his neck and around his angular jawline to his cheeks, which were blazing in a matter of seconds. "There's enough to take care of whatever you want done. I can work for you for a whole year and not lose a dime."

"Good! Then, yes, I want all the paint taken off and the wood stained and shining."

"High gloss?" he asked.

The color in his cheeks began to fade. Maybe the mustard took it away. Hmm, maybe it would work like that on cellulite. If I ate mustard and pickles every day, would the fat disappear off my thighs? Or if I rubbed mustard on my thighs and let it set until it was dried up like an old creek bed, would I wash away all the pesky little cellulite critters?

"What?" I belatedly asked.

"Varnish comes in flat finish, semigloss, and high gloss," he answered.

"I guess high gloss is the shiniest?"

He nodded.

"Then that's what I want. Does it look like a basketball court when they've just waxed it?"

He grinned. "That's about right."

When I finished chewing and swallowed the last bite of the sandwich, I brought out the cheesecake.

He groaned. "I forgot we had dessert. I shouldn't have eaten the third sandwich."

"Want to save it until midafternoon for our coffee break?"

"Yes, I do. But you go ahead. You only ate one sandwich."

"I think I'll wait too. It'll taste good with a cup of coffee in a couple of hours."

The window guys returned, and we all went back to work.

Put on stripper. Take off blistered paint. Do it again and again.

"Do you remember Mrs. Dorry in the first grade?" I asked. He'd remembered that I colored hair purple and the sky green. What else was hiding in that brilliant mind of his?

He nodded.

"I was terrified of her," I said.

"I know. When she called on you, I always wanted to answer for you. You looked so scared that I felt sorry for you."

"You were shy too."

"More like bored. My grandmother taught me to read before I went to school. I was reading the newspaper when I was five. And Grandpa taught me to do math and figure. They believed in living simply. Grandpa grew a garden, and Grandma canned food for the winter. They taught me to work and to love to learn new things. I wasn't really afraid or shy. I was just bored and different."

Suddenly it mattered to me very much that Billy Lee was my friend. He'd said I looked nice on Sunday; that he liked my hair; that I wasn't a whiner. He'd brought supper the day after Gert died. Not one of my old friends or acquaintances had even called or come by my house to see how I was faring with the loss and the divorce, much less brought barbecued ribs.

I tried to remember if I'd said anything nice to him since the funeral. Other than standing up for him with Drew—and I'd have done that for the real village idiot out of anger—I hadn't. Some friend I was!

That night I ran a warm bath and only whimpered a few times when I sank down into the water. The old claw-foot tub had a nice, sloped back made to lean against. I promptly fell asleep and awoke an hour later sitting in a tub of cold water.

After I'd toweled off and slipped into underpants and a comfortable old cotton gown, I stepped into the bedroom and actually shivered. God bless the woman who'd invented air-conditioning. Okay, it might have been a man, but I'll bet you dollars to earthworms that a woman nagged him into it.

I held the bottom of the nightgown over the front of the air conditioner for a few minutes, not caring if it produced chill bumps. Then I crossed the hallway to the room that would eventually be my bedroom and switched on the light to look at the progress one more time.

My bedroom. Mine. Not mine and Drew's but mine. I was as possessive as a little girl on Christmas with a brand-new doll. I turned the light off and noticed a yellow glow coming from across the yard, so I ventured to the window and looked out toward Billy Lee's place. His small house was dark, but light flowed from big open garage doors at both ends of his enormous shop building out in the backyard. Did the man ever sleep? As I watched, the lights went out, and the doors rolled down. Billy Lee made his way across the yard and into the house.

Alone isn't a bad place to be, especially when it's the alternative to distrust and unhappiness, but alone brought loneliness as the darkness surrounded me. I wished for the nerve to go downstairs and call Billy Lee. Just to hear his voice. Just to talk about the day. Just to be a nosy neighbor and find out what he was doing every evening in that big shop building.

Chapter Seven

I awoke in a royal pout.

Life was not fair.

It could have given me what I'd thought I had all along, but, oh, no! It had to wait until forty was bearing down on me to play show-and-tell with the truth of what had happened in my life.

Before the day in the ladies' room, the worst thing in my life was facing my fortieth birthday in July. I had a lovely home, a healthy, grown daughter, a loving husband, and friends by the dozens. That was BTF: before the funeral. Now I had an old house filled Aunt Gert's past, a daughter who was married to a boy I'd never met and who hadn't talked to me since the funeral, and an ex-husband who'd evidently never loved me. And the only person who'd come to my rescue was Billy Lee Tucker.

In the middle of the stripping job, I took a moment to really look at him. He was talking with the crew of men who'd arrived to put in my new central air-conditioning unit. The window men would finish their job by noon, the electricians were out of the attic and working their way through the bedrooms upstairs, and the plumbers would arrive Monday morning.

By the end of the next week the people crawling all over my house would be gone, and it would be up to me and Billy Lee to do the finish work. We wouldn't even have to work in the backyard once the air-conditioning was installed. But that morning the house was so hot, it sucked the air out of my lungs, so we were outside. Billy Lee had taken the doors off the bedroom and laid them across sawhorses under a shade tree. My job was to strip all the paint off one closet door. Billy Lee worked on another one when he wasn't supervising any workers. He kept everything going smoothly, and I was glad. I couldn't have done it even with a day planner at my fingertips.

He must've felt me staring at him, because he looked up and raised an eyebrow in question. I shook my head and went back to work. He gave the fellows a few more instructions and crossed the yard to me.

"Did you need something?" he asked.

"How do you do it?"

He picked up his paintbrush, loaded it with stripper, and slathered a section of the door. "Do what?"

"Keep everything going at once and organized."

He shrugged. "It's not so hard. Visualize the end, and start at the beginning."

"You are a genius."

He grinned. "Never been called that before."

"I'm adding it to your resume."

"Thank you."

"No thanks necessary. The truth is the truth whether you serve it up plain or top it with chocolate frosting. It's still the truth."

"So now you're a philosopher as well as a stripper."

I laughed aloud. "The first I might be. The second would be a physical impossibility."

"Why? You're doing a fine job," he said.

"Think, Billy Lee! You just called me a stripper."

He blushed. "Why would that be a physical impossibility?"

"I'm over the hill. Strippers are young and built well."

"You are stripping and doing a fine job of it," he teased.

"Oh, hush. I can't win a fight with you. So, what's next?" I'd gotten the hang of paint removal and hadn't dropped any of the lethal stuff on me in a couple of days until that moment. I dropped a glob onto my bare left foot, which I hurriedly wiped away. And I did not whine!

Billy Lee smiled and changed the subject. "Alford should have the bedroom and landing floors sanded by noon. So after we get these doors ready, we'll stain woodwork in those areas.

We wait until the plumbers, electricians, and air-conditioning men are finished to apply the sanding sealer and varnish. We can go ahead and work on some more doors if we finish before they do."

"Speaking of varnish, I've changed my mind. I want the floors so shiny you can see yourself in them but not the woodwork. I want that to look softer. Does that make sense?" I said.

Billy Lee nodded. "Yes, it does. You're making a wise decision. Satin finish will give it a classy look. High gloss could look cheap."

My temper flared. He would have let me ruin all our hard work without saying a thing? What was the matter with the man? Did all genius-level people have trouble speaking their minds? "Why didn't you tell me that?"

"Are you going to put the same furniture back in that room when it's all ready?"

I put the brush down and popped my hands onto my hips. "No, but don't change the subject. I want to talk about varnish."

"Are you upset?"

"Why didn't you say that high gloss would look cheap? You would have just let me make a big mess after I'd worked hours and hours on stripping the old paint off? I'm not working on this house to have it look cheap. I want it to be warm and beautiful."

He folded his arms across his chest and set his jaw. "You're mad at me because I was going to let you do what you wanted with your own house? It's your house. You didn't ask my advice, so I didn't give it. When you did ask, I was honest. So don't be mad at me because you almost made a bad decision."

"You should have told me high gloss would look ugly. We made a deal to be honest, and if you are my friend, then we have to be honest. I don't care about being nice. Look where that got me before."

He gritted his teeth. "Don't compare me to Drew. I never would have treated you that way. If you want me to tell you what I think, all you have to do is ask, and I'll be honest every time, but I've learned the hard way not to put my two cents in where they are not wanted," he said.

"From now on I want your two cents. If I don't like them, I'll tell you, and we'll discuss it."

He nodded.

"Tell me what you think, and be honest."

"High gloss on the floor and satin on the rest," he said.

"And you'll tell me what's best from now on?" I asked.

"No."

I jerked my head around to find him grinning. "Then we just had a big fight for nothing?"

"You call that a fight? I call it a minor disagreement."

"Why? I was blunt and not nice. It was a fight," I argued.

"A fight is when we don't talk to each other for a whole hour."

"Why won't you tell me what's best?"

"Because you can make decisions for yourself even if they're wrong. Mistakes can be corrected. Life is too short to have everyone else tell you how to live. Make a few mistakes, and learn from them. At least they'll be real, and you'll be living, not just existing."

"Are we talking about varnish or life in general?"

"Life as a whole," he answered.

"Who died and made you God?"

"Gert," he said.

A giggle started in the bottom of my heart and rose to escape out of my mouth in a guffaw. I could never stay mad at Billy Lee for a whole hour, so how could we ever have a real fight?

He grinned but didn't laugh. "Now, tell me what kind of furniture you want for your new bedroom."

"Gert was pretty high up on the ladder, wasn't she?"

That's when he chuckled. "One more step and she'd have been right up there with Saint Peter and the angels."

I laughed hard enough that the men working on the central air unit looked my way. I didn't even care. It had been years since I'd found anything so funny. *Poor Trudy, bless her heart!*

"What's so funny?" he asked.

"Saint Peter has his hands full with Gert, don't you imagine?"

"Probably so, but then, maybe she's got her hands full with Saint Peter. You going to answer me about that furniture?"

I wiped my eyes on the corner of my shirtsleeve. "I want a sleigh bed, queen-size. A dresser with a big mirror to match and a chest of drawers. Two nightstands, one for each side of the bed, and a thingamajig to put quilts inside."

He cocked his head to one side. "Quilts?"

"I've always loved quilts, so I'm decorating with them. I'll hit the antiques fairs and begin a collection, so I'll need a shelf thing to keep them in and one of those things that hangs on a wall to display one at a time and maybe even a quilt rack that holds six or eight to sit on the floor in the living room."

He nodded.

"Maybe next week we'll go find some of that kind of furniture. Or is it infringing on our friendship too much for you to go furniture shopping with me?" I asked.

He kept working. "Nothing can ever infringe on our friendship. It's solid."

"Are you sure about that? I'm not Gert." So our friendship was solid. I liked that idea.

"No, she died and made me God, remember? Come on, Trudy, if we're going to be friends, you've got to remember your place."

That brought on a whole new set of delicious giggles. I vowed to find something to laugh about every day for the rest of my life. I finally got my amusement under control, but a smile stayed with me most of the afternoon when I thought about Gert making a misstep and Saint Peter giving her soul to the devil. Bless Lucifer's little red heart, he'd have to keep Gert tied to his forked tail and make sure Lonnie was exiled to the back forty if he wanted to keep any kind of order in his fiery abode.

Several minutes later Billy Lee said, "When we get the doors done, I've got a surprise for you."

At noon everyone took a break, and Billy Lee and I stood our bare doors against the tree to dry. They looked pitiful, but he assured me they'd come to life with the stain we'd put on after lunch. We had sandwiches in the kitchen. Ham and cheese on rye bread with mayonnaise, Fritos, icy sweet tea, and the last of the cheesecake for dessert.

I pressed my fingers to the plate to gather up every last graham-cracker crumb. "If life was truly fair, cheesecake wouldn't have a fat gram or a calorie."

"Why do you worry about such things? You're perfect the way you are."

Well, knock me down with a sneeze, and beat me to death with a feather. Me, perfect? Was Billy Lee making a joke? I was thirty pounds overweight and looking forty in the eye.

"Thank you, but you are legally blind," I joked.

"We've had this conversation before. I can see perfectly. Evidently better than you can, because you're always putting yourself down. You are a wonderful person and a beautiful woman, Trudy."

I'm sure even my scalp was red from the full body blush. I couldn't remember the last time anyone had paid me a compliment. He would never know how much I'd treasure him from that moment forth.

He wiped down the cabinet top and hung the dishcloth on the edge of the drain board. "I promised you a surprise."

"I believe you did." I'd wondered about the surprise all morning and come up with dozens of ideas.

He led the way into the living room, back down the short hallway, and slung open the door into a storage room. He pulled a light cord and lit up the room, and I saw rows and rows of folded quilts arranged neatly on shelves—at least fifty, and the whole room smelled of dryer sheets instead of mothballs. I squealed and grabbed him in a bear hug. When I stepped back, he was grinning, and his ears were red.

"They won't fall apart if you touch them," he said.

"Promise?"

"I promise. Gert pulled one out of here to show me once. Said her mother made it. We were talking about birdhouses, and she remembered the quilts."

I was so tickled, I wanted to take them all to the living room. "It's a gold mine."

"So it's a good surprise. You aren't disappointed."

"I could kiss you."

His eyes lit up. "Then I guess you really are tickled with them."

I settled on one and carried it to the living room, where I laid it out over the sofa. I sat in a rocking chair, afraid to blink. He brought another rocker across the floor and sat beside me. Sitting there beside my friend, gazing at a fan quilt with black hand-embroidered edging, I figured out a big life lesson. I had two choices. I could be bitter, or I could get on with life. Drew could drop dead or marry Charity tomorrow. Crystal could grow up or stick her head in the sand for twenty years. Those were their decisions. Mine had been made. I had a whole closetful of gorgeous quilts, two doors out under the shade tree, and a friend to share it all with. I wasn't going to be bitter.

"You've got your stash of quilts without going to the antiques stores, and they've got a history. What do you think of that?" he finally asked.

"Unworthy," I said.

He frowned. "What?"

"This morning I was wallowing around in a whining pity pool, feeling sorry for myself, and now I realize that I'm blessed, not cursed."

A brilliant smile replaced the frown. "I told you."

"That I'm not cursed?" I asked.

"That you are wise. You recognize that you are blessed. That makes you wise."

"It makes me a fool for wasting a single minute wading around in a pity pool."

"A fool keeps wading. A wise person gets out of it. You got out of it, Trudy," he said.

"Okay, point taken. Now, which one will I put on my bed?"

He shook his head. "That could take hours and hours to decide."

"I need a couple more of those shelf things to set in corners. These are not going to stay hidden away. I'm going to display every one of them in this house when it's finished. Quilts will be the new theme of my house. The past meets the future. And thank you, Billy Lee, for this wonderful surprise. I seem to be saying that more and more."

It was the first time I noticed that his smile was crooked, and it made him look a little bit like Harrison Ford.

"I've always been your friend, Trudy. We just took different paths that led us away from each other for a few years."

"Well, I'm glad we got back onto the right path."

"Me too," he said softly.

Together we folded the quilt back up, put it away, and headed upstairs to take paint off the woodwork on the landing. I was beginning to love my new life and all its surprises. Betsy and Marty didn't have a clue what they were missing.

That afternoon Alford finished sanding the floors in the two bedrooms and the stairs. He left with a promise to come back when we were ready for the floors to be varnished. Workmen were in the attic putting ductwork into the upstairs rooms and down in the basement to vent air to the first floor. I hadn't built up the courage to venture into the attic or the basement.

Molly and Joe, my great-grandparents, had moved into the house right after they married. Her father had passed on, and her mother gave them the place with the stipulation that she could live there until her death. So my great-great-grandmother Elizabeth lived there with Molly and Joe until she died. They raised a family, and all those people with all their possessions over all that time, plus all those junk sales Gert had frequented—it all gave me the willies. Angels would hide in the back corner of Hades to keep from wading through the attic and the basement of this house. And I was no angel.

I was managing without Drew, and some days a whole hour or two passed when I didn't think about my former perfect shell of a life. Poor Trudy's big bubble butt was not pointed skyward anymore. I was existing quite well in my new world, working on a project that would net me a lovely home someday. I had Billy Lee right next door—my friend who could fight with me and still enjoy sitting and looking at a single quilt for half an hour. That night after a hard afternoon of work,

I fell asleep with a smile on my face. Life was good when I counted my blessings.

Heavy knocking on the front door awoke me. I sat up so fast, it made me dizzy. A quick look at my new digital clock said it was eight thirty. Billy Lee and I had agreed to take the weekend off. So what was he doing waking me up on the only day of the week I could sleep in?

I grabbed a ratty old robe of Gert's that had lost its buttons years before from the end of the bed, wrapped one side over the other, and plodded downstairs in my bare feet. Billy Lee had been there the day Gert's ancient alarm clock had startled me awake; evidently he didn't realize I'd have no qualms about taking the hammer to his head for the same thing. I unlocked the door and swung it open with a speech already on my mind that would scorch the hair out of Lucifer's ears.

It wasn't Billy Lee at all.

It was my daughter, Crystal.

"What are you doing here so early?" I asked bluntly.

"Good morning to you too," she said sarcastically.

"Come in. I'll put on a pot of coffee."

She followed me into the kitchen, where she pulled out a chair and slumped down into it, propping her elbows on the table and her chin in her hands and looking at me with disgust. "You look horrid."

I made coffee and rubbed my eyes. "You look like a breath of spring. You want me to cook you some breakfast? If not, I'm going to have cold cereal."

"Daddy took me to breakfast. I didn't come here to have a nice little mother/daughter breakfast and forgive you for tearing our family apart."

I laced my fingers together tightly to keep them from slapping fire into her cheeks. Physically she was a combination of three people. She had Drew's straight blond hair, my mother's clear blue eyes, and my short height. In attitude, she was often too danged much like Drew's sarcastic mother.

"Aren't you going to say anything?" she shouted.

I took two steps toward her, leaned forward until she was blurry, and whispered, "You will not speak to me like that ever again, Crystal. Either respect me, or get out. I haven't torn our family apart. Go ask your father about the divorce. He's got all the answers, not me."

Her voice instantly went back to normal. "Oh, come on, Mom. You had to have known about his affairs for years."

I went back to making coffee. "Sorry, doll. I didn't have a clue. If I had, I'd have left years ago."

She gave me one of those looks that I'd seen from her paternal grandmother many times. "I've known for years. How could you not have known? Besides, obviously he wasn't getting what he needed at home, or he wouldn't have strayed."

I gritted my teeth and poured Cheerios into a bowl. "Tell you what: when your new husband has a fling, you remember those words. And when you realize your worst nightmares and suspicions have become reality, you come on back here, and we'll talk again. There will come a day when you'll need a mother—trust me."

"Jonah and I are in love, and I'm never going to be your friend after what you did to our family," Crystal declared.

"Momma said to give a man everything he wanted and to make his life wonderful and he'd stay close to home. It didn't work with your father."

"Evidently you didn't work hard enough at it. Daddy says you're sleeping with Billy Lee Tucker. How long has that been going on? From Daddy to the town's oddball? That's awful." Her pert little nose wrinkled into a snarl.

"Billy Lee is my friend, and you will not call him names, Crystal. He's the only one who's stood beside me in this mess."

She threw her blond hair over her shoulder and pursed her lips. "Daddy says he caught the man in your bedroom, and I believe him."

"Believe what you want. Live the way you want. You are of age according to the laws of Oklahoma. You can even get married without my permission. You don't have to answer to me at all, do you?"

She stood up so fast that the chair almost went over backward. "I'm old enough to make my own choices."

I nearly smiled. "Likewise. I do not have to answer to you for any of my actions." I sat down at the table and started eating Cheerios. "Sure you don't want some breakfast?"

"I told you, I already ate. Has your mind gone along with your style and class?"

"Guess so. You got anything else to say?"

"Just that I'm ashamed of you."

She'd grow up someday and regret saying such mean things. Maybe I'd forgive her. Maybe I wouldn't. But I was sure that whichever way it shook out, the sun would come up, and the world would keep spinning on its axis.

"I'm sorry you feel that way. Did your father consult with you about Charity?"

She stuttered and stammered, but the words wouldn't form. Finally she slapped the table so hard, the milk in my cereal slopped out in big drops all over the plastic place mat.

"I don't have to listen to this," she said with clenched teeth.

"You know the way to the door, honey. This is my house. From now on I do what I want, and no one sends me on any kind of a guilt trip. Not even you, as much as I love you."

Her sweet little world had shattered into pieces, and she couldn't force me to put it back together again. "You're not my mother. She wouldn't say those things to me."

"Oh, I'm your mother, all right. And I should've been more like this the whole time you were growing up. It would have been a much better role model than who I was in those days. I should have confronted my doubts instead of burying them. I'm going to get dressed and go out to the nursing home to see your grandmother. Want to go with me?"

"Not on your life. I'm not going anywhere with you. If it were possible, I'd file for a divorce from you."

"Someday you'll grow up. Until then have a wonderful life and know that I love you." Surprisingly enough, I wasn't crying. I couldn't begin to imagine having this conversation before the ladies' room day without shedding enough tears to flood the Pacific.

"I might love you back if you'd give up this crazy lifestyle and go back home to Daddy." Her voice had turned into whining.

"Did he send you here to ask me that?"

"He hoped I could talk sense to you. He misses you. I guess he was wrong." She raised her tone a few octaves as she started toward the door.

If she was waiting for me to break into tears and throw myself at her feet, she'd better get ready to grow roots down through the floor, the basement, and even deeper, because I didn't care if Drew missed me.

"Guess you never know how much you like the water until the well runs dry, and if I can't have your love unconditionally, then I'll just have to do without it until you grow up. Drive safely," I said.

She slammed the door so hard, it rattled the pictures on the wall. I poured myself a cup of coffee and carried it upstairs without a tear and without looking back. Both of which surprised me.

Chapter Eight

The next morning I started to put on the yellow dress to wear to church, but I remembered that Momma had said I looked good in red when I'd visited her in the nursing home the day before. Even though I'd worn the red dress to church the week before, I put it on again. This could easily be my new look: a straight dress that didn't bind me up in the middle, a jacket to cover a multitude of eating sins, and simple shoes with no panty hose. Oh, yes, this was my style, and red was my new signature color.

There was one parking space left on the east side of the church, and I had two minutes to get inside before the service began. With any luck Marty and Betsy would not be sitting in my pew for the second week in a row.

Guess who didn't have any luck that morning?

Betsy and Marty were already seated, and their mourning season was clearly over. Betsy wore a yellow dress at least two sizes too small. She kept tugging on the skirt hem to keep her thighs covered. Marty's skintight purple top was so low that she kept pulling at it to keep a disaster from happening right there in church. I could picture Aunt Gert's eyebrows drawn down and her mouth set in a firm line, the look that she always had just before she crawled up on an imaginary soapbox and commenced to lecturing one of us girls. The words *an abomination unto the Lord* came to my mind as I settled into the pew with them.

"Good morning, Trudy. Didn't you wear that dress last week?" Marty asked.

"Yes, I did."

"No hose?" Betsy looked at my feet.

"That's right."

My smile and cockiness faded when Drew slid into the pew beside me. He stared at my toenails, which had been painted the night before—bright red to match the shoes. He then scanned the abominable goods all the way up to my ultrashort, kinky, curly, dark hair.

"You look horrible." He spit the words out as if they tasted bad in his mouth.

"Thank you," I whispered.

"I haven't filed the papers yet. I'm giving you one more chance."

"I thought I had used up all my chances when I didn't march my 'fat rear end' out to the car last weekend." I didn't whisper, and several people sitting in the pew in front of us turned to stare.

"You are making a fool of yourself." His tone was colder than an iceberg.

"File the papers. I'm not changing, and I sure don't want to be married to you anymore."

"I will tomorrow morning. Then I'm sending someone to pick up my car." He spoke in low tones, but they were as bitter as gall.

"You gave me that car for my birthday," I argued. My mind had a will of its own, and it was not bashful and did not stutter.

"The papers say that what is mine is mine and what's yours is yours. The Impala is in my name. I'll send someone to get it first thing in the morning."

"And they won't touch it. You want it, you come get it," I said.

"We'll begin by turning to hymn number . . ." the choir director was saying.

I stood up, deliberately stepped on Drew's toes, and walked out of the church. It's a good thing Oklahoma law doesn't allow liquor stores to open on Sunday, or I'd have driven straight through town and bought a bottle of Jack Daniels just to get the bitter taste of Drew out of my mouth.

Instead I drove to Billy Lee's church on Broadway Street.

Momma always said it didn't matter which church you went to on Sunday morning. The church wouldn't take you to heaven or fling you down to the devil, either one. All it did was provide a place of fellowship with others so you could worship God. I didn't see Him making a change, and I didn't intend to share a pew with Drew ever again. Betsy and Marty could take turns sitting beside him for all I cared.

The congregation was singing "I Saw the Light" when I walked through the doors. They finished the last word, and the preacher smiled at me. A few people turned to look at what was taking his attention, and they smiled too.

With a flip of one hand, he motioned me to come forward. "I do believe Gert's niece, Trudy, has come to visit us today."

I didn't know if they were going to pray for my soul or tack me to a cross, but I marched right down the center aisle, my kitten heels sinking into the carpet.

The preacher beckoned me forward. "No one has claimed the place where Miz Gert sat every Sunday morning, and it has looked empty without her. I'm sure she'd be delighted for you to take that seat, Trudy. Third pew from the front, there on your left. Please have a seat, and sing with us. We'll sing Gert's favorite song, since Trudy is here. I don't even have to tell you the number. Let's sing loud enough that the angels in heaven can hear us without straining their ears."

They began to sing "Amazing Grace" with such volume that I jumped. The person next to me tapped me on the shoulder to share a hymnbook. I nodded a polite thank-you and looked into Billy Lee's blue eyes. They held mine for just a moment, before I looked down at the words and added my alto to the mix.

He wore the same suit he'd worn to her funeral, and he looked like a lawyer or a preacher, certainly not a handyman. When we finished singing, the preacher opened his Bible to the verses in Jeremiah 51 where God was sending down his judgment against Babylon. I'm sure he meant for the congregation to realize that God takes care of his own, but what I heard was something about rendering vengeance.

The rest of the sermon was lost as I thought about Drew's

taking the Impala the next morning. Vengeance could belong to the Lord; I wouldn't argue that issue for a minute. If God wanted to baptize Drew Williams with vengeance, I'd sure be the one behind Him, egging Him on. I didn't hear much more of the sermon as I figured out ways to help the Good Lord out.

The preacher wound down his sermon and announced, "We're having a social lunch in the fellowship hall today. Everyone is welcome, whether you remembered to bring a covered dish or not. I think Billy Lee brought enough ribs to feed the multitude Jesus talked about in Matthew. So if you'll bow with me in a final word of prayer, we'll adjourn to the kitchen."

"Join us?" Billy Lee said after the benediction.

"I didn't bring anything."

"I brought more than enough for both of us."

"You aren't going to ask me why I'm here?" I asked him.

"Don't care. Just glad that you are. It would make Gert feel right good to know you're sitting in her spot. And I'm glad to have you here too, Trudy," he said.

"Then I'd be glad to eat with ya'll, and thank you for the invitation."

I helped the ladies set out the food and wound up sitting beside Billy Lee for the meal. The ribs he'd brought were delicious, and someone had brought a potato salad that was scrumptious. I had to have the recipe for Thanksgiving. It was creamy and had fresh green onions and lots of bacon in it.

"I heard you and Billy Lee were doing a number on Gert's place," Elsie Goodman said from across the table. "She would like that. Maybe you'll have an open house when it's all done so we can see it?"

"I hadn't thought of that, but I suppose I could. It would be fun. But it'll be a while, Elsie."

"I reckon it will. A person doesn't undo fifty years of neglect in a few weeks."

She turned to talk to the lady next to her, and Billy Lee leaned over toward me. "You look pretty today," he said.

"So do you. Why are you all dressed up?"

"Men do not look pretty," he said.

"Didn't mean to offend you. What is in this potato salad? Who made it?"

"I made it, and I'm dressed up because I felt like it."

"Are you mad at me?" I asked.

"No, ma'am, I am not."

"Children!" Elsie shook her head at us.

I had to smile. "Elsie, I think I'm too old to be called a child."

"Not to me. I'm ninety. Not much difference between me and Gert. She just went on ahead of me to get things ready. Kids your age will always be children to me. Stop fussing, and enjoy this lovely day. You are as pretty as a picture in that dress, Trudy, and whether you like it or not, Billy Lee, you are pretty in that suit. It becomes you and makes your eyes look even bluer. Now, what were you saying?" She turned to the lady beside her again.

"Fight settled?" I asked.

The corners of his mouth turned up ever so slightly. "Better be, if we don't want to stand in the corner."

"Tell me about the potato salad recipe."

"I'll bring it over later this evening."

"I'll make sandwiches for supper," I said, quietly enough that only he could hear it.

He nodded.

I talked to more people that day than I'd visited with in years. Everyone had a story to tell me about Gert and what a blessing she'd been in their lives. My cantankerous, bossy old aunt had had another side that I'd never known, one that reminded me of my mother. By the middle of the afternoon, I wished that I'd spent more time getting to know her.

When I got home, I changed clothes and crawled into the middle of the bed with a dollar-store spiral notebook, writing down every story that I could remember about her. My legs, crossed for a long time, went to sleep, and when Billy Lee knocked on the door, I was hobbling like an old woman.

"You okay?" he asked.

"I was writing down some memories Momma shares with me when she's lucid, and all the things folks told me about

Aunt Gert today. I didn't realize I'd been sitting cross-legged so long," I answered.

"Well, I brought the potato salad recipe and a six-pack of Coke. Want to sit on the swing and have a cold soda pop? I'll tell you why I wore a suit to church today if you'll tell me why you came," he said.

That was enough temptation to take me out the front door and to the porch swing. He popped open a Coke and handed it to me.

"Well?" I asked.

He grinned. "Impatient, aren't you?"

"You said you'd tell me. It must be something important. No one died, and you weren't the preacher, so why did you wear a suit?"

He tipped his own Coke up and took a long swig before he began. "On the anniversary of my granny's death, I always pay my respects by putting flowers on her grave. Roses because she liked them and never could get them to grow in our yard. So she gets a dozen roses on that day. Other times I just put out whatever I think is pretty. And I wear a suit to church that week in her honor. It's crazy, but that's why."

"I don't think it's crazy. I think it's sweet. I'll have to remember to keep flowers on Gert's grave."

"Now I'm pretty *and* sweet," he groaned.

"Billy Lee, you are sweet and sensitive, and those are qualities every woman looks for in a man. Why the devil aren't you married?"

"I can run fast."

We both laughed.

"Seriously," I said.

"It's complicated," he said.

I pressed on. "Haven't found the right woman?"

"Maybe the right woman but at the wrong time. Can't seem to get the two done at the same time."

"Fair enough."

"So tell me now, why were you at my church? What happened?" he asked.

I told him the story. "I'm really mad at him. That is my car."

"Give him the car. You don't need it. Use Gert's, or buy another one. Don't hang on to the past."

"Pretty, sweet, and wise. You'd better run really fast, feller," I said.

He downed the rest of his Coke. "Guess I'd best get on over to my place. I've got a couple more things to do before bedtime."

"Thanks for the Coke, the recipe, and the company," I said.

He smiled and waved as he disappeared through the hedge.

I sat in the swing for an hour while God and Lucifer had a battle. I have to admit, Momma would have been ashamed at the one I championed. Or maybe not. She might have been right out there in the dark helping me pour coals of fire upon my ex-husband's sorry, cheating head. I don't know if Lucifer won the battle or if God got tired of arguing with me and him and just let us have our way. I may still have to answer for what I did that night, but I'll go to my grave with a smile because of it.

I opened two cans of sardines and smeared a healthy dose of the oil on the underside of the mats on the back floorboards. One sardine found a new home in the glove compartment. Another one fit perfectly in the CD drawer. A nice film of Vaseline shined the driver's seat, giving the leather a brand-new glow. In case he brought Miss Charity along, I greased up the passenger's seat too.

I thought of her marrying Drew and got an instant visual of the two of them leaving the church in my car. So I rustled through the recycling bin outside for soda cans thrown in there by the men who'd worked on the house. I took down the clothesline and tied the cans in bunches of three to about fifty feet of rope. It took almost an hour to poke holes in those cans and tie them to the rope, and I had to lie on my back to find a part of the vehicle to attach the rope to, but I got the job done.

I found shoe polish under the sink in the kitchen and with it painted two perfect hearts on the windshield, so if Charity came with him, their faces would be framed as they drove through town. I used two rolls of toilet paper like crepe-paper streamers coming off the radio antenna, tucking the ends loosely into the back doors. The final touch was writing *Just Hitched* in black shoe polish on the white trunk lid in a lovely scroll, with a cute little heart dotting the *i* in *Hitched.*

If Drew didn't come to get the car, I'd have it towed and sitting in his front yard when he got home the next day. Aunt Gert's little thirty-year-old blue Ford Maverick—still in perfect condition, garage-kept, and rarely driven—would do fine for me. It had a stick shift, and I might jackrabbit it around getting used to driving it, but I'd get the hang of it again. Hey, I wasn't "poor Trudy, bless her heart" anymore. I was a force to be reckoned with, and if folks didn't believe me, they could crawl inside that white Chevrolet.

The next morning at seven thirty I carried my coffee to the porch, sat down in the swing, and waited. At a quarter to eight, Drew, Charity, and Georgia pulled up in the driveway beside my car. Drew and Charity got out of the backseat, and Georgia drove away in Drew's Lincoln.

Drew stared at the decorated car waiting for him. "You are certifiably crazy."

"She's not crazy! She's a certifiable witch," Charity said. "I can't ride in that thing."

"Keys are in it. You could walk back to town, Charity, but you'll ruin those cute little high heels." I watched as he helped her into the slick passenger's seat. I couldn't hear every word, but from the expression on her face and the way she threw her hands around, she wasn't happy about the way the Vaseline felt on her bare legs below her skintight miniskirt.

"You are crazy!" she screamed out the window when the aroma of eau de sardines hit her nose.

I held my coffee cup up in a toast to her.

Drew quite literally slid into the driver's seat, and the words that came from his mouth would have set a tropical rain forest on fire. He slammed the door, started up the engine, and quickly rolled down all four windows. Charity was gagging. Guess she didn't like sardines.

Vengeance had been very sweet and left no aftertaste of guilt. I giggled like a second-grade schoolgirl as they drove away.

"Guess you and God served up some retribution," Billy Lee said from the yard.

"Pretty childish, wasn't it?" I said.

"A whole lot childish but worth it, if it did one of those exorcism things on your heart. Was that sardines I smelled?" He sat down on the swing beside me.

"Two cans full, and I didn't waste a bit of the oil. And, yes, it purged my heart. I'm glad he took the car back, and I'm glad God and I had a bit of revenge. It's over. You want some breakfast, or did you already eat?"

"I'd love French toast and hot chocolate," he said.

"From scratch?"

"Is there any other kind?" he answered.

"Guess not, if you want the good stuff."

He followed me into the kitchen, where we set about making breakfast.

Chapter Nine

Billy Lee gathered the apricots.

We'd finished stripping all the woodwork in the hall, the banister, the stairs, and a gazillion little lathe-turned rails, not to mention the newel post, which was intricately carved. The electrician had finally finished. Air-conditioning was installed. The man who would varnish the floors was scheduled to come the next day. My body was worn to a frazzle with weeks of hard work behind me, and there was plenty more on the way.

And Billy Lee gathered the apricots.

The small orchard behind the garage had one apple tree, one peach, an apricot, a pear, and two pecan trees. Peeling little-bitty apricots was not my idea of a fun evening after putting in a final hard day of getting everything ready for the floor man. My fingers were stiff from using steel wool in every little crevice on the banister rails. It was asking too much to wrap them around a paring knife.

"Why in the devil are you gathering apricots this evening, and what are we supposed to do with them?" I asked when he brought them in the back door.

"Gert said last year that she had enough apricot preserves to last ten years, so I reckon we'll just peel them, throw in some sugar and Fruit-Fresh, and bag them for the freezer."

"And we have to do this tonight?"

"I reckon so. They're ripe, and they won't keep three days."

I must have looked puzzled, because he said, "Trudy, the floor man is coming to do your bedroom, the hall, and the stairs tomorrow morning, bright and early."

He set the bushel basket on the kitchen table, found two paring knives in a drawer, and started sharpening the blades. I'd never seen Drew sharpen a knife, but then, Drew had never gathered apricots, either. It mesmerized me: the quick motions, the way his rock-hard biceps tightened as he flipped the blade back and forth across the whetstone.

"Would you get a big bowl of water to wash them in? Then we'll each need two bowls—one to put the peelings in, the other to slice them into. I'll get the plastic bags, sugar, and Fruit-Fresh from the pantry. This won't take an hour with both of us working. We can't let this fruit go to waste."

This had to be a ritual he and Gert had adhered to. Bring in the apricots and either make preserves or freeze them for fried pies. I'd never made a fried pie in my whole life. Maybe Momma would have a good thirty minutes in the next few weeks and could tell me how to go about it. I set two serving bowls and a slightly bigger crock on the counter.

"Not a bowl like that. The white dishpan hanging on the nail beside the back door is what we wash them in," he said.

"What's three days got to do with anything?" I fetched it and filled it with water.

His look was one of pure exasperation. "I told you. The floor man is coming tomorrow. Spar varnish is an old product, but it's marine grade, which means it'll keep its shine even when you mop it. It's a long time drying and a longer time smelling. Everything will be wet for seventy-two hours," he said.

I was glad he didn't roll his eyes, or I might have slapped him.

"So?"

He grinned. I could have thrown an apricot at him or maybe the paring knife.

"So where is your bathroom?"

"Oh," I gasped.

The only bathroom was upstairs, off the landing, which would be wet for three days. Why hadn't I thought about that? But what did that have to do with the kitchen, where we could put up apricots whether the stairs were wet and smelly or not?

"That's right. You've got to clear out of this place for three days each time the floor man puts down varnish."

"Every single time?" I heard the whine in my tone and couldn't do a thing about it.

His lightning hands sliced the small fruit into the bowl. "Maybe not when he does Lonnie's room . . . I mean, your office . . . or Gert's old room, which will be a guest room. We could shut the door and chink it with pillows to keep the smell out of the rest of the house fairly well. But when he does the downstairs, yes, you'll have to leave."

Where was I to go? Momma's house had been sold years ago. Crystal hadn't returned any of my calls this past month. Marty and Betsy thought I'd caught a terminal disease, possibly from Billy Lee. All my old friends and acquaintances had avoided me like I had the plague. I'd attended church on Sundays, but I didn't know anyone well enough to ask if I could sleep on their sofa for three nights.

"Where do you have in mind?" he asked.

"Got a spare room over at your house?" I said before I thought.

"Yes, I do, but I've got another idea. I should have told you before now. I just figured you'd already made some kind of plans. Like a big shopping trip or off to see your friends. You've been awfully busy this past month. You might like three days to visit family."

"Friends and family are overrated. I'll check into the Western Inn motel," I said bluntly.

"I need to make a run to Dallas to pick up some specialty lumber, and there's a little town over by the Louisiana border that's pretty neat. Want to go with me?"

Could I go away for three days with him?

"I threw my cell phone into a ditch and haven't replaced it. I don't have a way for Momma's nursing home to get in touch with me other than this landline."

"Give them my cell number in case of emergencies, or go down to the dollar store and buy one of those prepaid Go-Phone things."

I tried to think of the last time I'd been away from Tishomingo on an overnight trip. We'd gone to see Disney On Ice when Crystal turned seven. Then there was a trip to Washington, D.C., the year she was caught up in American history—when she was eleven. After that she didn't want to go anywhere in the summer. She'd wanted stay home and swim in her own pool with her friends.

He went on. "I thought maybe we could stop at the Galleria Dallas before we pick up the lumber, if you'd like to shop a little. Jefferson, the town I mentioned, is only a little over two hours east of Dallas, so we could drive there, stay a couple of nights at a nice B and B I know, and drive home on the Fourth of July. Probably get here in time to go see the fireworks at the football field. Yes or no?"

"Yes," I said quickly.

"Then let's get these apricots done so we can pack."

By the time we washed up the knives and bowls, I was getting plumb giddy at the prospect of going out of town on a three-day jaunt. When we finished, we went to the dollar store and bought a disposable, prepaid cell phone that included three hundred minutes with the purchase. Billy Lee brought over his laptop and took care of programming it. I didn't even know he was computer-literate, but then, there were lots of things I didn't know about him.

He went on back to his house once he had the phone working; he'd told me to be ready bright and early the next morning. The floor man would be there by eight, and we'd need to be ready to leave right after that. I didn't tell him that I'd probably wake up every hour all night long to check the clock.

I was in the tub, bubbles up to my chin, thinking that I might have time to run to a salon at the Galleria and have my hair trimmed, when suddenly I remembered I'd left my old house without a suitcase. All I had was a multitude of plastic grocery bags. But I'd use them before I gave up a shopping trip to Dallas.

Surely somewhere up in the attic I could find a suitcase. It might not be a seven-hundred-dollar Samsonite Black Label like the one I'd left behind, but it would hold enough clothes to last two days. I jumped up from the bathtub. I dried quickly so I wouldn't leave footprints on the sanded floor and raced to my bedroom, where I pulled on underpants and a nightgown.

I should not have opened that attic door after dark. There I stood, barefoot, waving a hand back and forth, searching for the light cord, when a mouse ran across my toes. My screams sent it scurrying down the steps in a blur. I jumped straight up and tried to Velcro my hands to the ceiling. Gravity sucked me back down to the floor with a thud. Adrenaline sent me into a second jump, which is when I found the light cord. The light came on, but the old cord broke, and I fell on my butt.

I let out a string of words that could have blistered the paint off the woodwork, then checked to make sure I hadn't sprained an ankle or broken anything. If a rotten mouse kept me from my trip, it would be a sorry varmint when I caught him. Everything was fine except for my dignity, so I started up the steps, only to walk into a spiderweb that stuck to my face like superglue. No amount of grabbing at it dislodged that hateful web. In desperation I grabbed the first thing that came to hand, which was an old pillowcase, and wiped the gunk from my face. The grocery-store plastic bags were looking better by the minute. Who needed a suitcase, anyway?

But I was there, so I figured I might as well try to find one. Everything was covered in white canvas, and I could almost hear the theme music from a scary movie playing in my head as I carefully peeked under each tarp. There were lamps, roll-top steamer trunks that would be perfect to house some of my quilts, and gorgeous small tables for the living room, but not a single suitcase.

I was about to give up the search when someone pounded on the front door. It was nearly ten o'clock at night, and no one even came to see me in the daytime, so who on earth would be beating down my door at that hour? I reached for the cord to turn out the light and realized it had broken. I unscrewed the hot bulb by holding the pillowcase in my hand and hurried down the attic steps on tiptoe. I ran through the bedroom, grabbed up a housecoat, and yelled that I was on my way from the top of the stairs.

Billy Lee was on the other side of the door with a big grin

on his face. He held up a small suitcase, one of the new ones on wheels with a handle that popped up and down. "I brought over an extra in case you need it."

I unlatched the screen door and opened it. "Come on in."

He took two steps back. "I don't think so. Not at this time of night and with you already in your nightgown. Look across the street. Viola is peeking out her curtain. Probably heard me knocking on the door."

"I really don't care. We aren't teenagers, and you can come inside if you want. Besides, you're over here all the time. Day and night," I said.

"No, really, all kidding aside, I've got to get things ready for the trip."

He left, and I toted the case upstairs. The grapevine would be on fire the next morning. Billy Lee had delivered a suitcase to Trudy. Gossips would be speculating about whether I was packing my things to move back in with Drew. But after that stunt with the car, would he even take me back? And I'd be gone two whole days, so if someone was nosy enough to call, I wouldn't be there to give out answers. I smiled the whole time I folded shirts and jeans—and my two good Sunday dresses in case I needed them.

I slept poorly. I made mental lists of what I'd buy when we stopped at the Galleria. Billy Lee surprised me the next morning when he parked a big dark blue van under the shade tree in the backyard. I didn't know he owned anything other than a rusty old work truck.

I had the door open before he knocked. "Hey, where did that van come from?"

"Keep it in the garage part of my shop building. I customized it to haul eight-foot pieces of lumber so the wood won't get wet if it rains."

I settled into the bucket seat and wrapped the seat belt across me. "I like it. Sits up high."

"Someday when I'm not buying wood, we'll take my car somewhere."

That was the first inkling I had that he owned a car. Life did have its little surprises. What else did Billy Lee have out there in that big old building with its big old garage doors? My curiosity was piqued, but I didn't want to pry.

"What kind of music do you like?" he asked.

"Country," I said.

"George Strait?"

"Love him."

He put in a CD, and we listened to George for almost an hour. That alone was a treat. When I rode with Crystal, she listened to rock music. I'd learned to tune it out and go deep inside myself to think about other things while she bobbed her head and tapped on the steering wheel. When Drew and I went anywhere, he listened to classical. I treated it the same way and let it flow in one ear and out the other while Drew tapped on the steering wheel and hummed along. The only time I got to listen to country music was when I went anywhere alone.

"What kind of specialty wood are we going after?" I asked, when he took the CD out and handed me the case to pick out another one.

"Aspen."

"What is that?" I flipped through and found an Alan Jackson that I liked and handed it to him.

"It's very expensive and the new in-thing for furniture and cabinets. Got pretty grain in it." He slid the CD into the slot, and Alan started singing "Livin' on Love."

"How expensive?" I tried to ignore the lyrics, but they sank into my soul when Jackson sang that without somebody, nothing ain't worth a dime.

Did I believe that? Yes, I did. But I had Billy Lee, so life was worth more than a dime!

Billy Lee talked above the music. "What I plan to buy today will easily fit in this van and will run about two thousand dollars."

"What in the world are you going to build?"

"This and that. I'd rather talk about you than wood, Trudy. Tell me why you didn't finish college. You were always so smart. I figured you'd be running NASA or the FBI by this time in your life."

"I got married. Actually, I wanted to teach, but Drew wanted a baby right away, and then he wanted me to stay at home and raise her. We didn't need the money, so I did. When she started school, I got a job as a teacher's aide just to keep from dying of boredom, and that's what I've done ever since. Smart as *you* are, I'm surprised you don't run NASA or at least a Third World country."

"I like what I do and where I live. What would you do differently if you could undo and redo?" he asked.

I thought about that for maybe a mile. "My first thought is that I wouldn't have gotten married at all, but if I hadn't, then I wouldn't have Crystal. I might have been more aware of my surroundings. I don't know. What would you have done differently?"

"Not one thing."

I must have had a quizzical look on my face.

"Anything different might have kept me from being where I am today, and I'm happy to be riding down the road with you."

I smiled. Alan was singing that you couldn't give up on love because that was the thing we had to keep us going.

"You going to answer that comment?" Billy Lee asked.

"I'm sorry. I was listening to the song. If I could go back with the knowledge I have today, I would have spent more time with Gert and less with those who've tossed me away."

He nodded seriously. "I think I might have been a little bolder."

"So we both might have done a few things differently?"

"Maybe, as long as it didn't change the course of this day," he said.

The CD finished, and again he handed me the case. I chose an old George Jones, and we listened to it as we rode. It was eleven o'clock when we walked into Neiman Marcus. The young salesperson only snarled her nose slightly when she looked up at us. She wore her jet-black hair slicked back into a bun at the nape of her neck. Her neat black power suit could have been one of mine if she'd been Dumpster-diving in Murray County, Oklahoma, when Drew cleaned out my closets.

"May I help you?" she asked cautiously.

"No, ma'am. I can find what I need, but if you'd have a

dressing room ready in about thirty minutes, I would appreciate it," I said.

I expected Billy Lee to groan at the idea of thirty minutes,
but he just smiled.

The clerk was coolly polite. "I'll be right here in this section. You come on back and find me when you're ready, and
I'll be sure you get right into a dressing room."

She didn't give me a brilliant, I'm-going-to-make-a-thousand-
dollar-commission smile, but, hey, she didn't slap a hanky over
her nose, either. I was wearing a pair of jeans with a bleach
spot on the knee, a knit shirt with Donald Duck on the front,
and stained white tennis shoes. Billy Lee wore his usual bibbed
overalls and a chambray shirt. Sell us a pitchfork, and we could
rival Grant Wood's artwork.

I gathered clothing, and Billy Lee sat in a plush chair outside the dressing room.

I went into the dressing room with a ton of clothes draped
over my arm, and not one thing fit. I was relieved when the
salesclerk asked from the other side of the door if she could be
of assistance.

"Thank you so much," I said. "Everything I've picked up is
too big. I've worn a sixteen women's petite for ten years. Have
they changed the sizing?"

"Not that I know about. Throw everything over the door,
and I'll find you the same things in a fourteen."

I began tossing an enormous number of three-hundred-
dollar dresses and slacks suits over the door. I'd intended to
buy one pantsuit and maybe two dresses for church, but every-
where I'd looked, something else had caught my eye—and
none of it was black.

"I took the liberty of bringing a few more items. You have
such lovely skin and beautiful eyes and hair that I thought
you'd look good in a clear red."

I stuck a hand out and hauled in a dozen hangers. She was a
smart cookie. Flattery would get her a nice commission that
day.

"What size shoe do you wear? I could look for something

that would go with the outfits for you, so you can see what they'd look like," she said.

I'd just acquired my own personal gofer-clerk. I'd had them before but had never appreciated a single one until that moment. "That would be wonderful. Size seven and a half. B width."

I picked out red slacks and a matching top, a lovely floral summer skirt and mint-green cotton short-sleeved sweater, a nice Capri set in bright yellow, two Sunday dresses, and shoes to match each of the outfits.

She carried the whole pile to the checkout counter and flinched slightly when I pulled out my checkbook.

"That's an out-of-state check, so I'll need to see some ID."

I could read her mind. She was thinking that she'd spent two hours with me, and now I was about to write a check that could bounce all the way to the moon.

I flipped open my wallet to show her my new driver's license—short hair and all—and my bank card. "I realize this is a big sale and I'm from out of state. Please feel free to call my bank if it will make you feel better. I wouldn't want you to get into trouble."

She swallowed hard, trying to decide whether to offend me or take a chance.

I smiled brightly. "Go ahead and make the call. Phone number for the bank is right there in small print."

It was worth the wait to see the look on her face. By the time she hung up the phone, she was almost singing. "Thank you for being such a good sport about this. I'm sorry I had to keep you waiting. My name is Desiree. Be sure to ask for me next time." She carefully hung the clothing in garment bags.

Billy Lee carried the bags when we left the store and waited until we were completely out into the mall before chuckling under his breath.

"What is so funny? Did you not like what I bought or the top dollar I paid for it?"

"You looked lovely in all the outfits. I liked it when you came out and let me see you in them. And I wouldn't care if you'd paid double what you did for the clothing. I don't even care if you need it or just want it. It made you smile, so it was money well spent."

"Wow," I muttered.

"That was fun," he said.

"Fun? You had to sit there and watch me try on clothes for two hours, and you call it fun? I don't know another man in the world with that much patience."

"Didn't take patience. You want to shop some more?"

"No, I'm finished," I said. "How about you? You want to visit another lumberyard or hardware joint?"

"Only thing we need is lots of paint remover and sandpaper. We can get that in Tishomingo and not haul it all over the country. Hungry? We can grab a burger or have lunch anywhere you want."

"How about just a plain old McDonald's burger and then on to our B and B? Do we have reservations?"

"We sure do," he said.

Chapter Ten

Except for boasting more two-story homes that were in beautiful condition, the little town of Jefferson, Texas, didn't look all that different from Tishomingo. All the same, I felt like a sugared-up six-year-old on Christmas. Freedom surged through my veins as I tried to see everything at once.

Then Billy Lee parked the van in front of an antebellum home, and I saw that there was definitely something in Jefferson that Tishomingo didn't have. Looking at that gorgeous place practically made me hyperventilate. I know it raised my blood pressure twenty points. The sign out front said it was *Scarlett O'Hardy's Bed-and-Breakfast,* but it looked like Scarlett O'Hara's Tara. I'd read *Gone With the Wind* when I was fifteen and once a year since. It's my favorite book, and sitting there in front of a replica of Tara was like a dream come true.

"It's gorgeous. Can we tour it?" I whispered.

Billy Lee got out of the van and opened the door for me. "I made reservations for you to have Miss Scarlett's room. I'll be staying in the general's room."

"We're staying here?" I asked breathlessly.

"I thought you might like it, but there are other options."

"Oh, no! I want to stay here. Really, I do." I hopped out of the van and walked beside him up to the porch. The reverence in my heart was akin to what I felt walking into church on Sunday morning. This was Tara rebuilt. Scarlett's spirit probably lived on in the walls, along with Rhett Butler's.

I didn't drool all over the front of my shirt when we walked up onto the porch, but that was an absolute miracle. If I'd had to

107

speak or stand in front of a firing squad, I would have put the blindfold on and said my last prayer. We were met at the door by a man dressed like an antebellum butler who took our luggage straight up the stairs. As we followed him, I noticed green velvet drapes like Miss Ellen's po'teers at Tara in a sitting room.

The butler swung open the doors to Miss Scarlett's room and stepped aside. Billy Lee leaned on the doorjamb and watched me make a complete fool of myself. I squealed like a little girl and didn't care if Mamie rose from the grave and scolded me for acting like a heathen. I was right in the middle of a copy of Scarlett's bedroom.

"Cammie King slept here many years ago. She played Bonnie Blue in the movie," the man said.

"Like it?" Billy Lee asked.

"Oh, Billy Lee, I love it. It's absolutely wonderful. I feel like a southern belle."

"I'll show you to your room now," the man said to Billy Lee.

Before I could say another word, Billy Lee and the man were gone, and the door was shut. I shut my eyes and turned around slowly. I opened them to see a room filled with antique furnishings, including a plush bed with an elegant headboard, a fainting couch in the bay window, antique light fixtures, and an oak mantel. Wallpaper with Scarlett-red background covered the walls, and the bathroom had a grand tub plenty big enough for two people.

I ran a hand over the gorgeous bedspread and eased down onto the fainting couch, watching the sunset for a few moments with the back of one hand thrown dramatically over my forehead. Every word that went through my mind had a heavy Georgia accent.

It was my birthday. I was officially over the hill, and no one had remembered, but I didn't care. I'd just been given the most wonderful accidental birthday gift in the whole world. Someday I would tell Billy Lee what he'd accomplished but not for a long time. I was going to savor every single minute of the time in Jefferson, Texas, and make memories to revisit time and time again.

Momma used to say that I'd missed being a firecracker by

only two days. I'd always wondered, if I'd been born on the Fourth, if I'd have had more spunk and brains. I stared at the woman in the mirror hanging above the dressing table. Dark, curly hair. Nondescript green eyes with a few crow's-feet settling in around them. A square face with full lips. It shocked me to realize I was the image of my grandmother. No wonder Momma sometimes confused me for her mother when she wasn't having a good day.

Though it was my birthday, I hadn't thought about my customary dozen red roses all done up in a big vase from Drew until that moment. Momma would have thought I was a new maid coming around to clean the toilets if I'd gone to see her that day. She hadn't had a good day now in a long time. The only way Crystal remembered my birthday was if I reminded her. Then she'd run out to the jewelry store with her father's credit card. I had at least half a dozen little gold pendants with *Mom* scrolled diagonally across an open heart. They were in a silver jewelry box on the dresser at Drew's house.

Had Charity found that box yet? Had she held her breath, hoping to find diamonds and rubies, since that precious red gem is my official birthstone? If she'd opened it, all she'd found were little gold Mom necklaces bought at the last minute and a promise ring Drew had given me six months before we were officially engaged. I'd inherited his mother's engagement ring, which he'd replaced with a wide gold wedding band when we were married. Before we'd been married a year, the engagement ring went to the safe deposit box at the bank. It was one of those things "in his possession."

I was in Miss Scarlett's bedroom. My heart was floating six feet above my body, and I couldn't care less about roses, necklaces, or anything else. Nothing could erase or diminish the joy of that moment. A knock on the door jerked me back to the present. I opened it just a crack to see Billy Lee in a pair of khaki slacks, a blue short-sleeved shirt that made his eyes sparkle, and dress shoes. His sandy hair was combed straight back, and he smelled heavenly after a fresh shave.

"Can you meet me down in the parlor in half an hour? I thought we'd go to supper," he said.

I'm sure my face was a lesson in pure shock. Unable to speak for the second time in an hour, I nodded. I took the quickest shower I'd ever had, promising myself that later I was going to take one that lasted until the hot water went stone cold. I chose the swishy floral skirt and cotton sweater that brought out the green in my eyes, ran a brush through my hair, and slapped on a smidgen of makeup. I didn't rush down the staircase but took my time and wished I had a green velvet dress with a petticoat, maybe a parasol, and definitely a deep southern accent. I didn't look or sound a bit like Scarlett O'Hara, but I liked to think that my new fiery spirit was the same as hers.

The parlor did not disappoint. Whoever designed it must have loved and studied Tara. Billy Lee was sitting in one of the red velvet wing chairs flanking the fireplace, and he stood when he noticed me. He was even more handsome than Rhett Butler that evening, and he had eyes only for me.

"Ready?" he asked.

"Where are we going?"

He looped my arm though his. "To supper. I hope you like Italian. That's where I've made reservations."

"Love it. This is so . . ." And then I saw the horse-drawn carriage waiting at the curb.

"Thought you might like to go back in time." He smiled.

"Oh, my!" I gasped.

The driver held the door for us, and Billy Lee helped me into the carriage. I wasn't Trudy Matthews; I was truly a southern belle. As we rode down brick streets, past the Christ Episcopal Church, the museum, and hotels, I imagined it as it was in pre–Civil War days. I envisioned a time that offered a quieter, more genteel way of life. The driver kept up a steady chatter about legends and lore about everything we passed. I didn't need a notebook to write down every word. The whole experience was branded deeply on my heart and mind.

When the carriage stopped at the Italian restaurant on the west side of town, Billy Lee was a true southern gentleman and offered his hand to help me out. He opened doors and pulled out my chair at our table. He ordered a bottle of vintage wine, and I was amazed at his ability to pronounce the name. I would have stumbled and stuttered, and the waiter probably would have brought us Kool-Aid instead of a smooth, wonderful, deep red wine. I had veal parmesan. He had lasagna, and we talked about how the movie and the book were different. I'd never known a man who had read *Gone With the Wind,* and I had never had so much fun in my entire life.

I glanced out the window at the carriage several times during dinner. We weren't far from the O'Hardy place, and a nice stroll on a summer's evening would be fun, but I wanted another ride in the carriage to relish a few more minutes of the slow life that Scarlett had experienced before the war.

"It's not going anywhere. I ordered it for the whole evening," he finally said.

I smiled. "If this is my prize every time the floor man comes around, I may hire him to varnish something once a week."

"So I did good, did I? Am I now sensitive, pretty, and what else?"

"Just plain great," I said.

He grinned. "Hey, now, I like that word best of all."

"Finally, one we agree on," I teased.

He raised his wineglass. "To Trudy, who's beautiful in her new outfit and with her curly hair."

I clinked mine with his. "Thank you, Billy Lee."

"Shall we order a tiramisu to go so you can have a midnight snack if you get hungry?" he asked.

"Honey, usually I could eat two of those things, but it'll be sometime tomorrow before I'm hungry again."

"If you want one later, we'll have it delivered to the hotel."

The waiter laid the check on the table. Billy Lee put some bills inside the thin black folder and waved the waiter away when he said he'd return with change.

When we were back in the carriage, he told the driver to give us the grand tour of town. I could give someone the grand tour of Tishomingo in exactly five minutes. In a carriage it might take fifteen, and that would allow time for the horses to stop and nibble on Daisy Black's rosebushes that stuck out over the sidewalk.

Jefferson was a different story. The driver took us east of town, over a bridge across the Big Cypress Bayou. He told us the history as he kept the horses moving along at a steady pace. He talked, and I listened with one ear, but mostly I just let the words flow through my brain. All the history didn't appeal to me as much as did the frogs, crickets, and other creatures of the night setting up a chorus that sounded exactly like "Happy Birthday to Trudy."

The bayou had a peculiar smell to it, not anything like Pennington Creek in Tishomingo. Not even that year when the water got so high that they had to close off the old wooden swinging bridge did Pennington smell like the Big Cypress Bayou.

"What are you thinking about?" Billy Lee asked.

"The old swinging bridge that used to be across Pennington Creek when I was a little girl," I answered honestly.

He chuckled. "I take you on the grand tour of Jefferson, and you think about the swinging bridge back home?"

"I'm sorry. It's so beautiful, and the evening is enchanted. I was listening to the crickets and the frogs and thought of the creek at home. I didn't mean . . ."

He patted my hand, leaving his on top of mine instead of moving it away. "You don't have to apologize. I was thinking of getting a carriage so we could do this in Tishomingo, while we listen to the crickets and frogs. Shall we buy one?"

"Great minds must think alike." I smiled up at him. I'd never realized that he was that much taller than me.

"So you like my secret little town?"

"I love it. I can't wait until tomorrow to look in all the antiques stores we're passing."

"Has anyone ever told you how much fun you are? Honest, funny, hardworking. Gert was right. You're the best thing that came out of that whole family," he said.

My eyes popped open so wide, every crow's-foot must have stretched out tight. "Gert said that?"

"Yes, she did, and I believe it. Give you a problem, and you learn how to operate a bulldozer so you can plow it under."

"You sure you've got the right Trudy?" I asked.

"I'm more than sure. You've always been that way. It's what I admired from the time we were little kids. My first memory of you is when we were four. Your momma brought you to dinner at Gert's place. And Lonnie mesmerized us by eating peas with a knife."

"I do remember sitting on the back porch and watching him eat. Everyone else had left the table, and he wa, still eating. But I don't remember who all was on the porch with me."

"Marty, Betsy, and me," he said. "You said you could make peas stay on the knife without falling off. All you had to do was paste them on there. Marty and Betsy made fun of you and called you silly. I thought you were pretty smart."

"You did?" I was amazed that anyone had ever put the word *smart* into the same sentence with my name.

Billy Lee remembered a lot more about me than I did him. Suddenly it was important that I know more.

"So tell me about you," I said.

"Born in the house I live in now. Lived there my whole life. Went to school all thirteen years with you, then to Murray State and lived at home. Finished my degree at Southeastern in Durant and commuted. Got my Master's the same way. Didn't get the doctorate, though."

Six sentences told Billy Lee's whole life. "Is that all?"

"All I'm willin' to talk about tonight," he said seriously. "It's not my day. It's yours. Happy Birthday."

I was shocked. "How did you know it was my birthday?"

"Must have been something Gert mentioned once."

Billy Lee's face turned crimson enough to glow under the streetlights. I'd never seen a man do that before, and I couldn't stop looking at him.

"Did she also mention that I'm obsessed with *Gone With the Wind*? Billy Lee, did you do all this for me because you knew that?"

"Guilty as charged," he said.

"It's the nicest thing anyone has ever done for my birthday. Thank you."

"You are very welcome," he whispered.

The next several moments were awkward. He was more

sensitive and thoughtful than any man I'd ever known, and I was tongue-tied. I knew I should say something either profound or funny, but nothing passed from brain to mouth.

Luckily the carriage ride ended, and Billy Lee walked beside me to the door and into the house. He followed me up to the second floor and motioned toward a wicker settee. "Have a seat, and let's talk."

I sat down on one end and patted the spot beside me. "Okay, what are we going to talk about? Not remodeling tonight. Right now I don't even want to think about high gloss or satin varnish."

"We can talk about anything you want. I'd like to talk about you, since it's your birthday," he said.

I felt like he'd put a crown on my head.

"But first I want to . . . well . . . just wait here." He stumbled over the words. Then he jumped up and disappeared around the corner.

I leaned forward and caught a few glimpses of the dining room where we were to have breakfast the next morning. I felt Billy Lee's presence when he sat back down, and I turned to look at him. He was holding out a beautifully wrapped present. "For you on your fortieth birthday. May all the ones ahead be better than those that have already passed."

My first reaction was to let the tears welling up go ahead and flow down my cheeks. But he thought I learned to drive bulldozers just to plow my problems under. I wasn't about to let that image die and be replaced by a whimpering forty-year-old sentimentalist.

The present was too pretty to unwrap. It was done up in slick red paper that matched the walls in Miss Scarlett's bedroom, and it was tied with a big satin bow. I held it on my lap and stared at it.

"You going to open it or just hold it?" Billy Lee asked.

"It's too pretty to destroy."

"But you'll never know what's inside if you don't open it. Take it off gently if you don't want to tear the paper."

"You won't laugh at me?"

He pulled out his pocket knife and said, "I promise. Use this to slit the tape so you won't ruin the paper."

I carefully untied the bow and laid the ribbon beside me. The knife was sharp and cut right through the tape. When I folded the paper back, I was holding an antique copy of *Gone With the Wind*.

"Do you like it?" he asked.

"I love it," I whispered, and tears flowed down my cheeks. I wiped at them with one hand and held the book with the other. Forget the bulldozer. I was holding a vintage copy of my favorite book. I could cry if I wanted to.

"Open it up," he said.

With reverence I looked inside to find I was holding a first-edition volume of the book, and right there before my eyes was Margaret Mitchell's signature. The book was in perfect condition with a flawless dust jacket. Published in 1936. All one thousand plus pages in my hands, and it was mine.

To talk aloud in the presence of such a treasure would be next door to sinning, so I whispered, "This is too precious for human hands to touch. I'm going to have one of those special tables built for it in the living room. You know, one of those with glass on all four sides and the top, so I can open the book up to this page and let people look and yet be selfish enough that no one can touch it but me."

"Well, happy birthday one more time. We've got a big day tomorrow. There's a *Gone With the Wind* museum here in the house. Then we'll tour the haunted hotel and do some shopping," he said.

"You can't leave me now. Sit here a while longer while I take this all in. It's not midnight, so my birthday isn't over," I said.

"If you want me to, I'll sit here until dawn," he said.

"Be careful what you agree to do. Billy Lee, I'm in awe that you did all this for me. There aren't enough words in the world to tell you what it means to me. When is your birthday, so I can give you a wonderful surprise?" I leaned across the settee and kissed him on the cheek.

"You already did. My birthday was the day of Gert's funeral, and I thought it would be the saddest day of my life. Turned out I got the best present ever. A new neighbor and friend."

"I'm the blessed one," I said.

When the clock in the parlor struck twelve times, I finally let him go to his room after kissing him on the check once more, wishing I had the courage to really kiss him. But friends and neighbors didn't do that. Besides, I was so newly divorced that I sure didn't need to be looking at Billy Lee as any more than that.

He touched his cheek where I'd kissed it. "I enjoyed the day as much as you did."

"Impossible," I said.

Chapter Eleven

It was dusk when we piled into Billy Lee's old truck and headed east to the football field for the fireworks show. He circled the parking lot twice, ignoring several open spots.

I pointed. "Right there is one. If you don't park soon, we're going to miss the whole show."

"But you can't see the fireworks from there. I'm looking for a good vantage point so you don't miss anything, and I want to be able to hear the National Anthem."

"We don't need to see from here. We're going to be sitting in the stands. Fifty-yard line, halfway up, if there's room."

Billy Lee parked and looked at me a long time. "You sure about that, Trudy?"

"Polish up that bulldozer. It's time for us to do some plowin'," I said with a light heart.

A few seats were left front and center, so we climbed the bleachers and claimed them. Billy Lee wore a red-and-white-striped short-sleeved T-shirt under his overalls and looked almighty patriotic to me. I'd dragged out one of Aunt Gert's T-shirts decorated with the American flag done up in sequins— at least most of them were still attached—to go with my faded jeans, which I'd had to roll twice at the waist.

We listened to the National Anthem and heard a poem written by a local man, then a prayer from a preacher. It was after the prayer that Marty and Betsy settled in behind me. Daisy Black and her daughter were to my right. I pretended none of them were there. Maybe if I didn't officially see them and smell the smoke on Marty's breath, they'd all disappear.

It didn't work.

Daisy nudged me with an elbow. "I heard you're doin' a right nice job on Gert's house."

"Yes, we are," I said.

"Heard Billy Lee was helping you. What's that boy know about remodeling, anyway? Never knew him to work a day in his life."

"Billy Lee is a man, not a boy, and he's quite knowledgeable about carpentry, Miz Daisy," I whispered right back.

Billy Lee whispered, "Problem?"

"Miz Daisy was admiring my bulldozer."

"Bulldozer? I didn't know you bought a bulldozer. What are you going to do with a piece of equipment that big?" Daisy said.

Billy Lee and I both giggled.

"So you finally came to your senses and decided to bulldoze that place?" Marty asked from behind me.

Momma always said that a true lady never lets someone know when he's riled her; otherwise, she's giving away her power and her crown. My crown might be a bit tarnished, but I was not about to give it to Marty or Betsy. It was Independence Day: I was free. I could say whatever I wanted and live however I wanted. And I had a signed first edition of *Gone With the Wind*.

"No, I'm not thinking of tearing down the house. I plan to live in it. Billy Lee and I are working on refinishing every piece of woodwork in there. It's been fun."

"So you've been Dumpster-diving for friends since Drew divorced you?" Betsy said.

She and Marty both laughed as if she'd just cracked the next biggest joke to make the Internet rounds. Billy Lee stiffened beside me, and it hit me like a bolt of lightning. He had known there would be talk if we went to the fireworks together. That was the reason he'd wanted us to watch the fireworks from the parking lot. Chalk one up for Billy Lee. Take one away from smart old Trudy.

I pasted a big smile onto my face, not unlike that of a second-grader when the school photographer urges her to grin, and

I said, "Oh, no, Betsy, the only things I find when I Dumpster-dive are loudmouthed relatives."

Billy Lee let out a lungful of air and said, "You do a fine job of heavy-equipment operating, Miz Trudy."

"Thank you."

"I thought maybe you'd have gotten over that hateful spell by now," Marty said.

"I'm not sure I'll ever get over it," I told her as the first fireworks lit up the sky.

"Well, don't come around where I am until you do," Marty said.

"I was here first. If you don't want to be near me in this mood, maybe you'd best stay out of my space."

She hopped up and grabbed Betsy by the arm. They stomped down the bleachers just as a colorful red burst lit up the sky.

"Those are your cousins. You need to make peace with them, instead of taking up for a man who can't even hold down a job," Daisy scolded.

"Why, Miz Daisy, are you going to throw stones from your glass house?" I asked, all wide-eyed and innocent.

She snapped her mouth shut and watched the fireworks without saying another word.

Billy Lee, I mused, worked harder than ten men. He'd keep at it all day, then go out to that monstrous-sized shop behind his house. As I watched the fireworks explode, I wondered what went on in that building. Whatever it was, it had to bring in big bucks, because that book he'd given me for my birthday wasn't a dollar-store sale item. The one time I'd checked on-line at rare-book sites for a first-edition copy of *Gone With the Wind,* the price had boggled my mind.

After the fireworks display we went home to sit on the porch and have a cold Coke right out of the can. The past three days had been a fairy tale, and we'd driven the whole way home without a single argument as we discussed the ghost in the haunted hotel, the price of the quilts in the antiques store on the main street of town, and even the next step in our refinishing job. Billy Lee and I had become best friends, and we were happy sitting on the porch in each other's company, listening to the tree frogs and crickets in our part of the world. They didn't sound quite as southern as their bayou cousins, but the concert was lovely.

"Glad to be home?" he asked.

"I had a wonderful time. It was three days of indescribable wonder, but the closer we got to home yesterday, the more excited I got. Sitting here, right now, I just realized that this old house has become home to me. It gives me those warm, fuzzy feelings I read about in big old fat romance books."

"That's the reason I live in the house next door. I don't need anything bigger, and it's home. Sharing Jefferson with you was wonderful, Trudy."

"Sharing it with you was beyond wonderful, Billy Lee."

He tossed his soda can into the recycling bin.

"That's a three-point basket for you."

"It hit bottom. Last week it would have made more noise when it hit all the other cans in there."

"Oh?" I remembered the cans I'd tied onto the back of Drew's car.

"Had you forgotten about vengeance?" he asked.

"Guess I had, at that."

"That's good. See you tomorrow morning, then?"

"I'll be up and ready to go to work. Especially now that I've seen what lies beneath all that ugly."

He brushed a quick peck onto my cheek and said, "Good night, Trudy."

I could hear him whistling all the way to his house, as I held my hand to my cheek to see if it was really as warm as it felt.

Momma was having a good day when I got to the nursing home the next evening. I'd taken a shower and put on the new Capri set I'd worn in Jefferson so she wouldn't be ashamed of me. She looked up from her recliner, where she was watching a *Golden Girls* rerun, and smiled. "Trudy, I'm so glad to see you. Did you have a good birthday? I'm sorry we didn't get to go out and have lunch."

I didn't notice Lessie sitting in the shadows until she whispered into my ear as she left. "She thought she was five years old the past three days. Played with a doll and sang nursery rhymes. It's just in the last hour that she's been right."

I nodded and mouthed, "Thank you."

"Well, did you?" Mother asked.

"Oh, Momma, I did have a wonderful birthday. Let me tell you all about it." I pulled up a folding chair, took her hand in mine, and told her everything, even about the book.

"Well, I suppose since it's an old book, it's not improper for you to keep it. Now, if it had been a personal item, like something you wear, then you'd have had to refuse it," she said seriously.

"You are so right, Momma," I allowed. "Do you remember anything about Billy Lee's relatives?"

She patted my hand and held her head high. "Well, of course I remember them, Trudy. They lived right next to Granny Molly and Aunt Gert all my life. Best neighbors in the world. They had one daughter named Wilma, and she was a couple of years older than me. She was really, really smart but kind of slow in another way. Book learning came easy to her, but she'd been born late in their life, and she was . . ."

"A nerd?" I asked when Momma stammered. I held my breath, fearful that she'd drift back into the gray fog.

Her eyebrows drew together as if she was trying to remember. "That's what you would have called her in your day. In our time she was just odd. Anyway, they lived in that little house right beside Gert's place. You did tell me she left that house to you, didn't you? I'm glad. You need a place to live, and it was a fine old house. You can make it nice again, but it'll take lots of work. Have you lost weight? Your face looks thinner."

"Yes, Momma, I have. You were telling me about Wilma Tucker."

She nodded and went on. "Oh, yes. Wilma was one of those girls who never, ever had a date. She wasn't a very big girl, but she dressed all wrong. She wore old-granny oxfords and her hair pulled back in a tight bun like her mother's. The rest of the girls were all wearing cute little bobs, but not Wilma. She graduated from high school before me, and we'd see her around town with her mother or at church. And that's about it."

I sensed she was leaving something out. "But when did she get married?"

Momma lowered her voice to a whisper. "She married a truck driver, and he died, and then Billy Lee was born. Most of us didn't even know she was expecting until he was already born."

She smoothed her hair back with her hands. "Looking back, it seems like one day she was skinny as a rail, wearing dresses that hung on her frame, and the next day she was carrying around a baby boy. When Billy Lee was about two years old, she took sick and died. His grandparents raised him. They died within a year of each other when he was in college. He just kept on living in that house. He's a hermit kind of person, but he doesn't bother anyone. Gert said he was the best neighbor a person could have."

I had to know more. "Why does Billy Lee go by Wilma's maiden name?"

"Don't know. I guess after the truck driver died, she decided to keep her maiden name and gave Billy Lee the Tucker name. He's a good man, just odd like his mother. He proved it on your birthday. Who'd give a girl an old book for a birthday present? He should've given you a bouquet of flowers."

I thought before I spoke because I was afraid any show of anger could set her back. "I like the book."

"I'm glad. You should have a nice birthday. Did I tell you Marty came by today? She was all up in arms about seeing you coming to the fireworks with Billy Lee. Said the whole town was saying you gave up Drew for him."

"Momma, I really don't care what anyone says. I only have to live with me and my heart."

"Well, I'm glad," she said. "I wish you'd had that kind of backbone when you were married. What on earth changed you?"

"Eavesdropping in the ladies' room at Gert's funeral on Marty and Betsy bragging about all the women they knew who'd slept with Drew. Remember? I told you all about it," I said.

She hugged me tightly. "Both of them act like their sorry

daddies. Now, tell me all about the house. When can we go see it?"

"Right now, Momma. We can go this very minute, and we'll go down to the Dairy Queen and get some ice cream while we're out. Would you like that?"

"I'd love it. Do I have to change clothes?"

She wore khaki slacks and an orange-and-white-checked shirt. Her hair was combed neatly, and her Keds were spotless, but I looked her up and down for effect, anyway. "You look lovely just as you are. Would you like to drive past our old place?"

"I would, but after we see your new house. I want to see for myself if those floors shine like they did when I was a little girl."

I drove straight to the house, fearing every moment that Alzheimer's would claim her before she saw the floors. She walked inside and clapped her hands together. "It's just like it was in the old days when Granny Molly lived here."

I floated on a cloud high above heaven.

She claimed a rocking chair in the living room. "Okay, now tell me again, how long have you lived here? I forget sometimes, you know."

"Since Aunt Gert died. I moved in the very day of her funeral. It'll take a year or more to make it all pretty again, but I've got lots of time. I don't think I'm going back to work at the school this fall."

"Looks to me like you've got enough to keep you busy right here. Wouldn't be any need to work anywhere else. Are you okay with this divorce thing?" She took my face in her hands and looked right into my eyes, the way she had when I was a little girl and she wanted nothing but the truth.

"You always told me when I was dating and broke up with a boy that I could only be sad for one day. I was sad that long and then mad for a couple of weeks. Most days I don't even think of Drew anymore. He's fading away pretty fast for a man that I lived with for twenty years."

She kissed me on the cheek. "That's real good. I'm glad. I'd like to see you married again, but be careful who you date. If it don't feel right, don't do it."

"Momma, I don't care anything about marrying again. Look what Lonnie did to Gert and what Drew did to me. We trusted them, and we got our hearts broken."

"You got Crystal out of the deal, so it wasn't all bad. Don't waste an opportunity for happiness. Just be wise," she said.

We visited for a while and then went to the Dairy Queen. Momma had a banana split, and then we took a long drive. The light was fading fast by the time we got back to the nursing home. We were walking down the hallway to her room when she stopped and studied my face. "Trudy, sometimes I don't remember things. I hope I remember today for a long time. It was so good to spend it with you."

I hugged her tightly. I didn't want to let her go or for the day to end. "I love you, Momma."

"I've loved you your whole life. Now I'm tired and ready for bed, so you run along home and get a good night's rest."

"How about I just sit with you for a while until you go to sleep? Then if you remember anything else you want to tell me, I'll be here," I said.

I stayed with her until she fell asleep, but she didn't say anything more.

Billy Lee was sitting on the porch when I pulled into the driveway. He brushed at his pants legs, but he still looked like he'd walked through a sawdust tornado. He held up a sweating can of Coke, and I took it without hesitation. If it got any hotter, the devil would be moving his furnace to Tishomingo.

"Have a good visit with your momma?" he asked.

"She had a good day. I treasure each and every one when she knows me." I rolled the cool can over my forehead and face before I pulled the tab and sucked in the first cool foam.

He sipped his. "I'm glad she was good today."

"So what did you do this evening?"

"Worked in my shop. Painters are coming tomorrow to start scraping and painting. You sure you want the house yellow? This is your last chance to change your mind."

I nodded. "Original as I can get it, so no plastic siding, thank you. Think they can save all the gingerbread?"

"What they can't, I'll duplicate. They'll be taking it down

and stripping it. Take a while, but it'll look better. You want to start in Lonnie's room next?"

"Guess we might as well. Gives me hives."

Billy Lee set his empty can on the porch. "Lonnie died, and he's gone. Ghosts don't live in houses."

"Why not? There's a ghost in the haunted hotel at Jefferson. If one can live there, why can't one live in Lonnie's bedroom?"

Billy Lee chuckled. I prized the times when he laughed as much as I did Momma's good days. He was pretty serious by nature. Maybe that's why folks thought he was odd. I wanted to lean across the distance between us and kiss him. I blinked a dozen times to erase that crazy notion. What was I thinking? Billy Lee Tucker was my friend, and one kiss could spook him and ruin our friendship.

"You ever miss your momma?" I thought it was a good, neutral question to get my mind off his lips.

He looked away, and I wished I could call the words back.

"I didn't know her. She died when I was just a little kid. Grandma and Gramps adopted me and raised me as their child. I didn't know my father, either. He died before I was born. He and my mother were only married a few weeks. I miss my grandmother the way a person would miss a mother."

I changed the subject. "Sometimes I worry that I'll get Alzheimer's."

"Trudy, don't worry about tomorrow or let the past ruin today. If you get Alzheimer's, we'll deal with it then. Don't fret about it today."

"You're right, Billy Lee. Life's too short for fretting." I didn't miss the "we" he'd mentioned. He was promising to stand beside me in friendship through thick and thin, and I appreciated it.

"Guess we'd best call it a day. Plumbers, scrapers, and painters will be crawling all over the house while we strip woodwork and start on another room. At least you can see what the landing and stairs look like for inspiration."

"See you in the morning, then," I said.

He didn't whistle that evening, and I missed it.

Chapter Twelve

I unlocked the padlock on Uncle Lonnie's room that morning. If there had been even a faint rustle of the old lace window curtains or a squeak of the ancient metal bedsprings, I would have lit a shuck for Billy Lee's house. But the room was empty of ghosts, and a sliver of orange peeked through the lace curtains. I went down to the kitchen and brewed a pot of coffee. Sitting at the kitchen table, a cup of black coffee in one hand, a piece of toast in the other, I flipped through magazines. It was time to think about furniture.

When I was younger, magazines had had glorious pictures of the inside of houses. Now every magazine had sixty ways to keep a man happy: been there, done that, failed in the long run. Forty-nine ways to lose weight: remodel an old house and be too tired to eat. Dozens of tests to see if you were compatible with the man of your dreams: didn't have one. Billy Lee Tucker was my only friend these days.

Speak of the devil, and he shall appear. Billy Lee rapped once on the back door and poked his head in. "You're up early. Not sick, are you?"

I shook my head. "No, just trying to decide what to do with my bedroom. It's so pretty, I can't decide for sure what to put in there, and these magazines aren't a bit of help. Pour yourself some coffee, and help me make some decisions. I don't even know where to start to find something good enough to go in there."

"I . . . I . . . ," he stammered. "Well . . . I've got something I want to show you before the workers get here this morning."

"You're being nice again."

"I am not. I'm just afraid *you'll* be nice and say you like what I've got to show you even if you don't, just because we're friends."

"I'm all through being nice. If I don't like it, I'll tell you."

"Promise?"

"You've got my word."

"Then follow me. And remember you promised."

I slipped my feet into a pair of rubber flip-flops at the back door and followed him across the yard, through the hole in the hedge, and into his yard. I'd crossed into the inner sanctum by invitation. I'm not sure anyone in town had ever been to Billy Lee's house. When we were kids, he'd always come to Aunt Gert's yard when we visited.

He didn't go to his house but made a turn to the left when we reached the gravel driveway, and he proceeded to that big metal building set down against the tree line at the back of his property. So much for thinking maybe he had biscuits and gravy on the table for breakfast.

He fished a remote-control device out of his pocket, opened one of the huge double doors, and stood to one side to let me enter first. Was this where a secret organization took forty-year-old divorcées to offer them up to some pagan god? Was that why he'd been so nice to me on my fortieth birthday? Like the last-supper request of a person on death row, I'd been given a couple of amazing days before being stretched out on a stone altar and a fire started under my chubby body.

If I'd realized I was going to be the guest of honor, I would have dressed better. Maybe worn the Capri set I'd gotten in Dallas. No time to run home and change, though. Billy Lee and his overall buddies would have to take me as I was. Hair a curly, tangled mess, paint-splotched stretch-denim jeans, and a shirt that looked like it had been around since Noah crawled off the ark.

I stopped dead in my tracks and stared wide-eyed at the biggest Harley motorcycle I'd ever seen. I couldn't see him sitting on that thing, much less riding it around town.

"Is that yours?" I asked.

He stopped and let me look my fill of the cycle. "Yes, it's mine. Do you like to ride?"

I reached out to touch it but drew my hand back. "I've never been on one but always thought it might be fun."

"You can touch it, Trudy. Your fingerprints won't ruin the paint. We'll go for a ride anytime you want to, but that's not what I wanted to show you."

I looked around to see if there was a Mercedes parked somewhere in the space we'd just entered, but all I saw were several doors and a glass wall in front of an office that held a computer, filing cabinets, a massive desk, and a couple of leather-covered chairs.

"What is this place?" I asked.

"My business."

"Well, pardon me," I snapped.

"No, I didn't mean that it wasn't your business and mine only. I meant it literally; it is my business, Trudy. This is Tucker Custom-Made Furniture. It is my place of business."

"You make furniture? For how long?"

"Fifteen years. After I got my degree, I figured out what I really enjoyed was building furniture. Gramps had a nice life-insurance policy, and it didn't seem right to squander it, but I gave myself a year to do what I liked before I made up my mind what to do with my life. One of my professors commissioned me to build a few pieces of furniture, and word got around."

"I'm amazed."

"Anyway, you said you wanted a sleigh bed for your new room, so before you go to the furniture store . . ."

"Billy Lee, are you offering to make me a special bedroom suite? That would be wonderful. I wouldn't have to waste time and energy and . . ."

He slung open a door off to my left and flipped on a light. My breath caught and held. There before me was the most gorgeous bedroom suite I'd ever seen. I didn't care if I had to sell all of Aunt Gert's good jewelry to the man in Oklahoma City. I had to own it.

"Can you make me one just like that?" I whispered. To talk

aloud in front of such splendor was sacrilege worse than taking the Lord's name in vain.

"No, I only make one-of-a-kind furniture. That's why it's called custom-made," he said.

I was unable to tear my eyes from the beautiful queen-size sleigh bed, hutch-topped ten-drawer dresser with matching chest of drawers, bedside tables, and even a tall, skinny lingerie chest. All of which was really too lovely even for the White House. Why had he brought me out here to show me the very essence of my dreams if he wasn't going to make me a set like it? I blew the bottom out of that commandment about not coveting right there and then. It wasn't my neighbor's donkey, which the Good Book said I shouldn't covet, but rather that bedroom suite.

I moaned. "Billy Lee, I could strangle you. Why'd you bring me over here to show me something I can't have?"

"I didn't say that. I said I can't make another one just like it, Trudy. If you want this one, it's yours," he said.

I grabbed him in a fierce hug and stopped just short of kissing him passionately right on the lips. "I was willing to make a deal with Lucifer to get it. How much? I'll write you a check when we get back to the house."

"You cannot buy it. It's already paid for. Gert said to help you fix up the house. This is part of the deal."

"*God* doesn't have that much money," I protested.

He finally laughed. "God doesn't need money. So you like it?"

"Yes, I do. I really, really want this furniture, and I want you to build more. I want my whole house filled up with your work."

"Honest?"

"Cross my heart."

"Good. I won't have to give back any of Gert's money. I could have the painters help me move it in today. You could probably get a good mattress and box spring down at the furniture store here in town."

"Yes, yes, yes," I singsonged as I ran my hands all over the furniture.

"I measured the spaces you'd have for the dresser and chest, and there was that little place over there in the corner beside the window I thought the lingerie chest might fit into."

"Billy Lee, you are an artist. The next thing I'm going to start talking about is my office. But is all this going to take away from your business?"

"No, the joy of having your own business is that you can take a sabbatical year whenever you want to. I reckon we'll have the house done in about that long. You ready for breakfast? We could make some omelets and French toast if you've got eggs over there."

I was hungry, but I hated to leave my new furniture alone. I wanted to sit there until the men moved it to my bedroom, then spend the rest of the day admiring it.

"There are plenty of eggs. Want biscuits and gravy to go with an omelet instead of French toast?"

He grinned, and I really wanted to kiss him, but I led the way back through the hedge and into my kitchen, where we fell into making breakfast together. He browned a handful of sausage in a cast-iron skillet while I made biscuits. We decided on scrambled eggs rather than omelets. It was as if he read my mind when we worked in the kitchen. If I needed a spoon, he handed it to me before I spoke. I melted butter to just the right temperature, and he had the eggs ready the moment I needed them.

"I bought the new wood, the aspen down in Dallas, for your cabinets in the office. That room isn't as big as the other two bedrooms, so we'll make the most out of all the available space."

I reached up and framed his face with my palms the way Momma did with me when she wanted the truth. "Billy Lee, be honest with me. Did Gert really leave you that much money?"

He looked right into my eyes and said, "Yes, ma'am."

The notion was crazy, but I wanted to talk about something a lot more personal than my office and had no idea how to begin the conversation. I dropped my hands and poured gravy into a bowl.

"Maybe we'd better measure the room," I suggested. "I've

been meaning to get a tabletop and a laptop, but I've been too busy to go shopping for either."

"It shouldn't be much bigger than the one in my office. Towers and the new flat monitors don't take up as much real estate as the old ones did. So we can measure my equipment and make the built-ins to fit them."

When had I begun to think of Billy Lee as more than a neighbor? When he'd asked me to stay at the church dinner? Was that the day a friendship had been born? It seemed as if it had evolved slowly from neighborliness to friendship. I vowed I wouldn't ruin it with coveting more, so I started loading my plate with food. But it would have been very easy right then to stop coveting the bedroom suite and start coveting my neighbor.

That evening after we'd stripped paint all day, I took a long bath and went to see Momma. I hoped she was having another good day, because I really, really needed someone to talk to about Billy Lee and my changing feelings.

Lessie shook her head when I opened the door into the lobby. It had not been a good day. I sat down beside Momma on the settee near the piano and patted her leg.

"Crystal came today," Lessie whispered.

My heart dropped all the way to my aching, tired toes. "Crystal was in town?"

"Ungrateful child," Momma said in a strong voice. "You raised her wrong, Trudy. Gave her everything, and now nothing is good enough. What's the matter with young girls today? Want the world laid at their feet. You should send her to Gert for six months. That woman could straighten out the spawn of the devil."

"Gert is dead. Remember?"

Her eyes brimmed with tears that fell down her wrinkled cheeks. "Oh, no, when did Gert die? I must shop for a new suit for the funeral. Is it tomorrow?"

"Momma, Gert died back in May. Remember? I inherited her house, and you came to visit me and helped me decide where to put the quilts." I tried to bring her back to the present gently.

She wiped at the tears and narrowed her eyes at me. "Why do you tell me things like that? Who are you? I thought you were my daughter, but she's dead. She and Gert died together. Oh, Crystal will be so sad. Excuse me; I have to go lie down. This is too much for me right now. Does Drew know?"

"I'll take her to her room, Miss Trudy. You might as well go on. Maybe tomorrow will be better," Lessie said.

It was dark when I got home. Billy Lee was in his shop. I knew because I could see the light out there. What was he doing? There wasn't a sign hanging on the hedge that prohibited trespassing, and he was the one who'd made himself indispensable at my house, so I could go over there if I wanted. Nothing jumped out of the twilight and attacked me when I stepped through the hedge. Sweat dripped off my jawbone and beaded up under my nose. My hands were clammy as I slipped inside the building. The Harley was still in the same place. The room where my bedroom set had been was now empty, but there were four other doors.

Leave me alone in a room, and I'm instantly curious about what's in the drawers or behind doors. Momma trained me early in life that it was bad manners to go prowling around in other folks' belongings, but it didn't keep me from wanting to slip my hand into the pocket of that coat lying on the bed or take a quick peek inside the bathroom vanity drawer. It was an exercise in willpower that had gotten only slightly easier as I got older.

Perhaps if she'd let me prowl around more, I would've caught Drew in those first years of our marriage. Not that I was blaming it on Momma. Who knows what kind of person I would have become if I'd been given carte blanche when it came to snooping?

Which door did I take? The noise had died down, leaving me with doors number one, two, three, or four. Did he keep tigers and lions behind door number one? I eased it open, only to find the beginnings of a headboard, one of those tall, antique cannonball replicas. I could see it in Aunt Gert's old bedroom, which was to be my guest room.

"Hey," he said.

He was close enough behind me that I could feel the warmth of his breath on my neck. I jumped as if I'd been caught snooping in a dresser drawer.

Scarlet crept into my cheeks. "I was bored."

He pointed at the starting of the cannonball bed. "You like it?"

"It's beautiful."

"Thought it might look good in your spare bedroom. Maybe with a nightstand and a little vanity dresser with a round mirror. Not many folks come to stay very long, so you wouldn't need a lot of drawer space in that room. You mentioned liking cannonball beds when we were in Jefferson." He looked at me.

The town flashed before my eyes, but the shy kiss on my cheek after the trip made me touch my cheek.

He went on. "So, you're bored. Want to help me work on the built-ins for the new office? I could use another set of hands."

"I would love to help you. I'm completely ignorant of anything mechanical or electrical, but I'll do whatever you can teach me." I followed him through door number one.

"Can you hold a sander and keep it going with the grain of the wood? This is the first room I work in. This is a table saw. That's a planer. Over there is a jointer. It gets the wood cut into pieces and ready for the next room. Here, put on this mask. You don't want a sinus attack because you breathed in too much dust." He handed me a white paper mask, and I slipped it over my nose and mouth.

He handed me a sander, told me to sit on a bench in front of a workstation, and gave me a five-second lesson. Not a single piece of gym equipment could give the arms a workout like that sander did. It took a while before I convinced it I was the boss, but after that we got along fairly well. When Billy Lee was ready to call it a night, I'd sanded several pieces of wood—some short, some narrow, some long, some wide. I didn't know how it would all fit together, but Billy Lee was the magician. I barely qualified to be in the show.

He inspected my work. "You did a good job. I'll hire you to work any evening you want to come out here."

"Hire me. I'm just privileged to learn from the master. I should be paying you."

He grinned.

I pulled off the mask and laid it aside. "You are a genius with wood. Where all have you sold your work?"

"Far and near," he said.

"Okay, details. Where is the most impressive place one of your pieces of furniture sits right now?"

"Your bedroom."

"I'm serious."

"Okay. I made a dining room table to seat twenty and chairs to match for the governor's mansion in Oklahoma City," he said.

"I'm surprised it's not in the White House. If the president ever comes to visit Oklahoma and sees it, I'm sure he'll order one. Want a glass of iced tea? There's a pitcher already made in the refrigerator."

"No, I think I just want a long bath and a good night's sleep," he said.

"Well, then, good night," I said.

"Good night, Trudy," he said softly.

I thought of him taking a long bath while I did the same. And even though I was literally tired to the bone, both mentally and physically, it took a very long time before I went to sleep.

Chapter Thirteen

A warm breeze rattled the wind chimes and added to the chorus of crickets and tree frogs. I wasn't complaining. It was the last week of July, and we had a breeze, even if it was a hot one.

The outside of the house was painted a buttery yellow. With the white gingerbread trim and new windows, it looked like a Thomas Kincaid picture. Billy Lee had made and hung a new porch swing on the east wing of the porch, back in the shadows of a mimosa tree. I enjoyed the swaying motion with my left knee drawn up and my right foot hanging close enough to the porch floor that I could push off and keep the swing moving.

The sun had fallen behind the treetops, and the last light of day filtered through summer leaves in fading rays. I loved sunsets and sunrises more and more, especially when doubts crept up. Most days I could keep them at bay; on others it was like being at the starting gate at a horse race.

One moment the doubts were behind bars, the next they were running full speed ahead. That night I worried. How many more sunsets would I enjoy before I was diagnosed with Alzheimer's? Would I be in the nursing home when I was sixty-five years old? Billy Lee had said that we'd cross that bridge if we ever came to it, but he was my dearest friend; I could never burden him.

Then there were those other two more pressing matters. Number one: whether or not to go back to work in two weeks. If I was going to quit my job as a teacher's aide, then I should resign in time for the school administration to find a replacement. I thought about the pros and cons. I didn't need the money, and we weren't finished remodeling. Lately I'd been going out to the shop with Billy Lee in the evenings and working until dark. The equipment and all that power terrified me. I didn't even like the sander. But I enjoyed finish work, staining especially. Billy Lee used a spray gun to apply the sanding sealer and coats of varnish, but staining was done by hand using a paintbrush and wiping rags. I loved the way the grain popped right out, every knothole and swirl coming to life when color was applied.

I pushed off with my foot again and contemplated going inside where it was cool. When I'd first moved into the house, I could hardly wait for the air-conditioning to be installed. And here I was sitting out in the hot night air, sweat beading up under my lip and on the back of my neck, trying to think my way out of my problems.

Without reaching a firm decision about school, my thoughts went to my other big concern: Crystal. It had been longer than I'd ever gone without talking to my child. When she was young and every other word was *Momma,* I would have gladly been Gussie or even Minnie Mouse if I didn't have to hear a three-year-old whining "Momma" again. Now I'd love to hear her say that one word.

Should I make the first move and reach out to her? Or should I wait? If she needed me, she had the phone number. But—in motherhood, there's always a *but* or two lying around in the wings—I should be the one calling the shots.

A dark-colored pickup slowed down and turned the corner, coming to a stop in my driveway. I figured someone had turned at the wrong corner and was using my driveway to turn around. The engine stopped, and the door opened. That got my attention, and I recognized Drew the moment he stepped out of the truck. Squared shoulders. Belly sucked in. Chin up. He wore confidence as casually as his dark, pleated slacks and a white long-sleeved, lightly starched shirt. An evening breeze carried the smell of expensive shaving lotion across the porch as he shook the legs of his trousers down and rang the doorbell.

My heart caught in my throat. Something was wrong with Crystal. She'd had a car wreck and was dying or already dead. That was the only reason Drew Williams would set foot on my property again after the stunt with "his" car. He rang the bell a second time, waited a moment, and rang it again. When I didn't answer, he knocked hard and long.

"I'm around here." I finally got words to come out of my mouth.

"Where?" he called out.

"Side porch."

He strolled around the porch and sat down beside me without an invitation. He didn't look too shook up, so maybe our daughter wasn't hooked up to every known medical device in an intensive-care unit.

He slid a look from my dangling foot up to my hair. "Good evening, Trudy."

Wonder how he liked the jeans cut off just below my knees and frayed at the hems. I hadn't had time to hem them. I had a house to work on, furniture to stain, a mother in the nursing home, a child who wasn't speaking to me, and decisions to make. If he didn't like my jeans, he could take his charisma and go visit with the devil about it.

"Drew?"

"I've come to ask you nicely to come home where you belong, Trudy."

If that didn't beat all. Drew Williams asking me to come back to him and saying it was where I belonged. Had Charity found someone younger with even more money? Or did he like cut-off jeans with paint splotches these days? And to think of all the lovely lingerie I'd bought through the years.

He laid a hand on my knee. "Well?"

I picked up his hand and dropped it.

He sighed and looked out across the yard. "Okay, I was wrong. I've been a fool. But I don't like coming home to an empty house in the evenings. I miss supper being ready. I miss everything you did to keep a home together."

Not a single endearment. He missed having toilet paper on the roller and pot roast on the table. I couldn't remember the last time Drew had told me he loved me. I think he'd said the words when we were dating, but, sitting there beside him, I wasn't sure he had actually said those three words even then.

He threw an arm across the back of the swing but was careful not to touch me. "What do you say? Let's call a truce. I'll forgive you for the car. I'll forgive you for taking my money. We can sell this property and reclaim most of it. You've done a pretty good job of making this old place decent, so it should bring a fair amount. We'll put it back into the savings account."

Still he didn't mention loving me or apologize for all the misery and embarrassment he'd put me through. I was being offered my old car that no doubt still smelled faintly of sardines. And Charity got one of those new Thunderbirds.

"I've got a bottle of wine in my new truck. We'll celebrate tonight. Go lock up the house, and come with me. Your clothes are still in the house. I'll move them back into your closet if you'll come home. Please, Trudy?"

"Back into my closet?" I whispered.

Were Charity's short skirts and skinny little size-extra-small shirts on my hangers? Were her red satin thongs folded neatly in my underwear drawer? The drawer would be offended if my Hanes Her Way white cotton briefs were put back in there after it had known such tasty little treats. I just couldn't do that to a perfectly good dresser drawer.

"No, thank you," I said loud and clear.

His tone changed. "Don't play hard to get. I know I made a mistake or two, but you were so busy with Crystal and your own life, I just wanted someone to make me feel special. I'm past that now."

So now it was my fault. I'd spent too much time with our child. He hadn't felt special. Poor baby. Bless his heart.

"Marriage is built on trust and respect, and when that's gone, it's like sticking dynamite under the foundation of a house and expecting it to go on standing. I could never trust you again. Every time you got a phone call, I'd be wondering if you were setting up a date. Every time you said you had to stay overnight on a trip, it would be in the back of my mind that you were with another woman. So no, thanks. I'm not interested."

"You are a fool, Trudy." His voice took on a sharper edge.

"I can be a happy fool for not living with you or a miserable one for living with you. I'll take happy."

He jumped up and folded his arms across his chest. "I gave you a place in society."

"Give it to Charity. I don't want it anymore."

It takes me a while sometimes to get the big picture, but when I do, it's an amazing revelation. Drew was in a bind, and I was the only way out of it. It must be serious for him to arrive all dressed up, freshly shaven, smelling good, and with wine waiting.

"She wants to get married, doesn't she?" I guessed. "I provided the fire wall between you and your young toys, didn't I? You couldn't leave poor old dumb Trudy, so you were protected from all those young twits. Now I'm gone, and you are in hot water, aren't you?"

He jerked his head around to glare at me. "So what's the price? I can't marry that girl. She'll ruin me financially. Give me a ballpark figure of what you want."

"Price? As in money?"

"Or cars or a new house or you name it, Trudy."

"What if I said absolute celibacy?"

"What are you talking about? Me or you?"

"Both."

"You are crazy. You can have your own room, your own bed, and whatever else it'll cost me to get you back home. But I won't . . ."

Oops! He'd gone too far, and he knew it the minute the words left his mouth.

"I wouldn't ask it of you, Drew. You need a good, stable woman, but I'm not that woman. Not anymore."

"It'll cost you," he said.

"Oh?"

"I'll turn Crystal against you. I've already started. You'll either take us both or you don't get her. She'll hate you."

I raised my voice. "Don't threaten me."

"Hey, Trudy." Billy Lee pushed back the hedge and headed straight for the porch.

His timing was perfect. I thought about kissing him right in front of Drew.

"Over here, Billy Lee. In the swing."

Drew completely ignored Billy Lee when they passed on the steps. "You've got until tomorrow morning. Think it over," Drew threw over his shoulder when he reached the truck.

"I've thought about it. The answer is no. Forever." Strangely, I wasn't even angry.

"Got any sweet tea made up?" Billy Lee sat on the porch, bracing his back up against the house and stretching his legs out in front of him. Sawdust clung to his hair and clothing, and he smelled like wood shavings. He needed a shave, and the way his shoulders sloped, I could tell he was tired. But he was handsome beyond words and smelled like heaven to me.

"Yes, I do. I'll get us a couple of glasses. I could use one too."

He followed me into the house. "The floor man called me a while ago. Said he had a cancellation and can get to the office and guest room tomorrow if we want."

"Guess I'd better reserve a room out at the Western Inn?" I thought aloud.

"Well, if you want to catch up on some rest, that would be fine. But I was thinking maybe a little two-night jaunt some-where would be nice for some of that rest and recuperation stuff. You up for another trip?"

Billy Lee hadn't even mentioned Drew. Plain old curiosity would have prompted a couple of questions about why he'd been there.

"Sure. Where are we going, and what kind of clothes do I need to pack?"

He drank deeply of the tea I set in front of him. "Well, just how tightly can you pack a small bag?"

"How little of a bag are we talking about?"

"If we leave tomorrow morning, and you wear jeans and a T-shirt and maybe wrap an overshirt around your waist and tie the arms in front, could you make it with just the bare necessities?"

"But why would I need to take so little?"

"Thought we might go on the motorcycle."

My heart skipped a beat. "Then I can pack in a grocery sack."

"Duffel bag will be fine. I've got an extra one if you need it. We'll take the back roads down to Nocona, Texas, and prowl around in that area for a couple of days."

"That sounds wonderful. Billy Lee, I've got a decision to make, and I need the help of a good friend, if you don't mind listening."

A smile twitched the corners of his mouth. "You callin' me a friend?"

"Guess I am. You got a problem with bein' my friend? I wouldn't blame you if you did. It comes with a lot of baggage."

"I'll take the baggage. I've got baggage too, you know."

My heart felt lighter than it had in a long time. "Oh, yeah, what's your baggage? I'll bet mine is heavier."

"This is beginning to sound like a television commercial. 'My dog's bigger than your dog,'" he said.

"So what is your baggage? You don't have an ex-husband who's a horse's butt or an obstinate grown child."

"I don't want to discuss it tonight. What's the decision your friend can help you with?"

"Actually, I've already made it, but I guess I just want you to be in agreement with me," I said.

He looked away from me. "What is it?"

"I'm not going back to school this fall. We're not nearly through in the house, and I really like the remodeling business. It's like resuscitating an old lady who's almost dead and finding she's got a lot of years left in her. Hey, did I tell you I found an old lamp up in the attic that I plan to use in my bedroom? It's got this strange shade. Maple leaves around the edge, and it's kind of like a leaded Tiffany lamp, but it's not."

He turned back to me with a big smile on his face. "I remember that lamp. It used to sit on a table in the living room when I was a little boy, back before Gert married Lonnie. I was afraid you were going to say that you'd decided to give Drew another chance after all."

"Drew has had all the chances he's getting. He can fix his own problems from now on," I said.

"I'm glad, Trudy. I didn't want you to go back to him. I like us."

"Us?"

"Yes, I like us right where we are in this moment in time. I hope if it has to change, it goes forward, not backward," he said. "Now, about that lamp?"

"You changed the subject, Billy Lee. Why?"

"Because I'm not sure I want to hear what you've got to say about our going forward."

"I think I'd like that."

"Good. Now let's talk about the lamp."

I smiled. That was enough for tonight for both of us. "I'd love to have another one just like it, but there was only one in the attic. When I buy a computer, I'll do some research and see if I can find another, but I bet it's the lone survivor of an era."

He rolled his neck to get the kinks out. "Can you be ready by seven thirty in the morning?"

"I can be ready in ten minutes if you want to go tonight."

I got one of his crooked grins and thought again of Harrison Ford. "Seven thirty in the morning is early enough. And I think you made the right decisions about work and Drew."

The next morning Billy Lee brought over a duffel bag, and I filled it very carefully, carrying only the barest of necessities to get me through the next two days. I carried it to the kitchen and handed it to Billy Lee. The Harley was parked in the backyard, so we went out the kitchen door. The floor man arrived as we were leaving, and Billy Lee told him to lock up when he left. Billy Lee shoved my duffel into one of the empty saddlebags on the cycle and helped me settle a brand-new helmet on my head. He brought out a tube of sunscreen from his pocket and said, "The wind and sun will blister your fair skin. Put on your overshirt. It will protect your arms from the heat as well as bugs. I'll put this on your face and neck, and you can use it like hand lotion to protect your hands."

His touch was as light as butterfly wings. I didn't know which I'd rather do—ride with the wind or just stand there in the yard and let him cover my neck and face with sunblock all day. He finished and climbed onto the cycle, then patted the backseat, and I carefully hopped up behind him. Suddenly I was embarrassed. What did I do with my hands?

Billy Lee solved that crisis when he reached around behind him and grabbed both my arms, wrapped them firmly around his midsection, and revved up the engine. By the time he got to Main Street and turned right, I was in love with the cycle. Too bad Drew hadn't offered me a Harley. I might be moving my clothes back into my old bedroom.

Yeah, right, I thought.

Not even a Harley was that good.

Ravia, what was left of Russet, Mannsville, and Dickson blew past at seventy miles an hour. I was definitely resigning when we got back to Tishomingo. There was no way I was ever going to be stuck in a classroom if Billy Lee wanted to take a two-day jaunt on a motorcycle and I had the opportunity to go with him.

Chapter Fourteen

Billy Lee took us out Twelfth Street in Ardmore, past the shops that held absolutely no appeal to me that day. I was a motorcycle momma. I had all I needed in the duffel bag, and the world was mine. I didn't need to shop for a single thing that day.

I glanced at the Santa Fe steakhouse while we were stopped at the red light, but once the light turned green, even food took second place to the wind in my face and the freedom. He stopped at McDonald's on the far side of the I-35 overpass, removed his helmet, and helped me do the same.

"Thought you might be ready for breakfast," he said.

I fluffed up my hair with my fingertips. "Tell me the truth, does it look all right?"

"You always look beautiful."

"Billy Lee Tucker, we promised to be honest with each other."

"Trudy Matthews, I am, and someday you are going to believe me."

"Someday I might listen to you, but believing you is another issue. I'm starving for good old greasy food. Let's go." I looped my arm through his.

Instinctively, he laced his fingers in mine. We must have looked like a real couple, walking across the lot and into the restaurant. I liked the idea. For the most part the breakfast crowd had cleared out, so we got our bacon, egg, and cheese biscuits, hash browns, orange juice, coffee, and two apple pies quickly.

"So, what do you think of the ride so far?" he asked as we ate.

"It's freedom in a soup bowl."

"Never heard of a Harley ride put just like that."

"Let's not stop in Texas. Let's keep on going until we hit the Pacific Ocean, then turn around and head for the Atlantic," I teased, but if he'd agreed, I wouldn't have looked back one time.

"Maybe someday we'll do that. But we've got a house to get in order by Christmas. Won't have the furniture or the kitchen done by then, but we'll get the dining and living rooms finished so you can entertain if you want."

"And who would I invite to a Christmas party?"

He looked at me strangely, and my heart seized into a knot.

"I'm not inviting you to holiday meals. You don't need an invitation. You are welcome anytime, and you should know it."

"Like you should know you're pretty?"

"That's a different story."

"Are you being nice?" he asked.

"No, I am not," I answered.

"By then this will all be blown over, and they'll all want to come around to see what you've done with the old, ugly house. And you will have earned the right to gloat, Trudy."

"Who are 'they all'?"

He sipped his coffee. "Marty and Betsy and their families. Your mother if she's having a good day. Maybe Lessie. You'll be surprised."

I shrugged. "I would be surprised if anyone comes other than you and me. Getting the dining room ready will be our goal. Did you and Gert have Christmas dinner together?"

He nodded.

Sitting there dipping apple pie into the last of the coffee in my cup, I began to look forward to the holidays. I'd bring Momma home no matter what kind of day she was having, and I'd definitely invite Lessie. I'd call Crystal, and if she didn't want to spend the day with me, I'd try not to whine. I would even be nice and call Marty and Betsy. Billy Lee and I would make a turkey and dressing and all the trimmings.

"What are you thinking about? You look like you're somewhere far away," he said.

"I was planning our menu for Christmas. You think we should get a turkey or a ham?"

"Gert always had turkey, the smallest one she could buy."

"Buy! You mean she didn't go out to some farm and select a live bird?"

"Not in the past twenty years."

The giggles started.

"What's so funny?" His face was as serious as it had been the day of Gert's funeral when we were in the sanctuary.

I finally got my laughter under control with only a slight case of hiccups. "Gert made me feel like I wasn't a real cook because I didn't buy a live bird and dress it for holidays. She fussed at me every year, saying that a good wife wouldn't mess with one of those frozen turkeys."

"You three girls never knew when she was fussing and when she was teasing. Her sense of humor was very dry," he said.

"Then we'll get a turkey, and you can make that potato salad you brought to the church social."

"And the pecan pies. I'm good at making them. Secret is in—"

"Chopping the pecans very fine so they make a crusty top." I finished the sentence for him.

"That's right. And in never substituting waffle syrup for Karo."

I nodded slowly. "Learned that lesson the hard way too. I'm surprised Gert let you do any cooking. In her generation, men stayed out of the kitchen."

"It took some doing and more than a couple of years to convince her."

"I'd bet it did."

"But she never let me fix the turkey. I offered to deep-fry it or smoke it, but she wouldn't have any part of that."

"You've got that big a smoker?" I asked.

"Big enough to do two turkeys and a ham all at once," he answered.

"Then we're having smoked turkey. But if you make the

potato salad, pecan pies, and do the turkey, what's left for me to take care of?" I asked.

"I can't make hot rolls. When I do, they're heavy enough to be considered a concealed weapon if I put one in my pocket," he said.

"How about pumpkin pie?"

"Crust is always soggy."

I laughed. "Billy Lee Tucker! Are you just saying that to make me feel important?"

"I'll make hot rolls and a pumpkin pie, and you can be the judge. I'm being honest," he said.

"Okay, I'll believe you. Are we ready to go again?"

"You might want to visit the ladies' room before we take off. The ride is more than an hour, and the last forty-five minutes there's only one convenience store with a bathroom."

I'd hated ladies' rooms since Gert's funeral. The scenario from that fiasco did an instant replay any time I shut a stall door. Any moment I expected Marty and Betsy to barrel into the room, spouting off about Billy Lee, and I'd find out he wasn't the person I thought, either. But nothing happened in the McDonald's ladies' room that day.

Billy Lee was already on the cycle by the time I got outside. He handed me the helmet, which I jerked onto my head without any help. I threw a leg over the backseat and wrapped my arms around his waist. We stopped on the Taovayas Bridge across the Red River separating Oklahoma and Texas. The Red was down slightly, with sandbars on both sides of a shallow, winding river. Widespread debris gave firm testimony that in the rainy spring it had pushed its way over the banks. Green trees lined both sides, and on the Texas side Angus cattle and one lonesome-looking donkey dotted the pasture.

Billy Lee propped his elbows on the edge of the concrete bridge. "Know why there's a donkey over there?"

"Because he's cute?"

"No, donkeys protect the young calves. They can't abide bobcats or coyotes. They'll kick and bite them until they're dead."

"Are you pulling my leg?" I asked.

"It's the truth. I got an e-mail last week about it. If I had cattle, I'd put a donkey in every pasture."

"Imagine that," I murmured. How could anyone think he was an oddball?

It must have been a good day for cycle riding, because three more cycles stopped on the bridge. The riders meandered across the two lanes and asked Billy Lee how the roads were on up ahead. They were on their way to Turner Falls in Davis for the night, and then they'd return to Dallas the next day.

"Looks like there's construction on thirty-five, but you'll be taking the back roads anyway, won't you?" he answered.

"We get all the traffic we want at home, so we stay off the big highways," one man said. "Where y'all goin'?"

"Down to Nocona for a couple or three days. Anything going on that way?" Billy Lee asked.

"Traffic is bad. We passed two pickup trucks." The man laughed at his own joke and slapped his wife on the back.

She laughed with him.

The men went to the other side of the bridge to see how things looked to the east. The ladies gathered around me.

"So, y'all going to Nocona? There ain't much shopping in that little town. Got a good western-wear store and a couple of specialty gift stores and an antiques store, and that's about it. But then, traveling the way we do, there ain't any extra room to take it home, anyway. Sometimes I think this man of mine started this way of travel just so I couldn't shop."

"But don't you love it?" I asked.

She whispered into my ear, "It's the best thing since microwave ovens. I just have to give him a hard time now and then. I get so excited every time he plans a trip, you'd think I was a little kid."

"I can believe it. This is my first time to ride," I whispered back.

"That's not your husband? Y'all look like you been ridin' together for years," she said.

"No, we're just very, very good friends."

"Then, honey, you'd better wake up and smell the bacon frying. It's serious when a feller shares his bike with a woman."

"Really?"

"You'll have a ring on your finger by this time next year, or I'll give you my bike," she said.

"I might come lookin' for it." I smiled.

"You won't have to. I'll park it in your front yard. Where do you live?" she asked.

"Broadway Street, Tishomingo, Oklahoma."

"I know that town. Love the ride up through the country to get there."

"I'll be looking for that bike."

"You won't never see it, honey," one of the other women said. "She's that good."

"I really am. Trust me." She nodded toward Billy Lee and the others.

We mounted up and rode off, all three of the other couples waving at us. Those motorcycle folk were a friendly lot, and the mommas riding on the backs weren't a bit skinnier than me. If I had their names and addresses, I'd definitely send them an invitation to our Christmas dinner.

After we crossed the bridge, we came to a T in the road. A bullet-pocked sign said if we turned right, we'd travel twenty-one miles to Nocona. Billy Lee turned that way, and the ride took us through gently rolling hills. At times I could see the river over to the right, but most of the time the view was of Angus cows, oil wells, and those big round bales of hay. We came up to another T in the road, and the signs pointed to the right to Spanish Fort and to the left for Nocona. I figured we couldn't be far from the motel at that point and wondered what on earth Billy Lee had planned, since Nocona didn't have much shopping. I was expecting to drive right into a small town somewhat like Jefferson, but he took a gravel road to the left and slowed down considerably. Ten minutes later he pulled into the driveway of a log cabin set on the edge of a big lake.

He got off the cycle, removed his helmet, and held out a hand to help me.

"We're here? Look at those ducks! And that boat," I said breathlessly. The view was spectacular: water, sky, and grass all in Crayola colors. "Who lives here?"

"I do. It's my place, Trudy. We've worked so hard these past several weeks, and we had such a good time in Jefferson together, I thought maybe you'd like a few days of rest, and maybe we could do some fishing."

"This is almost as wonderful as the surprise in Jefferson. Can I go fishing with you?"

"Of course." He grinned.

"And whose boat is that? Can we rent it and putt around the lake in it? Do you really own this place? Let's go inside and take a look at it. You amaze me, Billy Lee. You've got more sides than a diamond ring."

"And you've got more questions than a two-year-old."

"You love it. You know you do," I teased.

"Okay, I admit it. I do love it when you are all happy and ask a million questions. The place really is mine. I bought it ten years ago. Got to coming down here to Nocona on my bike because the scenery is nice and the traffic is light. One morning I was reading a newspaper, saw a picture of this cabin, and called the Realtor. The boat is mine too. And, yes, you can go fishing with me, and, yes, we can take it around the lake after supper tonight."

I clapped my hands. "Would you look at that water? It looks like a sheet of glass, it's so still. Can we come here often? What does it look like in the winter? Do you have a fireplace in there? I think I see a chimney."

Without answering any questions, he opened the back door. The kitchen, living room, and dining room all ran together to form a combination great room with natural log walls. A big soft burgundy leather sofa took up the west wall, a galley kitchen the east one, with a table for two shoved up against a glass wall broken only by sliding-glass doors that led out onto a deck overlooking the lake. I was already planning to sit in one of those Adirondack chairs out there to watch the sunrise. Plush rugs were scattered haphazardly on oak hardwood floors, with the biggest one in front of the fireplace.

No wonder Billy Lee had fallen in love with the cabin. It was a perfect hideaway.

"Bedroom is in here. It's small, but it's got its own bathroom," he said.

I stopped at the door and looked inside. A patchwork quilt covered the queen-size bed, and another neatly folded quilt was stretched across the foot of the mattress. A rocking chair placed under the window to catch the setting sun had green corduroy cushions tied on the back and seat. A small chest of drawers held a lamp and scented candle. The bathroom offered a shower above a tub and a vanity with a mirror.

Guilt washed over me. "Billy Lee, you take this room, and I'll sleep on the sofa. I could even sleep on the deck in one of those oversized chairs."

He shook his head. "No, you will not. No arguing. I'll win, and I'm not just being nice, either. We've got time to take the boat out and do some fishing. Might catch supper."

"Let's go. And thank you." I'd remembered my manners at the last minute. It seemed I had said those words to Billy Lee more in one summer than I'd ever said them to anyone in my whole life.

"No thanks necessary."

Riding on a Harley took second place to relaxing on the pontoon boat and watching a red fishing bobble dance on the still waters. Billy Lee insisted on smearing more sunblock on my arms when I took off the overshirt; then he concentrated on fishing. I hadn't cast a line into the water in more than twenty-five years. Daddy used to take me along once in a while, back before I found out dating was more fun than spending the day out on Lake Texoma with a fishing pole.

"I love your idea of rest and relaxation," I said.

"Do you like catfish?" he asked.

"Love it."

"I was hoping you'd say that, because here comes supper." He pulled back on the line and brought in a nice big catch.

"How'd you know?"

"He's been teasing my line for several minutes. It was about time for him to take the bait."

After he'd snagged a smaller one, he put his rod and reel away.

"Do we have to go?" I almost whined.

He put the fish on ice in a blue cooler and opened the lid on a red one. "No, I put up the equipment because we have enough for supper and some left for the freezer. I'm going to read for a while. You catch anything, we'll do a catch and release. Hungry?"

"Sushi?" I snarled my nose.

"No, sandwiches and Cokes."

"Did you think of everything?"

"Hopefully. Want something to read?"

"Got a John Grisham?" I asked.

"Oh, you like mystery, do you? How about J. A. Jance?"

I removed the plastic wrap from the sandwich he handed me and took a bite. "I do like mystery, and J. A. Jance is a favorite."

He opened a tote bag and handed me a book. "Okay, then you can have this one, and I'll read the new James Lee Burke."

"Who is James Lee Burke?"

"Another good author. He can describe Louisiana so well, I can hear the nutria screaming and smell the swamp water. You'll have to read one of his books. You'll be hooked if you like mystery and good writing."

We finished our sandwiches and spent three hours reading in comfortable silence. The sun had reached its high point and started falling toward the western sky when Billy Lee fired up the motor and steered us back toward the pier beside his cabin.

He cleaned the fish, and I made baked beans and cabbage slaw. While he fried the fish, I added chopped onions, baking powder, egg, milk, and a little salt to the leftover cornmeal and made hush puppies.

"Been a while since I've had fresh catfish. Smells good, doesn't it?" he said.

"I can't remember the last time I ate fish fixed at home. Daddy liked to fish, and we had it often, but he's been gone ten years."

"Did he put cayenne pepper in the cornmeal?"

"Momma did. Said it needed a little fire."

"I agree," he said.

We ate out on the deck. The zapping noise of the bug killer competed with Mother Nature's night sounds, but there were no mosquitoes to ruin supper.

When we finished, he carried the paper plates inside to the trash can and pulled a couple of cold Cokes from the refrigerator. "Think I'll read a little more before bedtime, unless you want to do something else."

"Actually, I left Sheriff Joanna in a bind," I said.

To anyone else it would have been a boring evening. To me it was the stuff cotton candy and dreams are made from. No tension. No boredom. Not even a trip to the refrigerator to find something to eat just to have something to occupy the long hours. My tummy was full. I had a good book to keep me entertained. And Billy Lee was right there. Life was truly good.

Billy Lee took a shower at about ten o'clock and came out of the bedroom wearing knit pajama bottoms and a gauze undershirt. He wasn't as scrawny as he looked in his overalls. His arms and abs were rock hard. I had to exercise a good measure of self-control to keep from reaching out and touching the fine brown hair on his chest to see if it was as soft as it looked.

My voice was a little hoarse when I said, "Good night, Billy Lee. You sure you don't want me to take the couch?"

"Now you're being nice," he said.

"Yes, I was, and I apologize. I really do want that bed, and I'm looking forward to a long shower."

He tossed a couple of cushions onto the floor and pulled a bed out of the sofa. He opened a closet door beside the fireplace and found two pillows. "See? It's a real bed, and I'll be just fine."

"Then sleep tight. Any time we need to be up and around?"

"When you wake up. Sleep as long as you like. When we start in on that dining room and living room, we'll be working from sunup till sundown. Gert kept more junk in those two rooms than any of the others."

I lingered. "She did, didn't she? But then, that was what folks saw when they came inside the house. She wanted them to notice all her collectibles."

"Collectibles? That's not a collection. It's rejects from forty years of yard sales."

I almost ducked and ran for cover. Surely lightning would come crashing out of the sky. Billy Lee had just said something derogatory about Gert, and that was even more surprising than the motorcycle momma's prophecy.

"Amen!" I hustled on into the bedroom.

I wasn't really sure how accurate lightning bolts were. Keeping a wall between me and Billy Lee might just save my life.

Chapter Fifteen

I fought back tears when we left the lake. We'd slept late. We'd eaten when we wanted. We'd fished. We'd trolled around the whole lake one day and fed the fish and turtles part of our sandwiches.

"I don't want to leave," I whispered as we got onto the Harley.

"I never do. But it wouldn't be nearly as much fun if we had it every day," he said.

"Bet me."

"We can come back anytime you want to, Trudy."

"Is that a promise?"

"It is. But if you had all the candy bars you wanted every day, you'd get tired of them."

"You don't know me very well." I managed a smile even though my chin was almost quivering. "Next time we need to leave for the floor man, will you bring me back here?"

He nodded, and I believed him. Billy Lee had never lied to me.

Riding on the back of a cycle for more than two hours gave me lots of time for thinking. If we hadn't put so many long hours and elbow grease into redoing the top floor, I might have gathered up some twenty-year-old newspapers from a corner, soaked them in ten-year-old gasoline from the garage, and set fire to the whole house. The only thing that saved the place was the furniture Billy Lee had built. That and the brand-spanking-new big deep Jacuzzi the plumbers had installed in the bathroom. I couldn't very well torch something that expensive. But the thought of having to do the whole downstairs was enough to make me tell Billy Lee to turn the bike around and take me back to the lake house, where I intended to live permanently.

It was dusk when we got home, and Billy Lee didn't even come inside. He said he'd see me the next morning bright and early and went on home. I was tickled with the new, shiny floors, but all that junk in the living room and dining room hadn't mysteriously disappeared while we were gone.

I wandered through the downstairs, which was almost a perfect square. The foyer and living room extended across the entire front, taking up half the downstairs. Whoever had designed the place hadn't been thinking of rowdy children who could slide down the banister into the living room and run circles from the living room, through the dining room, into the kitchen, and back to the living room. Visions of the lake house danced in my head, and it became the light at the end of the tunnel.

The next morning we had breakfast together, and Billy Lee went straight up to my new office, where he would be assembling the desk and cabinets. I would rather have been helping him than boxing up all the junk.

"Hey, when you get all that done, you can come up here and keep me company," he yelled down the stairs.

"You're going to die a lonely old man!" I yelled back. "I'll have gray hair before this is done. I'm not totally sure that doing this job won't *cause* Alzheimer's. Going through Grandmother Matthews' old stuff is probably what snatched my mother's memory. You've got time to construct a new home complete with three stories and a basement and attic in the time it'll take me to empty the dining room."

He went back into the office. "Then when I get done, I'll help you."

With one last little whimper, I steeled myself and took a step into the room. Flattened cardboard boxes were stacked on the table, along with duct tape, wide packing tape, and a Magic Marker. I popped a box into a square, taped the bottom, and started on the bookcase along the back wall. In the beginning the shelves had been installed to hold fancy dishes and shiny silver platters. Gert had long since packed away anything of worth, and the shelves were now covered with junk.

I wished Gert would appear like a hologram right beside me. First I'd ask her what gave her the right to buy a turkey from the store when she knew how to wring a neck and pluck feathers. And then I'd make her tell me what was worth keeping and what was junk.

The doorbell rang before I had time to put a single item into the first box. I didn't care if it was Marty or Betsy, just so long as I could procrastinate a few more minutes. I opened the door to find a smartly dressed woman and man on my porch, each with a briefcase. It was definitely not my day. It didn't matter if they were selling encyclopedias or religion—I wasn't interested.

"Trudy Matthews?" The man had a high-pitched voice with a lisp.

Maybe they'd been sent straight from heaven to punish me for thinking about burning down the house. How else would they know my name? Or maybe Crystal had really declared me insane, and the briefcases were filled with drugs to sedate me until they could get a straitjacket onto me.

"Why do you want Trudy?"

"Mr. Tucker called last night and made arrangements for us to come by. We are antiques dealers from Ada, and . . ."

I swung the door open and motioned them inside. "Please, come right in. I'm about to clean out the dining room."

"Hey, Trudy, I forgot to tell you I called an antiques dealer to . . . Guess it doesn't matter now," Billy Lee shouted from the top of the stairs.

I shook a finger at him. I'd deal with him later. He was full of surprises, and I truly loved most of them, but someday he was going to forget to tell me something that would cause a heart attack.

The woman made introductions as they followed me. "I'm Linda, and this is my husband, Art. Is it all right if we set up shop on the end of this table?"

They were the same height and age, somewhere around sixty, and all business.

He gasped at the dining room table. "It's oak. Late eighteen hundreds. Are you selling it?"

"No, we're keeping it," I said.

"Please let us be first to bid on it if you decide to sell. Now, what would you like us to catalog and make an offer on?"

"Oh, Art, look at these precious salt and pepper shakers, and they're clearly marked on the bottom. I can see a lot of items we'd be interested in purchasing, so let me explain our rates. We will pay sixty percent of book value on any antique. We will show you the item in the catalog, so you'll know we are not cheating you."

Heck, I didn't care what they paid me. Anything was better than the nothing I'd get when I took it all to the Goodwill store in Durant.

"Just keep a list, and I'll look at it when you're finished. What you don't want, please . . ."

"For the honor of getting to go through this stuff, we'll gladly box what we don't want so you can store it." Art popped open a briefcase, brought out several books, a yellow legal pad, and a calculator, plus a hardbound business check-book.

We all took a break at lunchtime. They asked about a restaurant, and I sent them out to the Western Inn for the lunch buffet. Billy Lee stopped work, and we made sandwiches in the kitchen.

"So, are they finding anything good?" he asked, as I looked over the paper where they'd listed what they had found so far.

"About ten thousand dollars' worth so far. That's six thousand to us." That last word came out so naturally, it scared me.

"And is it making a dent in the junk?"

"Not nearly enough. Could we take what's left to the Good-will down in Durant?"

"Anytime you want, we can load it up in the van and run it down there. Got any more of that coconut cream pie?"

I brought a frozen pie out of the refrigerator, cut off two slabs, and put them on paper plates.

He reached for his. "Gert used to tell me she'd had a fortune in this house right under Lonnie's nose. Guess she did know the difference between good antiques and pure junk. I thought she meant it was hidden in the attic or basement, but then, that wouldn't have been right under his nose, would it?"

"What else did she tell you?" I asked.

"That when she was dead she hoped . . ." He paused.

"What?" I pressured.

"Okay, I'll fess up. I knew she was leaving it all to you."

"And?"

"She said she hoped you went through things really slowly and didn't toss out anything valuable."

"I can see why, but was she talking about just the stuff in this house?"

He shrugged. "Don't know. She'd say something like that and then tell me what happened back when she and Eula were little girls or some other piece of her history. There at the end her mind flitted from past to present and back again during the course of one supper."

He ate, and I pondered, finally putting my untouched pie back into the carton. What on earth could she have meant? The jewelry? Maybe she was afraid I'd toss everything without taking time to really look at it.

"I guess she meant that jewelry."

"You might want to put it into the safe."

Thinking he meant a safe deposit box at the bank, I asked, "And where's the key to that?"

"Don't need a key. It's a combination lock, and I know the combination."

I must have looked puzzled.

"Come on, I'll show you. It's in the basement, and no one but me even knows it's there. She had it installed after Lonnie died. I should've told you about it, but there's been so much to do, and—"

"—and I trust you, Billy Lee." I finished the sentence.

He opened a door down to the basement and pulled a penny chain cord. Light shined down a very narrow staircase. I hate cellars and basements and caves and anything underground.

Let the tornado whistle blow, and I'll ignore it. I'd rather take my chances swirling through the air with all the other debris than spend an hour in a musty-smelling cellar.

He moved an old Victrola to one side and squatted down to slide a metal suitcase away, and right there on ground level was the door of a safe.

"There we go. Combination is seven right, thirteen left, eleven right."

Every day brought a brand-new surprise.

The inside of the safe was about eighteen inches square and filled with papers, money, and more jewelry in little black velvet drawstring bags. I leafed through the papers and jewelry before putting it all back.

"I don't have time to deal with this right now. I've got to get the upstairs cleaned out first. One thing at a time. We'll go through the rest of it later and put that jewelry down here," I said.

Billy Lee shut the safe, twirled the dial, and moved the camouflage back over it. "Ain't inheriting fun?"

"I could write a book."

"Why don't you?"

"Are you serious?"

"Sure. You are so smart. You *could* write a book. You're funny too. Tell it just like you see it. Only . . ." He waggled his eyebrows. "Change the names to protect the guilty."

It began with a smile, which became a giggle, and then a full-fledged belly laugh I couldn't control. It was so infectious, Billy Lee caught it, and there we sat like two first-graders laughing our fool heads off, when the doorbell rang. We still wore stupid grins when we opened the front door to find Linda and Art ready for the afternoon's work.

On my way upstairs to work beside Billy Lee, an idea popped into my mind like a lightbulb in a bubble above a cartoon character's head. I could use the money we'd made today to help underprivileged girls get an education. I could create a Gertrude Martin scholarship to be given to the Tishomingo High School female senior who needed help to pay for college.

Billy Lee and I could be on the committee to decide who would get the scholarship.

By suppertime Art and Linda had a van loaded top to bottom, and I had enough boxes to warrant a run to the Durant Goodwill store, but that would have to wait. The store would be closed by the time we could drive there that evening.

Billy Lee fired up the hibachi out on the back porch. I topped cut-up potatoes, onions, and fresh green beans with pats of butter, salt, and pepper and wrapped it all in foil to grill thirty minutes before he put on the steaks. I sat in the swing and watched him cook.

"What're you going to do with the money you made today?" Billy Lee asked.

"I'm thinking about a Gertrude Martin scholarship for a high school senior girl."

"That's a good idea," he said.

"What'd you think I'd do with it?"

"Pay for divorces for women who have cheating husbands. Or else set up scholarships to train them for jobs so they could support themselves."

"Hadn't thought of that, but it's a good idea. I like it better than a scholarship for a younger person. What makes you so smart? And, while we're at it, you have got to start telling me stuff."

He looked me right in the eye. "I do tell you stuff."

"You didn't tell me about Linda and Art."

"I forgot. I was thinking about the office and hoping you wouldn't be disappointed, and I forgot."

"Billy Lee, I love every single thing you've done in the house. It's as if you read my mind and produce what I want even before I know what I want."

"Then what's the problem?"

"The problem is, I'd been dreading going through all that junk today. If it hadn't been for all the gorgeous furniture you'd built, I might have torched the place just to keep from sorting and packing up all that stuff."

He chuckled, and the tension disappeared.

"You've really got to start writing some of this down, Trudy. You'd be good at it."

"I couldn't keep a train of thought long enough to write a whole book. Besides, we've got too much work to do for that right now. Are those steaks ready? I'm starving." I changed the subject.

Sometimes Billy Lee's confidence in me was just plumb scary.

Chapter Sixteen

By Thanksgiving we had the dining room finished and the living room semidone. The woodwork had been stripped and the walls painted, but we'd decided to wait until after the holiday for the floor man. Momma and Lessie were the only guests, but we ate in the dining room on Granny Molly's good china. Momma was off in la-la land and thought I was the waitress and Billy Lee was a movie star. She fluttered her eyelashes at him after he said grace and carved the turkey. "I swear I saw you play on that episode of *The Golden Girls*."

"Don't mind her. Just be glad she's not yelling and upset," Lessie whispered.

"This is new territory for me. I didn't know Momma could flirt," I said out the side of my mouth.

"You two should stop telling secrets. It's bad manners to whisper like that. You will upset Billy Bob and me."

"It's Billy Lee, Momma," I corrected her gently.

"I know Billy Bob Thornton when I see him. It'll hurt his feelings if you call him Billy Lee. He's been my favorite movie star for a long time, so don't try to play games with me. Now, get us some more tea. My glass is almost empty, and his is only half full."

"Yes, ma'am," I said.

Billy Lee followed me to the kitchen. "Play along with her. It's really kind of fun."

"For you. You get to be a famous movie star. I'm just a waitress who's allowed to sit at the table."

"But it is Thanksgiving, and you've got family," he said.

163

"Oh, no, you don't. You're not playing the orphan card with me today, mister. And if you're going to be Billy Bob Thornton today, then get on in there and keep her flirting and happy." I pushed him toward the dining room.

He patted me on the shoulder. "Yes, ma'am. I'm on my way. Did I ever play on *The Golden Girls?*"

"I don't know, but that's one of her favorite shows. If she says you were on *The Beverly Hillbillies,* don't argue."

"You got it," he said.

"Did you get the help straightened out?" Momma asked Billy Lee when we got back to the dining room.

"I sure did. She just didn't recognize me off the big screen. I look different without stage makeup. Tell me, what movies have you played in, Miz Clarice?"

"Oh, darlin' boy, I'm not an actress." She giggled.

"Woman as lovely as you, I'll bet you used to be."

Momma blushed and fanned the heat in her face with the back of one hand. "No, I wanted to be, but my daddy said no. He said his daughters were going to marry and be good mothers. So that's what I was. I have a daughter who's away at college. She's going to be a teacher. I wish she'd be an actress, but I'd never tell her that. My daddy didn't let me be what I wanted, so I'll just keep my mouth shut and let her be a teacher. But she's so pretty and funny, she could be an actress. I bet she could play Blanche's daughter any old day."

I was learning more about my mother than I'd ever known or imagined, and it was all because of Billy Lee.

"Is your daughter Trudy?"

"Yes, she is. Do you know her?" Momma asked.

"I've met her."

"Well, imagine, what a small world it is. Do you think you could get her a part in one of your movies?"

"I might. Tell her to come down to the studio and audition for me," he said.

I tried to give him my best drop-dead look, but it just couldn't get past the silly grin on my face.

Lessie poked my arm. "See? She's happy even if she's not 'here.'"

"Thank goodness." I nodded.

Momma shot us each a look, and we stopped talking.

"Now, I want to know what made you decide to go into acting," she said.

"It just seemed like it was the thing to do. I was out there in Hollywood and couldn't find a job doing anything else, and this scout asked me if I'd like to play on *The Golden Girls,* so I gave it a try."

She nodded seriously.

"I got that part and went on to get another. Pretty soon I was the star of a movie."

"Well, that's a wonderful story, Billy Bob, but I'm sleepy from this delicious meal. Would you take us home now?"

He played along and went to his shop, opened a side door, and drove out a 1970 Cadillac Coupe DeVille: a bright, shiny, red convertible with white leather interior. My eyes popped out of my head. He bundled the two old girls up in their coats and scarves, then helped Lessie into the backseat and Momma into the front. She held her chin up as if she were escorted every day in such style.

I didn't believe my eyes until he came back in the car. I met him on the back porch. The wind was chilly, and I hadn't taken a jacket. He threw an arm around my shoulders as we went inside.

"Where the devil did that come from?" I asked.

"The garage," he said.

"But . . . ," I stammered.

"I told you when we went to Jefferson that I'd take you somewhere in my car sometime when we didn't have to buy lumber," he said.

"You didn't tell me it looked like *that,*" I protested.

"So, you like it?"

"How many more sides to Billy Lee are there?"

"Billy Lee is just a plain old feller who likes different things. That old Caddy reminded me of one Gramps had when I was about four. He used to take me for rides with the top down. When I found one that had been restored, I bought it. I took your Momma and Lessie for a little drive, or I'd have been back sooner."

"Where?"

"Just up and down Main Street and out past the grade school. By then Miz Clarice was getting cold."

"You are an angel," I said.

"Me? Not old oddball Billy Lee Tucker."

"You've played on that, you rat. You know what people say about you, and you don't give a dang."

"You got that right!" He winked. "Now, how would you rate our first holiday in the house?"

"You're changing the subject, but I don't even care right now. It couldn't have been better unless Momma was in her right mind."

He picked up a tea towel and dried dishes as I washed them. "I didn't mind being a movie star."

"I'm sure you didn't." I couldn't keep the grin off my face. "Even though I was a waitress and without Crystal and with Momma living in a crazy world, it was happy."

"I wonder what set her off on that track today," he said, as we worked together washing dishes.

"Well, if I close one eye and squint the other one, I suppose you do look like Billy Bob." I pulled the plug on the dishwater and looked at him through squinty eyes.

He slapped the air beside my shoulder. "On that note, I'm taking a turkey sandwich home and taking a nap."

"See you later. And when you come back, you'll be plain old Billy Lee, so don't be thinking you're going to get any royal treatment now that Momma has gone home. And, Billy Lee, you really look more like Harrison Ford," I teased.

"I get royal treatment every day, Trudy." He was out the door before I could slip another word in.

Chapter Seventeen

Two days before Christmas, Billy Lee brought in a cedar tree and one of those stands that holds a gallon of water so the tree won't die and shed all its needles. He brought the decorations box down from the attic, and when he opened it, it revealed big antique lights and fragile ornaments in a whole array of bright colors. Linda and Art would have drooled over everything.

While Billy Lee put the lights on the tree, I drove to the dollar store to pick up a new tinsel garland. And that's when I ran into Betsy and Marty—and I mean smack-dab into them. They were coming out of the store as I went in, and there was no hiding from them the way they used to avoid Aunt Gert.

Marty smiled. "Enough of this. We only have one another, and I'm tired of not talking to you. I'm sorry I knew about Drew and didn't tell you, and I'm sorry for those things you heard in the bathroom at Gert's funeral. Forgive me?"

Betsy threw an arm around my shoulders. "Me too. We were awful. You have a right to tell us where to go, but we miss you."

"Forgiven," I said. I didn't tell them that it was Billy Lee's spirit sitting on my shoulder telling me to be good that made me do it. "On one condition," I went on.

They both looked at me.

"That you never say another mean word about Billy Lee. He's my friend, and if you say anything nasty about him, I intend to mop up the streets of Tishomingo with you both."

"Agreed," Betsy said quickly.

"Okay," Marty said.

"Then why don't you two come to Christmas dinner? We'd love to have you," I said.

"We'll be there. We were just moaning about our kids all having plans, and actually wishing Aunt Gert were still around so we could have dinner with her like when we were kids." Betsy grinned.

"Good. We'll see you at dinner in a couple of days," I said.

I bought three kinds of tinsel because I couldn't decide which one I liked best. I'd never had a real tree. Momma was one of the first generation white-tree owners with all red bulbs and tinsel, red velvet bows, and even a red angel on top. A few years later, white trees went out of vogue. Momma bought an artificial green tree and decorated it with white lights, gold tinsel, and multicolored ornaments.

When I married, we bought a fake green tree and updated it every couple of years as the new and better models arrived on the market. But they all paled in comparison to the cedar tree I gazed upon as I carried a sackful of tinsel into the house. I tossed my coat onto a rocking chair and watched Billy Lee string the rest of the lights, plug them in, and give a thumbs-up shout when everything lit up the way it was supposed to do.

"What's that all about?" I asked.

"Gert and I were always happy when the lights worked one more year. She kept saying they should be retired, but I always liked the big bulbs better than those little twinkling things. Guess I've got old-fashioned bones. Grandma always had a cedar tree even when other folks had those fake ones, and I loved the big lights."

"I saw Marty and Betsy at the dollar store and invited them to Christmas dinner." I rubbed my cold hands together and thought of that lovely fireplace in the house by the lake.

"That's great, Trudy. We'll have lots of people around the table, and it'll be a wonderful Christmas!" Billy Lee said.

"You actually like this holiday?"

He was grinning so broadly that his crooked smile wasn't even crooked. "It's my very favorite."

He wrapped a tinsel garland around his shoulder and forearm the way I'd seen him do extension cords before he put them away; then he handed me the free end. "It's your job to get it on just right. Fill in the holes where the limbs are sparse, and make it pretty. It's my job to keep walking around the tree until we have it all done."

I started at the top. Drape here, fill there, stumble over the light cord, bump into Billy Lee a dozen times. I hadn't had so much fun decorating a tree in my whole life.

"Well, dang it all, I dropped it again. I'm the queen of clumsy today," I said.

"Who cares? 'Tis the season to be jolly, remember?"

"Then we're right in tune with the season," I said.

We finished the garland, and I threw myself down into a rocking chair. "Break time. Let's rest a minute."

He went to the kitchen, took the quart of eggnog from the fridge, and poured two glasses. He handed me one and settled into a rocker. "It's looking good. Last year Gert just wanted a little two-footer, and we set it on the dining room table. She'd just gotten the news about the cancer, but she put on a good front. She probably wouldn't have even put up a tree, but she kept up appearances for me."

"You were good for her. I feel guilty that I didn't put forth more effort to be around her."

"Gert understood. She knew you a lot better than you realize. I might have been good for her, but it was a two-way street. She was good to me. I loved that sassy old girl."

I'd finished most of the eggnog when the doorbell rang. Figuring it was a salesman or a religious group playing on the season for a donation, I dragged myself up out of the chair and hitched up sweatpants that were hanging off my hips. That alone was a Christmas present. Just that morning I'd looked in the mirror and found the hip bones I hadn't seen in at least fifteen years.

A cold north wind whipped around the edge of the house and through the doorway when I opened it. Crystal stood there like a stone statue.

I stared at her as if she was an apparition.

"Momma?" she whispered.

Her pretty blond hair, usually cut and highlighted to perfection, hung in limp strands. Swollen, red eyes and a fresh blue bruise across one cheekbone were the only things that gave color to her face. She wore sweatpants cut off raggedly right below her knees and old rubber flip-flops. She hugged herself in an attempt to keep warm.

Her voice quavered. "May I come in?"

I grabbed her arm, pulled her inside, and slammed the door. "I'm so sorry. You surprised me. Get in here out of the cold. You want some hot chocolate or coffee? Here, let me get you a quilt to wrap up in. You're trembling like a leaf. Have you got a fever? Where is your coat?"

"In the car with everything else I own, which is precious little."

I yelled toward the living room. "Billy Lee, it's Crystal!"

He peeked around the edge of the door.

I turned back to Crystal. "We're putting up the tree. Let me make you something hot to drink, and then you can help us, if you're staying that long."

She hung her head, and my heart went out to her. Who on earth had broken my spirited child down like this? If I found the sorry sucker, he was taking a midnight swim in Lake Texoma with a pair of concrete boots and a .38 slug between his eyes.

"Hot chocolate, please," she mumbled.

I went to the kitchen, and they both followed me. "Chocolate will warm you up. You're frozen."

She sat down at the table. "I need to talk to you."

Billy Lee pulled out a chair and sat down.

She pushed her chair back so fast, it hit the floor. I expected the fight to begin. She'd yell enough to wilt the Christmas tree. But she took two steps toward me, threw her arms around my neck, and broke into sobs so hard, she could scarcely breathe.

I hugged her tightly and patted her back, soothing her the way I did back when she was a little girl and someone had hurt her feelings. "Shh. Shh. Stop that right now, and tell me what's happened."

"I don't have anyplace to go, and I've been so mean to you, and he left, and I quit school without telling you. Daddy said I was a disgrace and I couldn't live there because he won't be disgraced again, and I'm afraid, Momma. Jonah said he wasn't ready to be a father, so he went home to Pennsylvania, and he's divorcing me. I've lost my job at McDonald's, and I don't know what to do," she said between sobs and wiping her nose and eyes with the Kleenex Billy Lee handed her.

I maneuvered her across the room and back to the kitchen table. "Sit down, and start from the beginning."

She melted into the chair Billy Lee had set upright, laid her forearms on the table, and kept crying. "I'm such a fool."

Billy Lee reached across the table and touched her arm. I expected her to go up in flames and pull away from him, maybe even give him a royal piece of her mind, but she looked into his understanding eyes, stood up, and threw her arms around his neck and cried on his shoulder.

I hurriedly made microwavable hot chocolate and set it before her. She finally let go of Billy Lee and sat down but kept her hand on his right there on the table. When I sat down, she ignored the hot chocolate and grabbed my hand with her other one. "I've made a mess of my life. I'm being punished for treating you the way I did."

"Start at the beginning," Billy Lee said softly.

"Jonah and I had this big fight when I got pregnant. It was an accident, but he wouldn't believe me, and he's gone back to Pennsylvania, and he took everything we had with him." She looked so miserable that it broke my heart all over again.

"Well, that's probably a good thing. It would be wise for him to stay in his part of the world if he wants to live to see his next birthday," I said with absolute conviction.

"Don't worry. He won't ever be back," she blurted out.

"Keep going," Billy Lee said.

She sipped the hot chocolate, and a little color came back into her ashen face.

"When I told him I was pregnant, he said I had to get rid of it, because he wasn't being saddled with a kid."

Billy Lee patted her hand and waited patiently.

I still had visions of feeding a fifty-pound catfish the remnants of a pretty boy's body.

She continued in a broken voice. "The rent is due in five days. I got laid off from my job yesterday. The food is gone. I've got ten dollars and a tank of gas. I went to Daddy and told him about the baby, and he told me to get out."

Billy Lee's expression was pure disgust. "You did the right thing, coming here, Crystal. Your momma has missed you."

I patted her hand with my free one. "We'll get through this. I've got a lovely spare room upstairs you can stay in. Then, when the semester starts again, we'll go find you another apartment."

"I'm not going back to school. I hate it. I was on probation all last semester. My grades were horrible," she said.

That put a whole new light on the issue. I was barely getting my own life together. I had a mother with Alzheimer's, a fresh divorce, and it wasn't an easy job keeping my emotions in check with Billy Lee. But this was my child, and I loved her so much that her pain was tearing my heart out.

"We'll talk about that later. Right now, we'll help you bring in your clothes."

"There's only one suitcase. We've pawned everything I had to keep going. Daddy cut off my credit cards when I got married. I got a job at McDonald's, but Jonah said he wasn't working fast food."

That fellow wasn't going to be tossed into the lake. I'd think of something much more painful and longer lasting than a simple bullet or drowning.

"I'll go get your suitcase, then, and you finish that hot chocolate," Billy Lee said.

"You had any supper? Billy Lee and I made vegetable soup today, and it's still on the back of the stove," I said as I hugged her tightly.

"I *am* hungry," she admitted.

The tone of her voice sent chills up my spine. My child was scared, pregnant, and hungry, and her father had turned her out. Maybe he'd join this Jonah-whoever in a shallow grave.

"Momma, I am so sorry. I didn't mean to butt in on you and Billy Lee. You don't need me messing things up for you," she whispered when Billy Lee was out the door.

"What are you talking about? You're not messing anything up."

"But I thought he lived with you."

"Billy Lee doesn't live here."

"That's what Daddy said. He said you traded him in for the village idiot." She blushed.

"Billy Lee is my best friend and the most caring, kind man in the world, but he goes home at night, Crystal."

I set about heating a bowl of soup in the microwave and uncovering the leftover corn bread. "Milk or tea?"

"Milk, please. Momma, I can't believe you'll just take me in when I've been so mean."

"Do you want to get rid of that child you're carrying? Have you had a single doubt about letting it live, even though its father is a fool?"

She shook her head. "Never."

"I feel the same about you."

Tears filled her already swollen eyes and flowed down her cheeks. "I don't deserve this."

"You are going to be a mother. Congratulations. Once a mother, always a mother. You don't ever get to quit or retire. Soup's hot. I hear the front door. Billy Lee will take your things up to your room, and tomorrow we'll go buy whatever you need."

"Thank you, and I mean it," she said humbly.

She dug into the soup with gusto. When she finished that bowl, she asked for another and even washed the dishes when she was done.

"Now, was there something about a Christmas tree?" she asked.

"Billy Lee cut it out of the forest," I said.

Her eyes finally had a little life in them. "A forest in Tishomingo? Come on, Momma."

Amazing what a bowl of soup and the promise of a warm bed will do. Drew ought to be covered in honey and staked out on a fire-ant mound. Denying his own child a place to stay must have broken her as badly as Jonah's leaving had.

I amended my story. "Well, then, in the woods out behind his house. Tomorrow I'm going to the Dollar General and buying one of those ornaments for Baby's First Christmas. I'm going to be a grandmother!"

Crystal picked up an ornament and hung it on the tree. "Momma, are you sure you're all right with this?"

"What? A live tree? I love it. Always wanted one, but my mother said they weren't the 'in' thing, and your grandmother Williams would have gone into cardiac arrest if we'd brought a live tree in after all the money she'd spent on that interior designer."

"Not the tree. I think it's great. It smells like the stuff you spray out of a can during the holidays, only not as strong. About me living here and having a baby without a husband."

"Truth is, if you were the first woman to have a child without a husband, we could sacrifice you to the gods of the perfect, but since you aren't and most likely won't be the last, then I suppose we'll keep you and the baby both."

Billy Lee fairly beamed.

"What about you?" I asked him.

"Neighborhood needs a child in it," he said.

Crystal picked up another ornament and studied the tree. "I wasn't expecting you to understand, Momma. I figured you'd give me a lecture and tell me what it'd cost me to stay here."

"I'm a changed woman. Speaking of which, you are going to be a mother, my child. You're going to need to figure out what you're going to do. Mothering is a big, big responsibility. How do you plan on caring for this baby?" I hitched up my sweats again. I was going to have to break down and buy some smaller clothing.

Billy Lee kept putting one ornament on after another. "What is your passion, Crystal?"

She eyed him carefully. "Passion? What are you talking about?"

Passion to a kid had a different connotation than to us forty-year-old dinosaurs. It had to do with steamed-up car windows in a parking place. She wasn't sure what he was talking about, and it showed in her face.

"As in, what makes you the happiest? You said you hate college. What makes peace in your heart? That's your passion."

"Digging in the dirt and making things grow," she said, and she put a red bell-shaped ornament on a bottom limb.

I jerked my head around to stare at the child I'd birthed twenty years ago. She wouldn't pick up fall leaves without gloves.

"I loved going to the garden with Grandpa Matthews. He used to let me plant all the marigolds around the perimeter of the garden, and I took some classes in horticulture in college. Daddy would have died if he knew I'd blown off pre-law and accounting and taken classes in plants. But that's the thing I liked. They're the only classes that kept my grades up high enough to even let me stay on probation. Someday I'd like to have a greenhouse and produce plants to sell to flower shops."

"You wouldn't rather own a flower shop?" he asked.

"Nope. For now I'll just get a job doing whatever I can, but my ultimate dream is to own a greenhouse. I'll have to save a long time for it, because even after I have one, it will be a year or more before it would support me and the baby."

This was my child, talking like an adult. Not once had she mentioned having her nails done or asked when we'd shop for a wardrobe.

"Sounds like a good idea to me. Job like that, you wouldn't have to take your child to a sitter. Never did like the idea of a baby being left with strangers," Billy Lee said.

"Me, neither. I don't know what I would have done if Momma hadn't stayed home with me. I didn't turn out too good even with that, did I?"

"I'd say you did all right. We're all entitled to a mistake or two in our lives." Billy Lee put several more ornaments on the highest limbs. "Gert would have liked the tree this year. I believe we're ready for icicles."

Crystal actually smiled when he handed her a fistful of long, silver-foil icicles. "Aunt Gert would have strung me up from the tree outside."

"I don't think so," Billy Lee said. "We aren't too judgmental here on Broadway Street."

He handed me the angel for the top of the tree and held the chair steady while I stepped up onto it and set her in her place.

"That's beautiful," Crystal said.

Billy Lee nodded. "I'm going home. I'll be around tomorrow morning to help start the holiday cooking. Seven all right?"

I didn't want him to leave, but I couldn't think of an excuse to keep him other than I didn't really want to be alone with Crystal. I needed his support.

Crystal's eyes bugged out. "Seven?"

"Seven in the morning, young lady, and you will be up with us. Whoever lives in this place works in this place," I said.

"Yes, ma'am," she said.

"You didn't think you were going to sleep until noon on Christmas Eve, did you? We've got pumpkins to clean and boil and a turkey to pluck," I teased.

"For real?"

"No, the turkey and ham are from the store, but don't say that too loudly. Gert will rise up out of her grave and haunt us," I whispered, and I waved good-night to Billy Lee.

"I'm dreaming."

"No, Crystal, you aren't. We'll get through this together. It won't be easy, and you'll face a lot of flak, but you'll live, and that which doesn't kill us makes us stronger. Now let's go to bed. I've got the most amazing Jacuzzi up there, and you're going to love it."

She looked around the room. "The old place is looking great. When are you buying furniture?"

"I'm not in a hurry about anything. But your room is furnished, so you won't have to sleep on the floor." I pulled the plug on the tree lights and flipped the wall switch. A night-light guided us up the stairs.

"Oh, my," she whispered when she saw the bedroom furniture.

"Pretty, isn't it? Billy Lee made it. Take a peek into my bedroom. It's just as gorgeous. If that man is an idiot, I'd love to see what he could have done with a brain."

Chapter Eighteen

We started Christmas off early with presents. Billy Lee gave me a gorgeous quilt rack that he'd made out of aspen, and I gave him a signed copy of James Lee Burke's newest novel. It seemed as if I was copying the idea he'd had for my birthday, but he was truly tickled with his present. Together we had a dozen packages under the tree for Crystal, most of them bought at the last minute and some pretty silly, like a new alarm clock with huge numbers. But she squealed at each gift like a little kid.

"This is the best Christmas ever," she said after each one.

"It really is," Billy Lee agreed. "Gert would've loved this day. Now, let's start cooking in earnest. I'll make breakfast," he said.

"I'll set the table. Can we use the good china for dinner?" Crystal asked.

"Of course. It's a holiday. Get out Granny Molly's pretty glasses too," I said.

She went to the dining room, and Billy Lee and I headed for the kitchen.

He touched my arm. "I want to thank you again for the book. I'm not too good with words, Trudy. I can talk all day about wood and refinishing, but . . ."

"Your face showed that you liked it. But there's no way you are as proud of that book as I am of the quilt rack," I said.

He smiled, and my heart melted. Billy Lee Tucker was the best thing that had ever happened to me.

At ten o'clock Crystal drove the Maverick over to the nursing home and picked up Momma and Lessie. Momma came

177

in the front door all dressed up in a velour jogging set I'd bought for her for Christmas the year before. She and Lessie each had presents under the tree, and they carried on like two little girls.

Marty and Betsy arrived at eleven with a basket full of home-made cookies and candies. They went straight to the kitchen to help and sent Crystal in to visit with Lessie and her grand-mother.

I couldn't have asked for a better gift than Momma's knowing everyone that day. We put the finishing touches on dinner, and Billy Lee sat at one end of the dinner table and carved the smoked turkey. Momma and Lessie were on his right. I was to his left, with Betsy, Marty, and Crystal across the table from Momma and Lessie.

Momma clinked her iced-tea glass with a knife and got everyone's attention, then raised it in a toast. "To Trudy, who has redone this house beautifully and who cooked this dinner for us." Everyone held up tea goblets and made some kind of "hear, hear," noise.

I didn't clink.

I stood.

"I can't take the credit for this meal or this house alone. Billy Lee has worked twice as hard and long as I have on the house. He's worked all day beside me, teaching me all kinds of valuable lessons. One in particular is that paint stripper will take the skin right off the knuckles if I don't get it washed off in a hurry."

Everyone chuckled.

I went on. "He's kept the carpenters, painters, plumbers, and electricians as well as all the laborers on schedule and organized. Then in the evenings he went to his shop and built furniture. You are welcome to tour the upstairs after dinner and take a look at his work."

Betsy and Marty glanced up the staircase. I bet they wished right then that they hadn't been so eager to plow the old place down.

I took a breath and kept going. "But most of all, Billy Lee has kept me sane through all my personal troubles this year.

He's been my true friend, and I couldn't ask for a better one. As far as dinner, I can't take credit for that, either. Crystal and Billy Lee helped all day yesterday and this morning. And she got up early both mornings, so that is truly a Christmas miracle."

That brought a round of laughter.

"So the toast goes to Billy Lee and Crystal also, not just to me. By the way, Crystal brought me the most wonderful Christmas present ever. She's having my first grandchild. So please raise your glasses to the next generation."

Crystal wiped her eyes, pushed her chair back, and stood up. "I didn't help that much. Billy Lee and Momma did most of it. I did get up early, but it was out of necessity. Morning sickness is horrible." She laughed. "To avoid a bunch of questions, I got married in Vegas a few months ago. The father of my child has chosen not to be a part of this baby's life. This toast is to Momma and Billy Lee, who have taught me more in two days than I'd learned in twenty years. And not just about how to make a pumpkin pie from scratch. I love you both."

A wide grin split Billy Lee's beaming face, and his blue eyes twinkled.

Momma leaned over and whispered, "When is Granny Molly coming out of her room? Are we taking a tray up to her later? She did a fine job on this sweet-potato casserole. I always did like it when she put in extra pecans. It's the only way to eat yams. Did Gert make the cranberry salad? She told me once that her secret is grinding up a whole orange, peelings and all, for it, but I think she was teasing. What do you think?"

"That's what she told me too," I whispered back, wishing she hadn't slipped away.

The table was silent for a while, but in a few minutes everyone was talking again. Momma kept right on eating, putting food into her mouth, laying the fork down between bites, her hands in her lap. Whether she could remember any more that day or not, the manners that had been drilled into her as a child had stuck. She'd always be prissy. What other constant was there in my life?

Billy Lee's name came to my mind without hesitation.

After dinner Momma and Lessie were both worn out, so Crystal offered to take them back to the nursing home. Momma shook her head. "When I come to this house, Billy Bob Thornton takes me home in his red Caddy. We leave the top down. Call him and tell him I'm ready to go home."

"Grandma, Billy Bob Thornton isn't here," Crystal said apologetically.

I touched Momma on the arm and smiled at her. "I will call him right now. I'm sure he's already on his way. He was really sorry that he couldn't be here with you today."

Lessie was the only one who smiled and nodded at everything I said. Everyone else looked at me as if I'd grown an extra eyeball right in the middle of my forehead. I kept talking to Momma about Billy Bob while Billy Lee slipped out the back door, and in a few minutes he drove the red Cadillac up into the driveway and honked.

"There he is, Momma, right on time. I'll help you get your coat on, and he'll take you home."

Marty, Betsy, and Crystal wasted no time getting to the back door to see who had honked. Poor little Crystal's face was a sight to behold, but Marty and Betsy's jaws hanging loose and eyes nearly popping out of their heads was just payment for the night they'd made fun of Billy Lee at the fireworks show.

"What in the . . ." Betsy got control of her jaw before Marty did.

Momma clapped her hands together like a little girl. "I told you. See there? It's Billy Bob Thornton in his red Caddy. Come on, Lessie. He'll give us a ride down Main Street and then take us to the home. He's a good man."

Lessie led her outside, where "Billy Bob" opened and closed doors with a flourish and then drove away.

"I know that's real, but I don't believe my eyes," Crystal said.

"God, that thing is beautiful," Marty said. "I had no idea Billy Lee had a car like that."

"It is gorgeous, isn't it? You don't think they'll catch pneumonia riding with the top down, do you?" I asked.

"If they did, they'd both die happy," Crystal said with a laugh.

Later that night when everyone had gone home, I sat in the living room in the dark, the quilt rack Billy Lee had given me for Christmas close enough that I could touch it. Tomorrow I'd find the perfect place for it in the sparsely furnished living room.

Billy Lee had asked Crystal what her passion was. I asked myself the same question as I sat there watching the ornaments sparkle on the tree. My first Christmas in my new house had been beyond wonderful. My daughter was home. Momma had been lucid for a little while. Billy Lee? Well, words couldn't describe Billy Lee.

But what was my passion? I'd jumped into remodeling with zeal, but the job was almost finished. We had some minor details in the new downstairs bathroom and the kitchen to finish up, but that didn't involve stripping wood or the floor man's putting us out of the house for three days. When that was finished, what then?

What was *my* passion?

Had I ever had one, even as a child? I had wanted to fly airplanes, but that dream had disappeared when I put my Barbie plane away with the dolls. I'd wanted to go to college and get a degree back when Drew and I first married, but that didn't appeal to me anymore. I'd enjoyed fixing up the house, but I didn't want to do that again. Billy Lee said I should write the story of the past six months or so, but who would believe such things?

My stomach growled, and I headed toward the kitchen to have a late-night snack. There was so little furniture in the dining room that there was no danger I'd fall over anything. Just the long table surrounded by chairs and a few choice pieces of glassware on the bookshelves. Gone were two rockers and two old overstuffed chairs with tables and lamps beside them, and the walls were bare except for a single quilt hanging from an oak rod.

From the dining room I went into the kitchen and flipped

the switch, bathing the room in soft light. I was still trying to figure out whether I wanted a sandwich or just a chunk of turkey when I stepped on a slimy, squishy slug with my bare foot. In horror, I hopped on the other foot to the sink, acrobatically stuck the first foot in, and turned the water on full blast to get the offending debris off me. Naturally, I soaked my pajamas and had to change into a fresh set.

Evidently I raised such a ruckus that a sleepy Crystal came downstairs to see what was going on.

She cocked her head to one side. "I heard some commotion. Are you all right?"

"I'm fine."

"But . . . wait. Aren't you wearing different pajamas?"

"Yes, I am."

She covered a yawn with one hand and grinned at me. "So explain, young lady. What did you do to warrant changing pajamas? Did you slip through the hedge to spend some time with Billy Lee? Am I going to have to give you the daughter/mother talk?"

Scarlet burned my cheeks. "Sit down, kid, and let me tell you all about it. And, honey, what I did wasn't nearly as much fun as sneaking through the hedge to steal kisses from Billy Lee, which, by the way, I've never done."

Okay, so I'd kissed Billy Lee. But I hadn't snuck through the hedge, so I wasn't lying.

She pulled out a kitchen chair. "Then we have to have a serious talk. If you don't get busy, someone, maybe even Betsy, is going to steal him right out from under your nose. Her eyes glittered when she saw the furniture he'd built, and I could see dollar signs in her eyes when he drove that vintage Caddy up into the yard. She had no idea he had that kind of thing going out there in his shop or that he owned a car like that. She's not stupid. I'm surprised he's outrun the women of Tishomingo this long."

"Advice noted and taken." I'd seen the new look in both my cousins' eyes when they realized what Billy Lee was worth and could do.

I went on to tell her about stepping on the slug, getting my pajamas wet when I stood on one leg and put my foot into the sink to wash it off, and having to change. By the time I finished, she was laughing so hard, she couldn't breathe. It wasn't all that funny to me, having just lived through the nightmare, but it was good to see her laughing the way she had when she was a little girl, from deep down in her belly.

She wiped at her eyes with the tail of her nightshirt. Could a baby really be hiding in that flat tummy? What would she look like when she was nine months pregnant and her tiny waistline was gone?

"Momma, you are so funny. You've got to write this stuff down, and don't leave out a word. I want to remember it just like you told it. And write down other things you've done too. In fact, you should write a whole book. Then, when I'm your age, I can look back and read about exactly how crazy and wonderful you were."

She yawned. "Look, it's past midnight. This has been the best Christmas ever in the whole wide world. It will go down in history, won't it, Momma? The Christmas of the Slug. The Christmas when Billy Lee Tucker made me get up at seven in the morning to cook, then gave me a handmade jewelry case. The one when we sat down to dinner with Grandma, and 'Billy Bob Thornton' drove her home in his red Cadillac." She looked into my eyes. "I love you, Momma," she said, and she hugged me fiercely.

"You should have seen your grandmother at Thanksgiving. That was when she first became convinced that Billy Lee was Billy Bob Thornton, and she flirted and laughed and told stories that I wished I'd known when I was younger."

"Funny, he doesn't really look like Billy Bob Thornton. He's a sight better looking . . . more like . . . like . . ." Crystal frowned, trying to think of who Billy Lee reminded her of.

"Harrison Ford?" I suggested.

"That's it exactly! Like he looked in *The Fugitive*."

"Don't tell your grandmother that. She really thinks he's Billy Bob Thornton."

"We've been through a lot, but we're in a good place, right, Momma?"

I nodded happily, and Crystal gave me a brilliant smile, then yawned again. "Okay, I'm going back to bed now. You stay out of the kitchen and away from slugs. Good night, Momma."

"Sleep well, pumpkin."

I thought about what Crystal had said about writing down stuff about the past year. If I did, then maybe someday when she was bone tired and her rebellious child had dealt her a week's worth of pure misery, she could read the silly slug story and laugh as hard as she had that evening.

She didn't have morning sickness the next day and was still sleeping soundly when I made my way to the kitchen. Billy Lee had let himself in the back door and was frying bacon when I got there. He picked up a mug featuring Maxine making a wry comment about mornings on it, filled it with coffee, set it in front of me, and returned to the bacon.

"Eggs or pancakes?"

"Both. I'm starving."

"I guess it was a pretty good Christmas if you're hungry enough the next morning for both eggs *and* pancakes," he said.

I'd started lifting the mug toward my mouth but suddenly spilled the coffee onto my white sweatshirt. I sighed. Coffee stains did not come out of sweatshirts.

"You going to let Crystal sleep this morning?"

I nodded. I didn't tell him that I didn't want to share him and that I treasured the moments we had alone.

"Good. I want to talk to you about something important, and I don't want her to hear."

My heart stopped. What could it be? Was something wrong? Or did he want to make sure that Crystal knew we were just friends?

"What?"

"Her dream is to have a greenhouse someday, and we could give her that now. It will keep her busy and give her something to keep her mind occupied while she's waiting for the baby. I figure we could attach one end to the shop and build it to the south. That way she'd have it right close to the house."

I'd been so busy with the holiday preparations, I'd given

little thought to actually acting on what Billy Lee had called her passion.

"What do you think? Or have I overstepped my boundaries?" he asked.

"I think you're a genius. It's a wonderful idea. When can we start, and is this the right time of year to do that? But would you mind having the greenhouse on your property?"

"I've got plenty of room for it. She can get started and begin lining up clients to sell to all year round, and she can do even more in the spring when people want to come straight to a greenhouse for their bedding plants. I did a lot of research online last night, and I've already drawn up some plans for her to look at. The only thing is, I don't know if . . . if . . ." He stammered, and his voice trailed off.

"Yes?" I asked, mystified.

"I've always wanted a family, Trudy," he blurted. "Gert was like my grandmother. Even though I'm not Crystal's father, would you be willing to share? May I at least be her friend and help her out in this way?"

"Share what?" Crystal asked sleepily from the doorway.

"You," I answered honestly. "Billy Lee and I would like to share in your future. How would you like to start building a greenhouse next door?"

That opened her big blue eyes wide, and they glittered like the lights on the Christmas tree. Her passion was digging in dirt, Billy Lee had discovered. His was working with wood—and making miracles. I think I found mine late the night before, when I couldn't fall asleep and actually wrote down the story of the Christmas of the Slug. It would be great if someday I actually wrote something that would sell, but if I never wrote for anyone but my daughter, that was all right too.

Chapter Nineteen

Brochures and a sketchbook were spread out over the kitchen table. It was day one of the planning stage. Crystal had visions of hothouse orchids and begonias dancing in her head. Billy Lee was designing and erasing as she told him what she had learned in her horticulture classes.

I sat in front of the cabinets on the kitchen floor discovering some of the aftereffects of being raised during the Great Depression. Aunt Gert had saved absolutely everything. I was sorting through stacks and stacks of plastic margarine containers, along with anything else that had a lid on it. The trash cans were still crammed to capacity from the Christmas detritus the garbage truck hadn't yet picked up on its holiday schedule, so the big black bag I was filling up would have to be stored in the garage until we could make a run to the dump. I stood up with a moan.

"You want me to take that out?" Billy Lee asked.

"It's not heavy. I can do it. Ya'll about to decide how big to make that thing?"

"Momma, I'd be happy with a plastic-covered bamboo hut to start with, but Billy Lee wants to make it permanent, with glass and steel."

"If this is truly your dream, then best to make it right," I told her.

I slipped on one of Gert's old jackets and threw the bag over my shoulder. If the jacket had been red, I might have looked like a Johnny-come-lately Santa Claus, but it was a faded green plaid. I probably looked more like a bag woman who'd had a good day Dumpster-diving.

I'd tossed the bag into the garage and was on my way back to the house when I heard a weird mewling beside the back porch. I stopped dead. After my recent experience with the Christmas Slug in my kitchen, I wasn't feeling very trustful about any unexpected critters. What if it was a rat the size of a mountain lion throwing off pitiful noises so I'd come nearer, and then it would scare the bejesus out of me?

I heard it again and carefully crept closer. If it was a rat, Crystal and Billy Lee could cart my carcass to the funeral home. At least the divorce was final, and Crystal would now be my only living survivor, so she'd get Aunt Gert's inheritance, and Drew couldn't touch a dime of it. I carefully peeked behind the scrap lumber the carpenters had piled up beside the porch.

It was not a rat but a cat—a big fluffy ball of gray and orange fur curled up around two baby kittens. She looked up at me with the same pitiful eyes that Crystal had had when she'd showed up on my doorstep a week before. Half expecting the momma cat to claw my hand off to nothing more than a bloody nub, I carefully reached down to pet her.

She purred, and my heart melted. I tucked her two kittens into the jacket's patch pocket and draped the momma over my arm. The purring got louder as I carried her into the house, as if she knew those babies couldn't survive outside in the winter, and I was their salvation.

Neither Billy Lee nor Crystal looked up.

"Hey, look what I found."

Crystal was on her feet and had that momma cat in her arms in an instant. "Oh, isn't she beautiful? But we can't keep her. Daddy is allergic to cats."

The look on her face was one of horror. "I'm so sorry. That just slipped out."

"Don't be sorry, Crystal. Drew is still your father. You can talk about him anytime you want," Billy Lee said.

She grinned. "Thank you. This really is an open house, isn't it?"

"It is," I said.

"Billy Lee and I decided from day one that we weren't going to waste time on 'nice.'"

"But you are," she argued. "I've never been around anyone as nice to each other as you two."

Billy Lee looked down at his papers.

I didn't know what to say.

"Can we keep her, please?" Crystal begged.

The cat purred as she stroked its fur, and both of them looked at me with the same pleading eyes.

"Billy Lee, you allergic to cats?" I asked.

I'd gotten quite fond of finding him in the kitchen every morning, coffee ready, bacon or sausage frying. Not even a momma cat with two kittens would stand in the way of me and my breakfast.

"I'm not allergic to anything. Got a cat myself. Used to hang around my shop, looking for handouts, and finally decided it was safe to wander inside. With the field behind us, there're always mice looking for warmth in the winter. Since old Lion started coming around ten years ago, I haven't seen a single one in the house or the shop."

"For real?" I asked.

"Absolutely. Lion would just love for a mouse to sneak in so he'd have something to pester other than me."

Would I never stop learning all the complexities of this man? He had a cat, its name was Lion, and he'd never mentioned it. But then, we were always in Gert's—*my,* I corrected myself—house, so how was I to know?

But that settled it. I'd adopt a dozen cats if they'd keep the mice—and, I hoped, slugs—from the house.

"We can keep her if she'll promise she'll never let a mouse into the house," I said.

"She'll be a good cat and scare them all away, won't you?" Crystal baby-talked to the cat.

"I've got some extra litter and an old pan over at the house. I'll go get it for you," Billy Lee said.

"Oh, I almost forgot." I reached inside my jacket pocket and brought out one fluffy yellow kitten and a black-and-white one. "This is a three-for-one day."

Crystal squealed.

I handed them to her. "You take care of them while I find a laundry basket and an old blanket."

In half an hour we were back to business. Billy Lee and Crystal had their heads together studying irrigation systems in modern greenhouses, and I was finding more remnants of "waste not, want not."

The only difference was that now a plastic laundry basket with a blanket and three felines in it was sitting right beside Crystal's chair, close enough that she could pet the mother, which she'd already named Mary, because it was the Christmas season, and there had been no room in the inn for her to deliver her babies. She wanted to name one of the kittens Jesus, but I wasn't about to start dodging lightning bolts. They could be Fluffy and Boots or whatever else cats were supposed to be named.

The morning got away from me quickly. I looked up at the clock to find it was straight-up noon at the same time Crystal declared she was hungry. Billy Lee organized their notes and put them into a folder. I pushed a second garbage bag to a corner.

"There's clam chowder in the refrigerator and still half a loaf of homemade bread," I said.

Billy Lee heated soup.

I sliced bread.

Crystal set the table and opened a jar of peaches for dessert.

"I reckon we could have the greenhouse built by the time the baby is born. You could have a grand opening," Billy Lee said as we ate.

"I don't want a big to-do. I want to do some advertising and start to work. If I'm good and my prices are reasonable, word will get around," she said.

Was this really my daughter?

"It'll be August when you open. Too late for bedding and garden plants," Billy Lee warned.

She had both kittens in her lap. "But just right for pansies and mums and bulbs and every other fall planting need. The cats can keep the mice out of the greenhouse too."

"Get ready for lots of hard work," I said.

"I don't see it as work, Momma. I can't wait to make things grow."

I fought back a bushelful of pure old jealousy when the two of them went back to discussing parking and office space; the latter would need room for a crib and a playpen. What was wrong with me? Crystal was my beloved daughter. Billy Lee was my dearest friend. But somehow I didn't want to play nice and share either one.

After lunch, Billy Lee went to his shop to work on the kitchen cabinets he had nearly completed. We'd spent *our* time at the table with brochures and yellow legal pads several weeks before. That's what had set me to cleaning out the old cabinets that day. Later that evening, after supper, I'd follow him out to the shop and do some staining. Crystal wasn't allowed in the shop because the fumes weren't good for a pregnant woman. For that little while I wouldn't have to share him, and I looked forward to it.

I'd finished cleaning out the lower cabinets by midafternoon. Before I tackled the upper ones, I took a break in the living room with a cup of mint-flavored green tea. I was sitting in a rocker sorting out my feelings when Crystal brought in the basket of cats and sat down on the floor beside me.

She used a forefinger to pet one of the tiny baby kittens. "Momma, could I talk to you about something?"

I'd made up my mind. She wasn't naming one of those kittens Jesus. It was pure sacrilege to name a cat after our Lord and Savior.

"What's on your mind?"

"It's Daddy. I called him on Christmas, and I don't want there to be secrets in this house. I want it to stay open and honest, and that's the way I want to raise my child."

That seemed pretty big compared to naming a kitten.

"Honey, if your father is still upset with you, that doesn't mean he doesn't love you and won't love the baby when it's born. You can call him and visit him anytime you want. You don't have to tell me."

"That's where you're wrong, Momma. I do want to tell you. Everything. I've lived in a house with dishonesty. Daddy had his affairs, and I think I knew about them from the time I was nine. If he hadn't gotten careless with Charity, we wouldn't be sitting here with these three cats right now. Jonah was a sorry rascal, but he taught me a lot. When he hit me and left, I sat in the middle of the kitchen floor all wadded up in a ball and cried my eyes out. You know why? Because I'd turned my back on you, and down deep I knew that Daddy wasn't going to bail me out of the mess. I knew what he would say before I ever went there."

"I'm sorry," I said.

"You were so trusting that you never knew about his affairs, did you? When I was a teenager I thought you were stupid one minute and hypocritical the next. Stupid if you didn't see what he was doing. Hypocritical if you did know."

"Marriage is complicated, and your father's unfaithfulness wasn't anything I could prove. I guess a part of me always knew that something wasn't quite right. Looking back, I can see that the signs were there. But I never looked for proof. I guess maybe I really believed that ignorance was bliss. Besides, in the past I always tried to avoid conflict, Crystal."

"Amen to marriage being complicated. I stayed long after I should have left Jonah, but I didn't want to admit I'd made a mistake. But you weren't hypocritical, you were just dumb."

"Thanks, I guess," I mumbled.

"That sounded better in my head. I love you, and I'm not going to let you down anymore. I'm sorry I didn't tell you about Daddy. I still love him, and I'll call him occasionally, but I'm not going to hold my breath for him to love me back unconditionally. He's always had his way—except when you left him and when I refused to get rid of my baby. He's even more spoiled than me!"

"Is that possible?" I laughed.

"Barely," she said. "But my eyes sure got opened the day I realized how low I'd sunk."

I laid a hand on her shoulder. "I'm glad you weren't too stubborn to come home."

"Home," she echoed. "It's crazy, isn't it, Momma? I used to hate it when you made me visit Aunt Gert. This house gave me the creeps. And it smelled funny." She laughed.

I raised an eyebrow. "It smelled funny?"

"Yeah, like a musty old cellar or soured milk."

"And it doesn't anymore?"

"No, now it smells clean and like fresh paint and varnish. Sometimes it's like Gert is here, but . . ." She couldn't find the words to finish.

I nodded. "I know. I think she'd be pleased with what we're doing."

"Do you realize you always say 'we'? That you always include Billy Lee in the planning and everything?" she asked.

"I guess I do. He was there that day I found out about Charity, and he's stood beside me through it all."

"Oh?"

"I didn't find out about Charity because your dad 'slipped up.' I was at Gert's funeral and overheard a conversation in the ladies' room about how stupid I was to let Drew get away with his infidelities. Later Billy Lee and I were the only ones in the sanctuary, and he consoled me."

Crystal frowned. "You told him what you'd just found out?"

I patted her hand. "Not about your dad. Billy Lee had no idea what I'd overheard, and I sure didn't blurt it all out. He was truly mourning Aunt Gert, and somehow that helped. I can't explain it. We were both miserable. For different reasons, but still grieving. He'd lost his friend and surrogate grandmother. I was about to bury a marriage. After that day he became my best friend."

"Wow! Is that the way it really was? I thought he'd been in love with you since you were kids or something."

Crimson filled my cheeks, and I stuttered, "Wh . . . Wh . . . What made you think that?"

"It's the way he looks at you. Like you've got a halo hiding under all that curly hair. Like you couldn't do or say a wrong thing if you tried. If some fellow ever looks at me like that,

I'm going to have him in front of a preacher so fast, he'll wonder how he got there."

"You're thinking about trying marriage again in the future?" I tried to change the subject.

"Yes, someday, when I find a younger version of Billy Lee. But we weren't talking about me; we were discussing you and Billy Lee."

"Then the discussion is finished. I'm forty, overweight, and getting wrinkles. Billy Lee isn't interested in being anything but a friend and good neighbor."

"We'll have to agree to disagree, then."

Smart girl. She knew when to hold 'em and when to fold 'em. Right now I had a mother who seldom had good days, an ex-husband who wanted to abort my firstborn grandchild, a pregnant daughter, and three new cats. I did not have time to deal with crazy notions about Billy Lee Tucker.

Chapter Twenty

I woke up New Year's Eve morning with a chip the size of a hundred-year-old pecan tree sitting on my shoulder. I didn't even know where the thing had come from or why. I tried to shake it off when I looked out the window into the beautiful morning. Bright sunshine poured into the bedroom, but my mood was as black as sin. My eyebrows lowered so fiercely that I was sure I'd given birth to a dozen forehead wrinkles. I forced myself to relax. Something had to have triggered the ugly mood. We'd had a lovely Christmas, and Crystal and I had cleared the air. We'd laughed over the Christmas Slug and talked about her father and her future. So what was wrong with me?

I hoped I'd shake it off by the time I got downstairs.

I didn't.

The kitchen was empty, but I could see Billy Lee and Crystal outside through the window. They were out beside his workshop with a steel tape measure and stakes, marking off where her new greenhouse would rise up like that mythical bird from ashes. Shouldn't she at least have to work at a job she hated for a couple of years before she got to dive right into her heart's desire? But, no, only I had to do that kind of thing. I was always the good girl. *Poor Trudy. Bless her heart.*

I dressed in a pair of jeans and a sweatshirt and grabbed the car keys. Billy Lee and Crystal waved when they heard the engine, but I pretended I didn't even see them. I drove straight down Broadway to Main Street and made a right turn toward the nursing home.

Momma was sitting in her recliner in her room. A rerun of *The Golden Girls* was on television, and she didn't take her eyes from it when I stomped into the room. I threw myself down into the other chair at the end of her bed, and she finally looked up.

"Who are you?"

"Momma, it's me, Trudy."

"Get out of here before I call the police. I'm not afraid to dial 911."

"Okay, I'll go." When I left, she was giggling at something Blanche had said. Why, oh, why couldn't she be lucid today?

I couldn't take the anger home, but there was really nowhere else to go. I drove slowly all the way out to the Y where the highway split, one part going to Madill, the other to Ravia and Ardmore. I stopped the car at the Western Inn's restaurant and thought about going in for a cup of coffee, but I was afraid I might commit homicide if Drew happened to be in there. So I drove to the park across the Pennington Creek bridge to where Billy Lee and I had gone to picnic that day in the summer. It was so cold, my breath came out in smoky puffs when I got out of the car.

I heard an old pickup rattling across the bridge, but I didn't look up until a door slammed. Crystal plowed across the dead grass with determination and more than a little worry in her eyes.

"What are you doing out here?" Crystal sat down across the table from me.

I shrugged.

"Tell me what happened."

I shook my head. How did I tell my child that I woke up that morning resenting her?

"What are you upset about?" she demanded.

Be honest! It was as if Aunt Gert was sitting right there giving me advice.

"It was there when I woke up this morning. I've loved you from the minute they laid you in my arms when you were born. But today I woke up resenting the heck out of you."

Tears welled up behind her beautiful eyes and spilled down

her face. "Why? I thought things were finally going well between us."

"They are, but I'm mad because . . ." I stopped.

"You might as well tell me," she said, regaining her composure. "We're doing 'honest,' remember?"

I sighed. "Okay, honest it is. I wanted to wait for a baby when your father and I married. I hoped to go to school and get a degree, but your grandparents really wanted a grandchild, and they pushed hard for that. I think they had visions of Drew going on to something big, like politics, and a stay-at-home wife and a baby would look good."

"Dad's no politician, Momma. He's a small-town lawyer. Politics might have been the Williamses' dream for their son, but Daddy never would have that kind of discipline or drive. He was way too spoiled, and he is what he is."

"How'd you get so smart?"

She smiled and reached across the picnic table to touch my hand. "Go on, Momma."

I went on. "Anyway, we had you, and I loved you to pieces, but I guess I always felt I'd been cheated out of my dreams. I basically had to walk two steps behind Drew and cater to his every whim. Then, when you were about two, I wanted another child, but your father said no way." I stopped. "I don't know why I'm telling you this."

"Because I asked and because you resent me," she said honestly.

"Oh, stop that. We both know I've always loved you no matter how spoiled and demanding Drew and I let you become—especially when you were a teenager, though I pretended that that was just a phase. And I allowed it because I couldn't stand fighting. I love you, and you know that, and that's all that matters. Now let's go home." My stomach hurt, and I had a headache.

"No, not until we've talked this through."

"I can't."

"Oh, yes, you can. Are you upset because of the baby?"

"It's not the baby. It's me. I'm forty, and for the first time I have a life all my own, and now . . ."

"I can get my own place. I don't have to live with you," she said.

"I like having you live with me. I love sharing our lives."

"Well, you have to decide. If I'm upsetting things in your new life and making you have these moods, then please tell me. Maybe you could give me a loan until I can get my business up and running. But if you want me to stay, then you have to remember that we're both adults now. You can come and go and do as you please, and you don't have to explain anything or answer to me or take care of me as if I was still a child."

That took me by surprise; my daughter was trying to meet me halfway, just as a grown-up would. I guess I'd figured she'd flounce back to Billy Lee's truck and throw gravel all the way home.

"How are you going to manage with a baby and a new business?"

"I'm going to be a mother who runs a business." Her eyes glittered at the prospect. "I'll have a crib and playpen in the greenhouse, remember? That's the beauty of having my own business. I can do both. I'm not asking you to take care of me or my child, Momma. All I need from you is to always be my mother. A real one. Not a perfect one. I don't even care if some days you hate me, as long as most of them you love me."

I almost cried at how smart and logical she had become. I stuck my hand across the table. "Deal."

She shook it firmly. "Now, let's go take care of the rest of this. Might as well finish up the year by throwing out the old and starting off tomorrow with a clean slate."

"What are you talking about?"

"Get into the truck. We're going to see Daddy."

My stomach did two flips, and my gag reflex almost lost the war. "I can't. Let's just go home."

She opened the passenger's door of the truck and literally shoved me inside. "Nope. He's at Grandmother Williams' place, and you can unload on the whole bunch at one time. Don't hold a single word back, either. Cuss, rant, rave, even throw one of her fancy-pants vases at him if you can get your hands on it. It'll cleanse the soul—believe me."

Later, I'd wonder how she knew where Drew was that day, but at the time I was so nervous over confronting him and my in-laws that I wasn't sure I could utter a word when we got there.

Crystal parked the truck in the circular driveway as if it was a limo and jumped out, motioning for me to follow. I made it to the front door of the house at about the time she pushed the doorbell.

The housekeeper, Elise, opened the door. "Miss Crystal. Miss Trudy . . . oh . . . my!"

My ex-mother-in-law, Ruby, peeked out the den door into the foyer. "Who is it, Elise?"

Crystal marched right in, and I followed.

"Neither of you are welcome in this house," Ruby said. "And, Elise, if you let her in here again, I will fire you."

"When she does, come see me, and I'll put you to work," I said.

"Tell me why we aren't welcome," Crystal said.

"Because you broke your father's heart."

"Is he here?" I asked.

"We are all in the den, but you aren't coming in."

"Yep, Grandmother, we are. Come on, Mother."

I followed her even though Ruby looked like she was about to drop dead of a heart attack.

"What are *you* doing here?" Drew's eyes shot pure hatred at me.

"Momma has something to say," Crystal said.

"We don't want to hear anything you have to say," Ruby said. "This is my home, so get out, and don't ever come back."

"You'd better sit down, because Momma ain't leavin' until she speaks her mind," Crystal said.

Ruby pointed a finger at me, but she didn't sit down. "You've changed. You are no longer the woman we chose for our son. You have been nothing but vindictive and mean."

"Me? *I've* been mean? Lady, you'd better wake up and smell the coffee burning. Your son cheated on me most of our married life. He's bought fancy cars and gifts for his bimbos and even coerced his daughter into covering for him."

"If he did those things, it was because you weren't a good wife. A man will find happiness. If not at home, then away from home," Ruby said.

That lit the fuse and loosened my tongue. I slapped her finger away. "I'll get to you later."

I pointed a finger at Drew. "I can't think of anything vile enough to call you, Drew Williams. I was a complete innocent when we married, and—"

Ruby's temper flared. "Don't you call my son any names!"

One look from me and she grabbed her mouth.

"I said I'd deal with you later. This one is between me and Drew." I raised my voice an octave or two or forty. It sure felt good to be standing in her living room yelling like a fishwife.

He opened his mouth, but nothing came out.

"Like I said, I was an innocent and thought you walked on water. I ignored the signs right in front of my nose and didn't face up to what you were doing. Right up until Gert's funeral, when my two cousins came into the ladies' room talking about all your affairs. How could you treat someone so badly? Why didn't you just leave me when you found out you didn't love me?"

"I never did love you! I never wanted to marry you!" he yelled back.

"Shut up!" Ruby whispered.

"Well, I didn't. I didn't want to be tied down to a wife or a baby. But Mother and Father thought I needed stability, that if I married, my law practice would be more solid. And it was. They were right."

"So you stole twenty years of my life to make your law practice solid?" I shouted even louder. "Did you ever give a thought to how I might feel?"

"I liked the way you took care of things, and you had a place in society. You had been trained well."

"You really are a coldhearted bastard," I said.

"Don't you call him that," Ruby said.

I shook my head in disbelief. How could I have been so naïve? "He's just like you."

"Be careful, Trudy. She's my mother," Drew warned.

"She had to have known what you were doing. Everyone knew."

"I didn't care what he did as long as he was discreet. I told him he could have all the mistresses he wanted, but he needed a good woman to serve as his wife. You were that, Trudy, until you went off the deep end," Ruby said.

"What about you? Did you know?" I asked my former father-in-law.

He shrugged.

I looked back at Ruby. "I suppose you'd be fine with Andrew flaunting a mistress and you being the good woman to serve as his wife?"

"Get her out of here. She's nothing but trash," Ruby said.

I shook my head. "I've said my piece. Now I'm leaving of my own accord."

I marched out of the house.

Crystal followed me. "Feel better?" she asked, when we got to the pickup.

"You will never know how much. Thank you."

Chapter Twenty-one

A cold north wind stirred the lake into frothy whitecaps. Wrapped up in blankets, Billy Lee and I sat on the deck watching the old year die after we'd feasted upon grilled steaks and stuffed baked potatoes. I loved the lake house and could live there forever, if only Billy Lee would sell it to me.

I was glad that Crystal had forced me to face my past and that Billy Lee had wanted to drive the Caddy to the lake house to ring in the New Year. Peace reigned deep inside of me in a way it never had before.

"It's because we were raised only children," Billy Lee finally said.

"What?"

"That's why we hate fighting. We didn't have siblings so we could learn how to do it properly. But sometimes we don't have a choice. You feeling better or worse for clearing the air earlier today?"

"Much, much better."

"Good. I'd hoped everything about Drew would go away and never bother you again, but that's unrealistic. You two share a child, so there'll always be that."

"I suppose so. What time is it?"

"Eleven thirty. Another half an hour and this year will be finished. What's been the good, the bad, and the ugly for you this year?" he asked.

I had to think about it for a while, but he waited patiently for my answers.

"The biggest ugly was the episode in the ladies' room at Gert's funeral, for sure."

"And that was?" he asked.

What is said in the ladies' room generally stays in the ladies' room. A guy would never understand. Still, I told Billy Lee the whole story, even about wiggling at the funeral and putting a hole into my panty hose.

"And you let them live and even invited them to Christmas dinner? I always pictured you as a take-charge, don't-mess-with-me woman."

"Billy Lee, you've pictured me all wrong. I'm a wimp."

"A wimp wouldn't have cut her ties as cleanly as you did. So you didn't want to know what was going on. At least when you found out for sure, you didn't sit around moping and feeling sorry for yourself. You walked out and started all over."

"But Gert made that easy to do," I answered.

"You'd have pitched a tent alongside Pennington Creek and used a public restroom before you'd have lived with Drew Williams after you found out he was cheating."

How had this man come to know me so well?

"The good?" he prompted.

There had been so many good things. To list them would take more than the time I had left in this topsy-turvy world that had spun my life in a hundred-eighty-degree turnaround.

"Good would be that Crystal and I are forming some kind of adult relationship. That Momma has had a few good days and that we got to celebrate the holidays with her. That I've got a house full of gorgeous things built by a new friend I cherish. Good would also be the mornings when I smell bacon and coffee as I stumble half asleep toward the kitchen. It's finding baby kittens and feeling safe. The good outweighs the ugly by far."

He smiled. "The bad?"

"Today," I answered honestly. "I hate confrontation. I still don't know how I had the courage or the anger to have that showdown with the Williams bunch. Dealing with Marty and Betsy was easier than that."

"If you could go back and redo any of it, would you?"

"No."

We sat there a few more minutes before I realized I'd just bared my soul. "Aunt Gert used to say that turnabout was fair play. So it's your turn, Billy Lee. The good, the bad, and the ugly of the whole year."

"The ugly. The way people acted at Gert's funeral. She was a fine lady, and she deserved to be mourned properly. You were the only one who was sad.

"The good. Gert leaving you the house so the hole in my heart was filled up again."

I was amazed beyond words. That was good in his eyes. He'd worked his fingers to the bone, and there was still work to do.

"The bad. Today."

I raised an eyebrow. "Why was today bad for *you?*"

"Because when Crystal and I came into the house and found you'd left without even touching your breakfast, I was afraid you'd gone back to Drew. It was a long day for me, until Crystal brought the truck home and told me what had happened."

He looked at his watch. "Ten, nine . . ."

He tossed off his blanket and held out a hand. I pushed aside my own quilt and took his hand to go inside. We'd watched the old year ebb out into history as the birth of a brand-new one came sliding into home base.

He kept my hand in his and nodded toward the other side of the lake, where fireworks lit up the dark sky. "Seven, six . . ."

"Five, four, three, two . . ." He pulled me close and looked deeply into my eyes, a faint smile on his face.

The man was going to kiss me. My thoughts were jumbled and my mind frantic.

"One . . ."

The kiss caused as many fireworks inside me as the ones showing their glory across the lake. Then he hugged me tightly and said, "Happy New Year, Trudy."

My ears were ringing so loudly, I wouldn't ever be completely sure what I said, or if I said anything. He kept my hand in his—surprisingly, it fit there as if it had been formed especially for that purpose—and led me through the glass doors into the living room.

"Good night. Sleep well." He leaned forward and brushed a sweet kiss across my forehead that was as passionate as the one on my lips.

I closed the door to the bedroom, sank down onto the bed, and stared at the ceiling, looking for answers to questions I couldn't even form. I began to rationalize. Billy Lee had wanted the day to end on a nice note and had felt obligated to give me the traditional New Year's kiss. There were just the two of us at the house, and I'd had a bad day. He was a good man and an almighty fine kisser.

I fanned my glowing face with the back of one hand. He'd made my toes, my lips, and everything in between tingle in ways it never had before. I wanted to kiss him again so badly, it was a chore to keep the bedroom door shut.

The next morning I awoke to the aroma of coffee and bacon but dreaded leaving the bedroom. I dressed slowly, made the bed, and invented a dozen things to keep me from going out into the kitchen to avoid the awkwardness that was sure to hang in the air like cigarette smoke in a cheap bar. Finally I opened the bedroom door and took a step out into the living room.

Billy Lee was the same as always. "Good morning. I thought I heard you up and around. Temperature is forty degrees, and the sun is rising, so we'll have a lovely day. What would you like to do with it?"

"Can we take the boat out and putter around the lake?" My voice came out sounding normal. Maybe I'd only imagined that he'd kissed me so passionately last night. Perhaps it was just a dream and hadn't really happened at all. No, not even my most vivid dream was that real.

"Sounds like a plan to me. I'll leave black-eyed peas cooking in the Crock-Pot, and we'll have them for supper. Have to eat our peas and greens today if we're going to have good luck all year. Did you bring a warm jacket? The wind can get cold out there on the water."

"I did," I said.

"I'll take along a quilt just in case you get cold," he said.

That was my Billy Lee, always thinking about me, and I loved it.

I set the table for two and found butter and jam in the refrigerator. Billy Lee had already whipped eggs for scrambling, and biscuits were in the oven.

"I'd better eat a double portion of peas and greens," I mumbled.

"How many did you eat last year?"

"Not a single bite, but I'm not jinxing what . . ." I stopped. I'd almost said, "what we have."

I cleared my throat. "I'm not about to jinx any good luck coming my way."

We had breakfast just as if we were at home in Tishomingo. We talked about the cabinets Billy Lee was finishing for the kitchen and the stain we planned to use. A rich cherry finish. Not as red as mahogany, but something that would enhance the grain and go with the white marble countertops. I could already see starched white curtains on the windows and pots of herbs on the sills.

It was as if we were two old, settled married people. Only we weren't, and if that kiss from the night before was any indication of what being married to Billy Lee would be like, it would be far from "settled," and there wouldn't be any dull moments.

I wore a pair of jeans, a red turtleneck, and a zippered sweatshirt with a hood. The sun was warm, and Billy Lee tucked a quilt around my legs so I was cozy as I propped myself up on pillows and read an old LaVyrle Spencer romance book. I'd read it at least a dozen times before, but it was like having tea with an old friend: same friend, same tea, still good.

I sneaked peeks at Billy Lee all day. His blue eyes were piercing, and I wanted to touch his hair. At that thought, high color flooded my cheeks. I felt like I was too close to an open fire. I went back to fiction; it was much safer than reality.

"You want the new baby to be a boy or girl?" he asked out of the clear blue.

"I don't care which or one of each. It's been a long time

since I've been around a baby. I'm looking forward to being a grandma."

"You sure don't look old enough for that title," he said.

"You are blind."

"I wear contacts, and they make my sight perfect. I'm excited about the baby. I looked at plans for building cribs this past week."

"You do too much."

He gave me another crooked grin and said, "I'll be the judge of that, Trudy."

"Today, I'll let you be the judge," I said.

"Be careful. What happens on New Year's is what happens all year long."

The kiss came to my mind immediately. I sure hoped he was right.

By the time we ate supper and got back to Tishomingo, it was fully dark. Crystal had left a note on the refrigerator that she'd gone to the nursing home to visit Momma. With luck she wouldn't be the cleaning lady that day or, worse yet, Marty or Betsy. Billy Lee said he had to check on his cat and headed out, leaving me to ponder the past two days over a cup of hot chocolate.

Chapter Twenty-two

Men are so frustrating; sometimes I think they really do come from Mars. That's the planet where they take boy babies' souls at birth to raise them with no feminine influence of any kind. They use John Wayne as the primary role model and make them mean and tough. Then they return their souls to them when they start puberty. That's why they are so obsessed with the female species at that time. After all, they've been living on Mars, where no such things exist.

For a whole month we went on with our routine. Billy Lee started breakfast every morning. Crystal and I meandered in when the aroma of coffee and bacon wafted up the stairs and into our bedrooms. She set the table for three. I helped Billy Lee finish cooking, and we ate together. He never mentioned that earth-shattering kiss on New Year's Day, so it must not have affected him the way it did me. I wasn't about to tell anyone that I dreamed every night of him kissing me again, or that when we were working side by side, I stared at his lips.

On the first day of February I awoke to nothing. No coffee. No rattle of pots and pans. I sat straight up in bed, my eyes open so wide, my face hurt.

Billy Lee was dead. I was sure of it.

Tears welled up behind my eyes and spilled over the dam into rivers down my cheeks. I brushed them away with the edge of the bedsheet. What would I do without him, and why hadn't I told him how much that kiss meant to me? I sniffed the air. Maybe I was getting a cold and couldn't smell the coffee or the breakfast.

Nothing.

Not one thing could keep Billy Lee out of the kitchen other than death, so that was proof of my suspicion. I grabbed a chenille robe from the closet. The only socks I could find were two mismatched ones: a blue with navy stripes and a black with red hearts. I grabbed two house shoes from the floor of the closet: a Clifford the Big Red Dog and a Minnie Mouse.

Peter, Paul, and Mary were all meowing in the utility room: further proof that Billy Lee was in his shop, graveyard dead. He always fed them first thing in the morning. I ran across the yard, through the hedge, and to the workshop. It was locked up tight.

I'd lived next door to him for months, and not once had I been in his house, but desperate times called for desperate measures. If he didn't answer the back door, I had every intention of breaking and entering. If he pressed charges against me, I'd pay the fine or sit it out in jail. Surely they'd seen women in worse attire than mine down at that place.

I knocked.

No answer.

I tried the knob.

It was locked.

The windows were covered on the inside with miniblinds and curtains, so I couldn't see a thing. That didn't keep me from trying. Concerned neighbor? Peeping Tom-ette? Who cared what they called it when they came to haul me down to the slammer?

I leaned on the front doorbell until the cat set up a howl, and still not a human sound came from within. I tried the storm door, and it opened, but the main door was locked. It was either kick it in, or the cat would begin eating Billy Lee by nightfall. Clifford the Big Red Dog was on the way to the first attempt when the door opened suddenly. I overbalanced, fell into the living room, and looked up at Billy Lee Tucker, alive and in the flesh.

His voice came out nasal and almost whiny. "What are you doing?"

He wore faded red flannel pajama bottoms and a long-sleeved gray shirt. His face was flushed, his nose red, and his eyes bleary. He might not be dead yet, but the devil was knocking on the door.

I pulled the robe around my naked legs and stood up, tightening the makeshift sash. "You look like the devil."

"So do you," he said right back at me.

"Yes, but I could get dressed and look better. You could put on a tux and still look horrid."

He headed toward what I assumed was his bedroom. "Go away. I'm sick, and I don't want you to catch it."

He slammed the door.

I heard a moan and bedsprings.

Standing just inside the living room, I took stock of the house. The living room was long and rectangular—with outdated furniture. The orange floral sofa with a coffee table and end tables were definitely not of Billy Lee Tucker quality. A matching chair with a side table and lamp seemed to date from the sixties. The only redeeming piece in the room was a nice, big, leather recliner facing a small television set.

Meandering toward the back of the house, I found a kitchen with a U of cabinets—still not made or produced by Billy Lee—an old chrome table with a yellow top, and four matching chairs. The window above the sink looked out over the sidewalk to his shop.

When I went back through the living room, I discovered a short hallway with a bathroom and two bedrooms opening from it. The bathroom door was open, and I love to snoop, so I stepped inside to find light green fixtures, a wall-hung sink, and curling, green-flecked linoleum on the floor. The spare bedroom invited me right in, where I found a bed covered with a white chenille bedspread, every inch of a dresser crammed with family pictures, chest of drawers with a brush and comb set, and nightstands with a Bible on each. Billy Lee's grandparents had slept in this room, no doubt.

I slung open his bedroom door without even knocking. "When did you get sick?"

He pulled the covers over his head. "I told you to go away. I thought you'd left."

"Humph," I snorted. "I was snooping around your house. Now I'm going to make you some toast and hot tea. I'm not ready for you to die."

"Trudy, trust me, you don't want to catch this. It's miserable, and it comes on fast." His voice came out muffled from beneath the quilt.

I jerked the covers back and touched his forehead. "If I get it, you can take care of me. What have you taken? Tylenol? Advil?"

"Not a thing. I hate medicine. As it is, one minute I'm burning up, and the next I'm freezing. Add a bunch of medicine to that, and I'll be dizzy and disoriented too."

"Stop acting like a baby, Billy Lee."

"Please, Trudy," he said.

"No. Even 'please' won't work. I'm staying and taking care of you."

I called Crystal, who was in the kitchen wondering where we were. I told her to look in the medicine cabinet and bring me a bottle of Tylenol and the vitamin C and leave both on the front porch. Then I told her to pack me a bag and to toss in a couple of books from the pile on my dresser.

"Keep those germs there," she agreed. "I don't think I could bear to be sick now that the morning sickness has passed. Whatever you need, you just call, and I'll put it on the porch," she said.

Need? What I needed was to bare my aching soul to Billy Lee. But he had to be well first. Hearing what I had to say might shove him right over the edge into eternity.

While I waited, I set about making a cup of my famous healing tea. Eight ounces of boiling water, a tablespoon of honey, and a fine dusting of ginger over the top. That and two pieces of cinnamon toast would be his breakfast. After he ate every bite and drank every drop, he'd have a Tylenol and a thousand milligrams of vitamin C. For lunch he'd get home-made chicken noodle soup and more pills. For supper it would be more of the same, and at bedtime a cup of very sweet hot lemonade.

The doorbell rang. The ordered items had arrived with a

note. I was to call after breakfast, and Crystal would make a run to the grocery store and check in on Momma. I changed clothes, and ten minutes later I was sitting cross-legged on the bed beside him, arguing over every bite or sip. I didn't care if he didn't like the taste of ginger or if the toast had too much sugar on it.

"You don't listen," he muttered.

"And you are not a good patient. That tea and toast will keep you out of the undertaker's hearse."

He sniffled. "I am not dying. I just want to be left alone, not badgered into eating and taking those stupid pills."

I handed him a tissue from the box beside the bed. "Blow your nose, and stop whining. I'm protecting my interests; if you die, I don't get my new cabinets." I didn't tell him my interest involved more than cherry stain and a new sink.

He huffed and puffed, but he ate the toast and drank the tea. If this was what they taught them on Mars, I hoped my grandchild was a girl.

"Now get up and go take a shower, put on some lounging clothes, and meet me in the living room," I said.

"I can't. I'll pass out in the shower," he groaned.

"If you do, I'll come in there and revive you," I threatened.

He almost grinned. "You are a drill sergeant."

"You've got that right. You'll get sore and weaker lying around all day. You need to sit up. We'll read or watch television or even work the crossword puzzle in the newspaper, but you are going to get well."

He narrowed his eyes at me. "Don't you touch my crossword puzzle. I'll take a lot of bossing, but don't you touch my puzzle."

"I'll do the whole thing in pen and cross out errors and make a big mess of it if you don't get out of bed."

He took a shower, shaved, and put on a pair of flannel bottoms and a shirt. He didn't faint dead away or even throw up the abominable ginger. He wasn't real perky when he plopped down on the sofa, but at least he wasn't kissing Saint Peter's ring or having a discussion with Lucifer about air-conditioning Hades, either.

If a portion of his brain hadn't been fried with fever, he probably could have finished the puzzle in fifteen minutes without a peep from me. Have to also fess up that I could have been a bigger help if he hadn't splashed that good-smelling shaving lotion onto his face. My thoughts weren't exactly on the capital of Peru or Nigel Julio's nickname in a 1941 movie.

"I'm feeling better. I'm going to get dressed and go out to the shop," he announced a few minutes after we finished the puzzle.

"Over my dead body. You are going to rest for at least two days; then we'll talk about it."

"Who died and made you God?"

"Remember when I asked *you* that? You said Gert. Well, the same answer applies to me today," I shot right back at him.

"Even Gert left me alone when I was sick," he snarled.

"I'm not God *or* Gert."

I picked up the remote and turned on the television. *Jeopardy!* was just coming on.

"Oklahoma," Billy Lee said between coughs.

"What?"

"Oklahoma is the forty-sixth state to enter the Union. After that was Arizona and New Mexico, then Alaska and Hawaii."

I switched my thoughts to the program. "Oh."

"What were you thinking about, anyway? I don't even like this show. I thought you wanted to watch it."

"I'd rather watch a movie. What have you got?"

"You didn't answer my question. What were you thinking about?"

I told a white lie. "The lake house."

"Let's go to the lake house, and I'll sit on the deck and watch the sun come up and go down. I'll even let you drive the Caddy."

"Nice try. Let's talk," I said.

"I'm sick. I don't feel like talking. It makes me cough."

"Then we'll read. Or, better yet, let's have a *Lethal Weapon* marathon. You own all four of them?"

"Don't own a single one. Don't even know what you're talking about. I don't watch much television," he said.

I went out to the kitchen and called Crystal on her cell phone. She was on the way to the grocery store from the nursing home. Momma was not having a good day. I told her to go to the video store and rent all four movies and leave them on the porch. And to also bring popcorn, a whole chicken, a package of noodles, and a gallon of vanilla ice cream.

"It's not fair. I'm stuck over here all by myself, and you two get to do a marathon. *Lethal Weapon* is my favorite, and now that I'm pregnant, that last item would be extra special," she whined.

"Rent two copies of each, and bring my new cell phone over. We'll talk later."

Billy Lee chuckled.

He was going to live.

Life was wonderful.

Chapter Twenty-three

I lost my nerve.

Billy Lee was well, but now that I wasn't taking care of him anymore, I wasn't so brave about telling him how I felt. I was terrified he'd tell me that all he wanted to be was my lifetime friend and neighbor. And I wanted so much more. I wanted to open my eyes in the morning and see him all squinty, trying to focus on my face. I wanted to hear him tell me I was beautiful.

February slipped into March. The crocuses and tulips peeked up from the frozen earth and put on their show. The kitchen cabinets were coming along very well, and the carpenters would start taking the present kitchen down to the bare studs in a few days. The greenhouse plans were finalized, and a crew from Oklahoma City would arrive the next day to start that job. We were in our normal routines and busy again.

But every time Billy Lee was in the room, and that was every single day, I wanted to sit in his lap and kiss him. I was sitting on the back part of the porch watching the kittens, Peter and Paul, romp around on the porch. Mary had spent a couple of days at the vet, so there would be no more children for her. Peter and Paul were just little boys intent on biting each other's tails and ears.

Billy Lee joined me on the porch swing. Sawdust clung to the legs of his overalls and his shirtsleeves. I flicked a piece from his left sideburn and asked if he wanted a glass of iced tea.

"No, thanks. Pretty day, isn't it?"

"Too pretty to be inside. Want to go to the lake house for a couple of days?" I asked wistfully.

"Got too much to do right now. Maybe in a few weeks. How do you feel about me, Trudy?" he asked.

I was stunned into muteness.

"As in?" Two words were my limit.

"What do you mean?" He frowned.

"As in friend, neighbor . . . as in . . ." I managed a few more, but my mind was racing.

"As in me. Plain old Billy Lee Tucker."

"Billy Lee, there's nothing plain about you. You are a wonderful person. A devoted friend who's brought me through tough times and made me feel alive again. A wonderful neighbor."

"Is that all?"

"Why?" I swallowed hard.

"Because I've been in love with you my whole life. I can't remember when I didn't love you. I'm not so good with telling you romantic things that are in my heart. We can talk about wood or refinishing all day, but I get all tongue-tied when I start to tell you how I feel. But I love you with my whole heart. I've got an idea about something, but I want to know how you feel about me. I don't want you to like my idea just to be nice," he said without looking at me.

I felt as if someone had jump-started my heart with a set of those orange cables they use on a car. Electricity set every hair on my neck and arms to standing straight up.

"You love me?" I whispered.

"You had to know that," he said.

"I've been scared to death that you were going to tell me you just wanted to be my friend and neighbor, that our New Year's kiss was just because of the holiday and . . ." I ran out of breath.

"So?" he asked, his voice barely above a whisper.

"Billy Lee, I can't say that I've been in love with you my whole life. But I can say that I intend to be for the rest of it. I don't even know when it happened, but it did. I can't get you off my mind or out of my heart," I said.

He gave me his best crooked smile. His gorgeous blue eyes sparkled. Before I could open my mouth to say another word, he'd slid across the swing and proved that all his kisses would set my heart to singing. He finally pulled his lips away but kept his arms around me.

I laid my head on his shoulder. "It feels so good to get that off my chest. I was afraid . . ."

"Hush," he said, and he kissed me again.

He held me tightly and whispered, "Trudy, I've waited nearly forty years to hear you say that."

I took a deep breath. "Billy Lee, are you going to ask, or do I have to?"

"Ask what?"

"If we're going to get married."

"I've waited almost forty years. I can wait until you're ready."

"We're going to have a church wedding at our church—you know, at our church on Broadway Street. How about in two weeks? That will give us time to plan a simple wedding, and the reception can be in the fellowship hall." I snuggled down into his chest. I fit there as if I belonged.

"You sure you want something that public?"

"You are the man I've fallen in love with. I love you and can't wait to be your wife. Two weeks is my limit."

He raised an eyebrow. "You plan whatever you want. I'll be there. I'd like a wedding at our church."

I cuddled down even deeper into his arms. "Then I'll tell Crystal, and we'll plan it for two weeks from today."

"Want to hear my idea now?"

"If it's got to do with more kisses, yes."

"Actually, it kind of pales in comparison to our kisses, but I was thinking that maybe Crystal could have my house, and it would give her and the baby more independence, and I could move in here with you."

"I love it." I pulled his lips down to mine.

He hugged me tightly, and then we broke apart. "Where do you want to honeymoon? I'll plan that while you and Crystal put together a wedding," he offered.

"The lake house."

"Trudy, I can take you anywhere in the world. Name it, and we'll go."

"The lake house. And bring a 'Do Not Disturb' sign."

He kissed me again, and I was very sure about my honeymoon.

Epilogue

We were married four years ago. Momma was good that day. Crystal served as my bridesmaid. I wore an ecru brocade suit, and Billy Lee wore the same suit he'd worn for Gert's funeral. We spent a whole week at the lake house.

Billy Lee and I talked about children for six months and decided that we'd just enjoy our granddaughter, Malee. After all, we were both over forty, and Crystal was grown with a child of her own, so we made up our minds and didn't look back.

It's said that when you set your plans in stone, God pitches in a monkey wrench to show you who's really boss. I thought I had the flu; then I thought I was going through menopause. Wil was born the day we were married eighteen months.

Malee is four now. Crystal hired a local man named Joshua Valdez to help her in the greenhouse when the business took off—like a bottle rocket, I should add. They had so much in common and became such fast friends while they worked together, it was no big surprise when they married when Malee was a year old. Now there's another little girl, Tess, over in the house next door. They talk of adding a wing to it, and I expect that'll be the next big project around here, since Crystal is pregnant again. So poor little Wil tags along with those girls and does the best he can. I'm reminded of Billy Lee having to make do with me and my cousins all those years ago.

Drew talks to Crystal occasionally. He isn't involved with the granddaughters and doesn't remember their birthdays or even Christmas. I don't think he'll ever change, but that's his problem. I'm too happy to waste even one precious moment thinking of him.

Momma had a couple of good days after Wil was born, and I'll always have those memories. But a year ago the disease progressed to the point that she didn't know any of us anymore. She died in July, a few days after my birthday, and I miss her terribly. Lessie joined her three weeks later. It seemed fitting in a way, since they'd become such good friends. But losing them both so close together wasn't easy.

Marty and Betsy come to holiday dinners. Both of them are recipients of the Gertrude Martin divorced-women "scholarship." Marty owns a doughnut shop and has stopped smoking. Betsy has a flower shop on Main Street and buys her plants from Crystal. She made a gorgeous piece for Momma's casket. I think Momma would have liked that.

At Crystal and Billy Lee's encouragement, I began to write in earnest. First it was just a column for the local newspaper, and then it became syndicated. It's just about everyday occurrences that everyone has lived or will live through. It had all started that Christmas night I stepped on that slug in the kitchen.

One day I was writing a column about Thanksgiving, when I remembered Aunt Gert's fussing at me for buying a turkey from the store, already plucked and frozen. A lightbulb flickered a few times, then shined brightly inside my head.

Until then I thought she'd left her fortune to me, but in that moment I realized she had done no such thing. In her own way she'd left everything to Billy Lee. If she had left him the house and all the money outright, I never would have moved in next door to him and figured out that I loved him. She'd known I would find out about Drew eventually. I wondered if she'd put it into Marty and Betsy's minds to follow me into the ladies' room that day of her own funeral. I'd put nothing past her when it came to giving Billy Lee Tucker what he wanted.

Billy Lee had once asked Crystal what her passion was, and she'd said she'd always liked digging in the dirt and growing things. She had then made her passion her success. We've all had our successes: Billy Lee's gorgeous furniture; Crystal and

Joshua's greenhouse; my writing; Marty's doughnut shop; and Betsy's florist business.

But none of that is really my passion. My and Billy Lee's passion is our love for each other. I will always be grateful to Aunt Gert for giving us that. And, much as I hate to admit it, I'm also grateful for that day in the ladies' room. It changed my life forever—and for the best.